Advance

LILY'S

"Cheryl Drake Harris beautifully demonstrates the ongoing power of Vietnam as a metaphor for complex aspects of the human condition. This universal story of love and loss and the longing for connection is played out brilliantly against the Vietnam War and its aftermath—and, moreover, through a woman's eyes, which gives the work an even wider resonance. This is impressive work indeed by a fine new writer."
—Robert Olen Butler, Pulitzer Prize–winning author of *A Good Scent from a Strange Mountain*

"One of the most intense renderings of a woman in Vietnam and in post-Vietnam America that I have ever read. . . . Few novels present Vietnam so thoroughly and completely with its aftershocks. A story of great courage and tremendous power."
—Robert Stone, National Book Award–winning author of *Dog Soldiers*

"The story of a woman who, as a doctor, served in Vietnam and was permanently changed by her experience. Skillfully weaving into her novel a story of romantic love and a suspenseful account of a mother's effort to remain united with her child, Cheryl Drake Harris makes a compelling, memorable debut." —Frederick Busch, author of *Girls* and *The Night Inspector*

LILY'S GHOST

Cheryl Drake Harris

DELTA TRADE PAPERBACKS

LILY'S GHOST
A Delta Trade Paperback / July 2006

Published by Bantam Dell
A Division of Random House, Inc.
New York, New York

Book design by Glen M. Edelstein

Delta is a registered trademark of Random House, Inc., and the colophon is a trademark of Random House, Inc.

Library of Congress Cataloging-in-Publication Data
Harris, Cheryl Drake.
    Lily's ghost / Cheryl Drake Harris.
        p. cm.
    ISBN-13: 978-0-385-33933-9
    ISBN-10: 0-385-33933-X
        1. Vietnamese Conflict, 1961–1975—Fiction. 2. Americans—Vietnam—Fiction.
    3. Women and war—Fiction. I. Title.
    PS3608.A7823L55 2006
    813'.6—dc22

                                                            2005056273

Printed in the United States of America
Published simultaneously in Canada

www.bantamdell.com

BVG   10 9 8 7 6 5 4 3 2 1

For the women who so valiantly served in Vietnam

In Memory of Frederick Busch

Grateful acknowledgment and my thanks to my agent, Wendy Weil, and my editor, Caitlin Alexander.

Without the support of the following people this book may not have been realized. Sincere thanks to Malcolm Harris, Jackie Cantor, Bob Drake, Shane Drake, Erin Drake-Prior, Clinton Prior, Cathy Mudge, Terri Cahill, Melissa Caron, Rob Caron, Nancy Boardman, Marianne Roth, Auta Main, Jaimee Wriston Colbert, and Gail Rowe. Special thanks to my friends and colleagues at Duy Tan University, Đà Nẵng, Vietnam.

LILY'S GHOST

CHAPTER 1

November 1978

Lily. That's my name. It has a certain implication: purity. I'm not sure I was ever pure. In fact, I railed against the tenets of purity: I lived with Ben for five years before I married him, only then because I was three months pregnant.

Marriage hasn't affected the fear. I hid even after Jaime was born. Slid under the bed with him held tightly to my chest. He snuffled, rooted for a breast. And I acquiesced, rolling a nipple between forefinger and thumb, remembering the tightly furled red buds of my mother's flowering quince. He grew frantic, sucking hard. He seemed to feel the rush of my fear, but he would sleep, finally. And I? Well, I felt safe. The wide floorboards against my back. Two-hundred-year-old pumpkin pine. Once the color of jack-o'-lanterns cracked open on wet October earth.

Jaime has just turned four and sometimes I still find solace under that bed. A spool bed. I lie on my side, head resting on my arm, looking out into the hall at the mahogany handrail and finely turned balusters that gleam like polished chestnuts. Through them I see the well of the hall papered in a floral print: thistles and mums, and coneflowers that look dramatically phallic.

It isn't the master bed. That is in the master bedroom on the second floor. Left front corner. Four windows. The old glass distorts the view, a wide lawn bordered on the east by a break of thirty-foot lilac trees and a lone spruce, and on the south and west by meadow.

I am in the third-floor guest bedroom. It is the Friday after Thanksgiving and Ben has left to take my mother back to Durham before heading on to visit his mother in Kittery. Jaime is along for the ride. It is early evening and I cannot tell you the relief I feel as I stand in darkness. I am at a window, one of the two in this most northern room. I slide back the gathers of lace and watch the stars above the trees, the sky as navy as the shadows, moonlight making the back orchard look unearthly. I could live comfortably like this forever, the only light cool and planetary. When Ben's out, I don't bother with the lights. Jaime, like me, has become adept at living in the dark, reaching for a slice of apple, knowing it's there by the sound of the paring knife cleaving the crisp flesh, the burst of apple essence in the air above the sideboard. And I feel him reaching up for a slice even before he asks, the shallow cup of his small palm radiating warmth.

I julienne carrots in the dark. It is all a matter of feel. I can see, through the tips of my fingers, the notch ends of avocado; the grain of sirloin; the width of a mushroom and the fragility of its pleated underside. I make pie dough by touch: pastry smooth and cool, overlaying mounds of apples fragrant with cinnamon; fluting the edges, pinching and turning, pinching and turning, piercing the top, creating miniature leafy branches.

When Ben is home I live with the light, the stark light of noon; the harlequin light of dusk; and at night the ubiquitous fluorescence: the anemic light bleeding from the overhead ring in the kitchen, and the horizontal tubes that pulse beside the bathroom mirror, spreading a funereal pall over the down-stairs toilet and tub.

Ben insists on making love with the light on. He is driven by what he sees and I try to imagine what that is, shadow deepening the wedge at my waist; the soft after-baby of my belly; the queer truancy I know invades my eyes. And after, while he sleeps, I close my eyes and see the mist that rises up from the valley, how the flares make it glow pink like clouds of cotton candy, as if it were spun high in the sky over Pleiku, and always with this image comes the smell of blood. It's under my fingernails, and I feel it, dark and arterial, bloodying the skin under the saturated cloth of my fatigues; aware of it only now, after the kid is gone. I watch as he fast turns to stone, blue-white granite, polished and cool.

It is Saturday morning. Ben calls from the New Hampshire toll. "Should I pick anything up?" he asks. "Milk or bread?"

"We have plenty of bread," I say, "but you could pick up milk."

I talk to Jaime. He's chewing jujubes. "I'll save the green ones for you, Mum," he says. "I promise."

I have a couple of hours or more before they pull into the driveway, gravel spinning out from beneath the tires of the twenty-year-old Mercedes that Ben drives, left to him by an elderly aunt who on hot afternoons parked it in the shade of trees so her collie could comfortably nap in the backseat. Though Ben is meticulous about the car, we still find long hairs that work their way up through the seams of the uphol-stery. I open the drapes. Shafts of sun warm the honeyed tones of the woodwork and floor. When Jaime's home he delights in this event, blinking at late-afternoon light, spinning in motes, the glitter of a billion particles of dust.

I will bundle him up after dinner and we'll walk in the moonlight, over the fields to the cemetery where the family who built this house lies: Jacob Woodman; Sarah Eliza, his wife; and their daughters, Martha, Florence, and Millicent, babies all, hardly out of the womb. Their graves look out over Browns Head. We play tag around the white headstones. I mean no disrespect. I think the dead want the living to cavort while they can.

I do as a good mother should do, but I do it with trepidation. I try to channel the fear underground. But it inevitably oozes back up, seeping into the breach between muscle and skin, invading, finally, my whole body, narrowing my throat, leaving my tongue lying like a stone on the floor of my mouth. I had Jaime at thirty-five because I wanted to change the defining experience of my life: I wanted blood to signify life, not death. Becoming a mother has given me untold joy, but it has not stopped the flashes of memory: the Marine who talked about the blue summer mornings of his native West Virginia and then quietly died. I'd laid my hand on his chest; it was smooth and hairless. I tried to convince myself I was wrong, that he was still alive, so I listened for a heartbeat, and when I could find none, I said, Fuck You, God. Fuck You.

By the time I hear Ben's car, I have been tempered by the light. I no longer feel like a wood louse whose log has been rolled over.

"It tastes great the second day," Ben says, "doesn't it, Jaime?"

Jaime nods enthusiastically.

I don't bother to tell Ben it's the *third* day after. His dish is laden with leftovers: turkey, gravy, creamed onions, squash, mashed potatoes, and green beans.

Jaime scoops out a quivering slab of cranberry jelly from the small cut-glass bowl and slides it onto his plate next to the pieces of turkey breast Ben has carved for him. He begins to build then, carefully pressing a spoonful of buttered potato into a small mound, and when it is shaped to his satisfaction, he pushes a bit of turkey into it with his thumb. I sip my wine and watch him. With intense deliberation and remarkable dexterity, he crowns it all perfectly with a slippery crescent of cranberry.

"Quite a feat, there, Jaim'," I say.

He smiles at me before spooning the exotically layered mound into his mouth. With cheeks slightly bulging, he chews with particular rumination, like his father. Not something he does, usually.

"You need to build your next culinary creation just a bit smaller," I say. And before I can get up from the table for more milk to facilitate his feasting, Jaime gags as if he's choking.

Ben stands and ineffectually pats him on the back.

Jaime's cheeks are now full to bursting, and his eyes are watering, but his color's fine.

With deliberate calm, and in order not to panic him, I say, "Just spit it out, sweetie."

He obeys me, bending over his plate. A masticated mess of food mixed with saliva splatters onto the chipped stoneware. I get up and kneel next to him. He begins to cry. I dab his tears with a napkin and wipe his nose.

Ben ruffles his hair.

"It's okay," I say, encircling his small shoulders with my arm. "You put too much food in your mouth, that's all."

He nods, still crying, more out of embarrassment now than fear. To make him understand the gravity of the situation, I say, "But you could have *really* choked, and I was ready to squeeze it right out of you, like squeezing toothpaste out of a tube."

He looks at me gravely. I hug him. "Like this," I say, "only a bit more energetically."

Through brimming tears he smiles at me. "I made it too big, Mum."

I dab his eyes again. "If it's not raining, maybe we can take a walk after we do the dishes. How 'bout you stick your nose out the door and check the weather?"

He nods, sniffs, and wipes his eyes with the backs of his hands, then slides out of his chair and, with a new sense of purpose, heads for the kitchen door. After he has opened it and carefully closed it behind him, Ben says, "You didn't need to get quite so graphic, did you? It sounded a little scary to me, '. . . like squeezing toothpaste from a tube'?"

"Choking is *more* than a little scary."

Ben shrugs and begins to clear the table, leaving Jaime's plate for last.

I feel like asking him if he *really* wants to know what happens when someone chokes, but I resist the urge. Decide not to tell him about the particularly speedy trach I'd had to do on a grunt as he lay on the floor of a chopper with a dead buddy wrapped in his poncho beside him for company.

Jesus, Lily, I tell myself, just leave it alone. Just damn well leave it alone.

Jaime comes in. He closes the door behind him. Emulating his father once more, he loosely splays his fingers out low on his hips. "It's raining, Mum," he says, "but not *too* much."

"Maybe not a good idea, then, a walk tonight," I say. "Maybe your dad'll give you a bath. And then I'll read you a story. How about that?"

An hour later, he comes downstairs dressed in mismatched pajamas, a yellow top with white piping and black-watch bottoms. Tucked under his arm is one of his favorite books: *Through the Looking Glass,* a delightful 1930's version my mother gave him on his third birthday. Flushed from his bath, he nestles next to me in the chair, smelling of lemony shampoo and Ivory soap.

" 'The Walrus and the Carpenter,' " he says. And he proceeds to give me the book, which I open to Tweedledum and Tweedledee. There is something about the oysters Jaime loves; maybe it's the shoes.

I read the first two lines:

"The sun was shining on the sea,
Shining with all his might:"

I continue, enjoying the rhyme and the bizarre characters, but Jaime is impatient through the next six stanzas, anxious for the appearance of the oysters. When they come, he chimes in, and slowly we say it together, enunciating each word:

"But four young oysters hurried up,
All eager for the treat:
Their coats were brushed, their faces washed,
Their shoes were clean and neat—
And this was odd, because, you know,
They hadn't any feet . . ."

By the time we finish reading, Jaime is sleepy, his thumb in his mouth. I put the book on the table and ease myself out of the chair. "Come on, sleepyhead, let's tuck you in."

His thumb stays in his mouth all the way up the stairs. But when I get him into bed, he pops it out. "They do have feet, Mum," he says. "I saw them in the pictures."

"You're absolutely right, Jaim', I saw them too, all in shoes." He nods, pleased with the affirmation. I kiss his hair. "I'll check on you later, make sure you're covered, okay?"

He hugs his plush blue octopus and nods, and with a sumptuous sound, he plugs in again, his mouth a cherubic seal at the base of his thumb.

We're going to have to work on that thumb, I think, but not for a while yet.

By the time I pick the turkey carcass clean and simmer the bones for broth, it is nearly ten o'clock. With doubled dish towels, I take the covered stockpot out into the shed and set it on top of the wood box where it can cool. For a moment, I watch clouds of aromatic steam float up into the cold air. Then I go in, lock the door, and head upstairs.

The dark of Jaime's room is palpable now; it seems to envelop me. His snore is a fine-tooth rasp filing rhythmically. I cover him and leave the door ajar so that I can hear if he wakes in the night.

I think how good a warm bath will feel.

Our bedroom door is open, and the lights are on. Ben is sleeping. I go in, lift my nightgown from the frayed boudoir chair near the window, and sit down.

The blankets lie in soft furrows at the foot of the bed. I gaze at his pale nakedness and think that I took the path of least resistance when I married him. He was dependable and stable, the kind of man who carried jumper cables in the trunk of his car and kept a miniature Swiss Army knife on his key chain.

We'd been in the same homeroom in high school. He'd dated my best friend, and I'd dated Christian Dunn, who, ironically, now lives next door to Ben's parents. We'd even double-dated, the last time after Christian had gone off to Bowdoin. The three of us drove to Brunswick to visit him and catch The Electric Flag in concert. We'd gotten drunk on sea breeze, a punch of vodka and cranberry juice, and sitting together in the stands of the gymnasium, as the bass of electric guitar thrummed and the strobe lights pulsed, Ben surreptitiously stroked my hip with his thumb.

When I saw him next, some years later, I'd just finished my residency and had volunteered for a commission as a Navy doctor. And by that time, Ben had broken up with my former best friend and had fallen into a long-term relationship with a woman who'd now decided it was time to find herself. He ended up back home after his father's death and was pressured by his brother into helping run the family business, a drycleaning establishment. Probably the last thing he had wanted to do. My love life had remained pretty constant all those years, until Christian Dunn decided to go to culinary school in

New York City, where he took up with some sous-chef and promptly dumped me.

Ben made me laugh. I was attracted to his attraction for me: the way he smiled, for instance, whenever he saw me, that goofy kind of grin that hijacks the face of the helplessly smitten. And always he'd say, "I can't believe how beautiful you are, Lily." And I'd say, "That and ten cents'll get you a cup of coffee."

We played this game, all talk and no action, until one drizzly November night, after a movie, a few days before I took off for Camp Pendleton. I wanted him to make love to me, because I was overwhelmed by a feeling of dread. At the prospect of going to Vietnam. I was suddenly terrified that I wasn't up to the commitment I'd made. So I forced myself to concentrate on the feel of his fingers tracing the line of my jaw, of the pleasant rasp of his beard on the small of my back.

I was grateful to Ben the way you are grateful to someone who is unexpectedly kind.

When I returned to Pointe Blue a year later, permanently freckled and too thin, hip bones jutting out below a concave belly, I was taciturn and jumpy. And just plain goddamn depressed. And having decided that I never wanted to see an open gut again, I was effectively out of work. Because Ben had known me before Vietnam, I suppose he thought, given time, I'd snap out of it, be myself, or at least regain some resemblance to the woman he'd known prewar. So for the five years I lived with him before we married, he didn't interfere, didn't question my eccentricities, my need for quiet, my longing for the dark.

And I, I was conflicted, by the decision not to do what I'd been trained for. I'd worked so goddamn hard for it. The gross anatomy lab my first year in med school had nearly done me in, the sheer violence of tearing the body down: the sound of the saw cutting through the skull, how the air grew thick with bone dust, and how when you pried the flap of bone up and pulled it back, it sounded like you were peeling a thick-skinned grapefruit with your fingers.

At first, I hadn't been able to look at the face of my female cadaver and kept it covered, but the condition of her body led me to it. Although she was eighty-six, I found when I delved under the skin that the musculature was supple and strong, something I hadn't expected. It struck me that she had really been *living* her life, almost to the moment of death. I imagined her walking her dog; carrying groceries; lifting a basket of sheets, snapping each one out before hanging it, pillow slips first, on the line. Compelled then by a desire to see her face, I lifted the piece of plastic sheeting. I got as close as I could, leaning over and onto the table. Her skin, spotted and finely wrinkled, her eyelids, lashless pouches of diaphanous blue, were all indicative of her age. But it was the structure beneath that fascinated me. I gently touched her face, tracing her forehead with my fingertips, the temporal bones, the aristocratically high cheekbones, the small straight nose, the delicately feminine chin. Clearly, she'd been beautiful. And from that point on, I felt a respectful ease with the human body.

But that seminal experience made what I saw in Vietnam even more horrific. Because the violence wrought there was of the coldly calculated kind that comes with war. And so instead of seeing the body being systematically reduced to its parts in order to reveal its miraculous secrets, I saw it defiled and blown apart: a sweet-faced boy without arms. A sweet-faced boy without legs. A sweet-faced boy shot full of human shrapnel, the bone shards of an atomized buddy.

Ben turns over onto his back. He snores, then stops. I listen. He doesn't breathe for what seems an extraordinarily long time. I wonder idly if he has sleep apnea. But he rolls over then and breathes normally again. I look down at the nightgown in my lap. It's the most beautiful shade of pale green. I feel its softness in my fingers, like cashmere. I realize that I have been sitting in this chair for a long time looking at Ben. His body is compact and muscular. But most amazingly, it is solidly intact.

I close the bedroom door before heading to the bathroom, telling myself that one day I'll wake up and forget to think about Vietnam.

And in the dark I run a tub. The beaded chain grazes the porcelain as I seat the stopper. When I'm satisfied that it will hold, I close the door and undress. Slowly, I lower myself in and slide down. The water shifts, sending wavelets over the shelf of my clavicle. I close my eyes and feel the heat of the water.

People thought I was crazy. After all, I had it made: I could look forward to the possibility of a six-figure salary. Why not reap the rewards? they'd asked. Many of those who'd survived grueling back-to-back shifts in the ER at Mass General would return to the suburbs they came from, places like Greenwich, Wellesley, and Cape Elizabeth; they would join established practices, their patients a mix of octogenarians who still had all their own teeth, housewives who belonged to the Junior League and complained of "tennis elbow," and trust-fund babies who suffered from cirrhotic livers.

But I'd grown up in a whole different milieu from my fellow classmates. I still had roots among people like those who lived in Fredericton: octogenarians who had few of their own teeth; women suffering from chronic obstructive lung disease, having spent years breathing the "fluff" that floated around the finishing rooms of the cotton mill; men who supported their families by physical labor, doing carpentry, or cleaning oil burners, or running new wires inside walls and under floors.

My father, a high-school math teacher, was a manic-depressive who suffered from delusions of grandeur. He left when I was six months old, after deciding to sell a substantial piece of riverfront land inherited from his mother. He thought

that he should become a venture capitalist, and when that
failed he traveled to Utah convinced he'd find uranium and
make his fortune. After a year of failed claims, my mother divorced him and a few months later developed a phone relationship with his new wife, a young woman who believed she
could Mormonize him, a woman to whom my father was irre-
sistible. Same old story. That marriage didn't last either,
though his former wives still maintain a long-distance friendship to this day.

He finally settled in Wyoming with a woman aptly named
Patience, a native of that spun-out, tipped-up land, a woman
who innately understood idiosyncratic behavior and was willing to accept the fact that my father wouldn't stay on his
lithium. Unlike my mother and her Mormon counterpart, this
woman gave as good as she got: She took my father out onto
the range to bed down with the sheep, her hair wild and wool-
like, the persistent smell of lanolin about her. And he, in his
manic reveries, recorded observations on the backs of labels
nimbly peeled from cans of shell beans and fruit cocktail.

When they came back to civilization, she carefully cata-
loged the labels, taping them in albums meant for snapshots.
She was fascinated by my father's flight of ideas, how in a
purely metaphorical way he made associations. The last time I
saw them, on my way out West to see my brother, she surreptitiously slipped me the latest volume. "Brilliance here," she
said. I took the Woolworth album and went off to the "sewing
room," where she had made up what she called the daybed,
an old camelback sofa covered with line-dried mismatched
sheets. After propping myself against a pillow that looked
pregnant, the foam-rubber pieces having migrated to the middle to form a lumpy mound, I opened the album, the skunky
smell of petroleum-based plastic overpowering. The profusion
of subjects on the glue-stained labels was mystifying, reflecting
my father's compelling associations: animal consciousness,
how sheep are aware of coming weather before it is apparent

and how the death of one affects the others. Then a real leap: the varied ways plastic refuse is carried on the wind; the specifics of air thermals and wind patterns, along with detailed drawings of plastic bags and the like caught up in trees, in barbed-wire fences, and even in the grilles of pickups. Arrows indicated wind direction; air temperature and wind speed were calculated by analyzing the specific way a plastic bag was caught up in fence or grille. My father even estimated the population density of the area from which the plastic litter had come and, consequently, created a map based on his calculations, which I have no doubt would concur with actual populations. So. From my father I inherited an affinity for math and an almost manic sense of possibility.

From my mother, a high-school English teacher, the oldest of ten children, and lover of all animal life, I got a strong sense of humanity, wavy chestnut hair (a little too wavy), blue eyes, a long waist, and a propensity for pickled eggs. I grew up in the town of Fredericton, Maine, a tiny place a few miles west of Pointe Blue, known for its modest set of falls that in winter froze an astonishing shade of yellow. My mother liked to complain, good-naturedly and with some pride, that we lived in genteel poverty. She made our clothes on an old Singer treadle, and canned quarts of tomatoes and string beans. Peeled zillions of apples from our orchard. Made countless jars of apple jelly, deep-dish apple pies, and pints of pink applesauce laced with nutmeg and cloves.

Sometimes I think that taking care of us was the sum total of my mother's existence. Her one respite came on Saturday nights when she liked to nurse a gin and tonic, and more than once my brother and I spied the glowing red eye of her cigarette as she sat on the back porch, sure we were fast asleep.

I'm sure my quirky genes played a huge part in my determination to go into medicine. My affinity for math and science had gotten me a full-boat scholarship to U Mass at Amherst and from there to med school at BU. My ability to empathize and my inclination to question authority gave me an edge, a fearlessness that came with youth, a quality that Vietnam honed and then nearly obliterated.

My blood connection with the town of Fredericton, where sulfur from a neighboring mill tainted the air, kept me humble. And I realize only now that my fate was tied up in that town because of an encounter with a former friend and high-school classmate.

I'd come home one spring weekend to escape, if only temporarily, the frenetic pace of my life in Boston. On Saturday afternoon, I decided to drive into Pointe Blue to pick up takeout at Doc's Lunch. I missed the beer-battered onion rings, and the homemade piccalilli spread over the cheeseburgers.

Doc's never seemed to change: booths upholstered in red vinyl, marbleized Formica tables, chairs with curved cushioned backs. Irene, the waitress, called me "dear" and asked about my mother as she slipped the candy-striped carton of onion rings into the bag with the burgers. "I'm surprised you haven't seen her," I said, "knowing her fondness for Doc's cooking."

"Well, dear," Irene said, "your mother does have her figure to worry about. Just like me."

"We're all in this together," I said. "Only right now I'm throwing caution to the wind." Irene's uniform showed off her attributes, smooth skin awash in apricot freckles, the shadow of a deep cleavage, a small waist accentuating her hips. It was obvious that she did not indulge in Doc's food.

She passed me the handwritten slip, her hands lovely, nails beautifully shaped and buffed smooth, flawless pale crescents above each cuticle. My hands were homely next to hers, utilitarian, nails cut short and square, knuckles red from scrubbing with Betadine. "Can you read it all right?" she said.

"Your writing's exquisite," I said. Her script was diminutive but distinct, each letter and number elegantly drawn:

$6.54. I didn't have enough money. As I scrounged in my bag for change, sure I had a handful of quarters at the bottom, I heard a man playfully ask: "Need a loan, Lily?" I turned to see the person speaking shrouded in smoke, sitting in a wheelchair set kitty-corner to a nearby table.

It took me a moment to orient myself, to recognize the man. I had glanced at him when I came in but I had thought he was a boarder from Pine Point Manor, a rehab facility across the way; the residents who could wheel or walk often spent time at Doc's. He looked more like a lopsided scarecrow than the young man I'd known in school. One leg had been amputated at the knee and his left arm hung slack over the side of the chair, like the limb of a dead man, the fingers contracted into a claw. He shifted in the chair, retrieving the dangling arm and with deliberate gentleness settling it in his lap as if it were a sleeping baby.

I said: "Leo Farley."

After some moments of awkwardness, Leo rescued me, answering the unasked question. "Fragged," he said. "But, hey, at least I'm here." He smiled then, raising his beer high with his right hand, making light of his infirmities, gallantly trying to put me at ease.

Jesus, I remember thinking, he still has that way of looking, of making you feel absolutely known. A way of looking that he had inherited from his father, a man who on more than one occasion had helped my mother, jump-starting our old Chevy or rebuilding our sump pump, or doing any number of other things that needed a man's hand.

I sat down across from Leo.

"And what about you?" he said. "I hear you're gonna be a doctor."

It was difficult for me to make the switch to my life, in which events seemed inconsequential compared to the circumstances that had affected his life, his ravaged body a testimony to the fragility, and the strength, of the boy I remember going to haul with his dad, setting and tending his own traps. I answered his questions and we talked about how the town had changed, what his father was up to, how my mother had survived twenty years as a high-school teacher. We did not talk about Vietnam. Amazingly, Leo had kept his sense of humor, joking with Irene, telling her that he was a big spender and to put my food on his bill. We hugged, his good arm tight around my waist, and promised that we would get together again soon.

I thought of Leo's father on my way home, how he must have been devastated by what had happened to his son. I remembered him bragging about Leo, saying he was "a goddamn good stern man" even at the age of ten. Leo's driving ambition had been to fish, like his dad, to be up at four, out on the water at first light, heating his breakfast on the manifold, smelling the brine; bitching about the whore's eggs, the urchins, whose spines stuck in his fingers. He saved almost every penny he got working for his father. He wanted his own boat, wanted it built at Stonington.

I remember seeing him in the summer on the dock; at sixteen, he had a man's muscled shoulders, an inherent dexterity, his hands all grace, his motion fluid as he worked on the traps. He had a curious way of concentrating. It seemed like a kind of meditation that profound physicality brings. I realize now, as I remember him, how purely beautiful he was even with the foul effluvium rising from bait bags stuffed with redfish. He had more depth at sixteen than most people have at fifty.

I didn't let myself think about Leo for a long time after that—never even said anything to my mother. But it must have been percolating in my subconscious, because it arose a year and a half later fully formed, the notion that I would go to Vietnam. A notion that became a commitment.

CHAPTER 2

My sister-in-law, Rachel, frowns as she watches Jaime and Nina squatting over Tabitha, an incredibly patient marmalade cat who allows small fingers to smooth, tweak, and generally annoy.

"Be gentle, you two," Rachel says.

Nina gives her mother a look. I see petulance in the way she tilts her chin and continues to rub the tip of Tabitha's left ear between forefinger and thumb.

"And she's only four," Rachel says. "What do you suppose adolescence will bring?" A question she poses more to herself than to me.

"What were you like?" I say.

"Don't ask," she answers.

I look at Nina. She has her mother's delicate features, but her sturdy frame is a contradiction: a fireplug of a body, short thick arms and legs, built more like Jaime, the Townsend side of the family, than her mother's people.

"She'll be fine," I say. "You worry too much." I gather my bag and keys and ask Jaime for a kiss.

"Have fun," Rachel says. "I'll drop Jaime off around four."

I pass the First Congregational Church. November sun

muted by the gauze of bonfire smoke diffuses the reds and purples of stained-glass windows, evoking an unearthly glow reminiscent of Pleiku: a vermilion sun burning through highland mist. I stop at a light just beyond the church and when I glance in the rearview mirror, I see the Montagnard child standing by the door of the parish house. She is as I remember her in Pleiku, napalm searing the thin flesh of her arms and legs, exposing fragile bone, its stark whiteness obscene in the hazy light. She beckons me, and I see her face as it was the day they brought her in.

It had been eerily quiet. At the 71st EVAC. I'd had the morning off. And I was focused on mildew. It bloomed voraciously in the pervasive jungly dampness. Like a green scourge it threatened to consume everything: clothes in my locker blighted, sandals I'd forgotten under my bunk unrecognizable, a horror of furry straps and soles. After I doused everything in bleach and tossed out what couldn't be saved, I showered and headed for the hospital.

By contrast, the compound was a wasteland of red dirt, with the exception of the grassy island upon which the hospital itself squatted. Silky red dust sifted through everything, settling into even the most obscure places: the fine pores of your skin, the roots of your eyebrows, the seams of your clothes.

Post-op was still quiet. There were only a couple of grunts, both casualties of friendly fire. One boy, an abdominal wound, was recovering from surgery, minus two feet of small intestine. He was trying hard to razz the nurse changing his dressing.

The other, an eighteen-year-old FNG (Fucking New Guy, an acronym I would become intimately familiar with), had suffered a noninvasive chest injury. His left lung had collapsed. I watched him sleep and found myself embarrassingly moved by his childlike face, dark eyelashes extravagantly thick against smooth skin, an angelic mouth perfect except for a few stray whiskers on his upper lip.

He'd been a trouper when I'd put the chest tube in. Had

closed his eyes tightly when I'd numbed the skin. There'd be a little pressure, I'd told him, but no pain; then I'd made a small incision and passed the tube, threading it carefully between his ribs. And almost at once it was in the pleural space, exactly where I'd wanted it.

I'd been relieved at my good luck. The procedure had gone perfectly, despite the fact that I'd done it less than half a dozen times. I'd praised the boy for his pluck. He'd smiled a little and nodded, almost bashfully, as if he were pleased at his own stoicism, a quality he hadn't realized he possessed.

The quiet ended abruptly, later that afternoon. There'd been a firefight, and napalm was dropped close to a Montagnard village. A corpsman brought the girl in. We had to cut out bits of clothing that had fused in the flesh of the burns. Never once did she cry. Her dark eyes took everything in. She held me with those eyes, held me until I had to look away.

A horn blares. The light has turned from red to green. I accelerate, following the faded Volvo in front of me over the South Street bridge, and at the Pointe Blue line I turn left and the Volvo goes straight. After a little maneuvering, a lane change, and a quick stop to let a guy on a bike cross, I pull into the IGA and park beyond the usual selection of station wagons and pickup trucks. I try to be rational: It isn't the first time you've seen her and it won't be the last.

I remember the girl's death and how from that point on it didn't let up. We experienced push after push, losing count of the grunts, the eighteen- and nineteen-year-old boys. We managed to put some back together, but too many died. I remember the blood, on greens and on masks, the sterile field around a gut-shot boy from Hope, Missouri, wicking it up, becoming darkly saturated. We sloshed around in it, slipped in it, yelled for someone to clean it up. And with a heavy string mop someone did, whipping up a red froth that flowed into a floor drain, a veritable sacrificial pit.

Tubes of fluorescent light, running parallel the length of

the store, flicker. I loosen the belt of my trench coat but decide to keep my sunglasses on. I push a cart down aisle B, stop at the dairy case for cream cheese and butter. When I round the corner to go up the next aisle, I pass a mirrored fruit carousel and catch sight of myself: I don't look crazy. No one would guess that I just saw a dead child who seems to have followed me ten thousand miles from the Highlands of Vietnam to Pointe Blue, Maine. I look straight ahead, pushing the cart mechanically, picking up the other things I need, conveniently stacked at the end of aisle C: paper towels, embossed tp.

I find the shortest checkout line, slide a magazine from a rack and leaf through it, trying to distract myself, to keep the panic from rising. I look up at walls of plate glass, papered with the weekly specials: *Bananas 29¢ a pound*; *Oreo cookies two pounds $1.19*; *Ban deodorant $1.39*. I close my eyes. I see the windows explode, stilettos of glass flying. I imagine it cleaving the flesh of the people closest, lodging in bone.

"How are you today, Mrs. Townsend?" the cashier asks.

"Fine, thanks, Gloria," I say. The dread grows in my throat, blooming as I write out the check. I watch Gloria pack the paper towels, the great white wattles of her upper arms swaying. I think of the flying glass, how it would lacerate her Crisco-colored flesh, paring it to slivers.

I make it out of the store to the car, where I stand digging in my pockets for the keys. Before I can find them, I hear a loud boom that seems to be coming from the sky up over the IGA; without thinking I go into a crouch, lean into the driver's-side door, eyes closed, hands fisted over my ears. After a time, my heart slows and I open my eyes. To see my shoulder bag lying open on the blacktop, things spilling out: a lipstick, a roll of butterscotch Life Savers, a barrette, a purple crayon.

It was a jet breaking the sound barrier, I realize. Before I can compose myself and get up, a man appears. He reminds me of a fellow student at BU, a Tennessean, who could scoop up an elderly patient from her bed and gentle her into a chair like a benevolent giant. This guy has the same quality of size and bearing, but is ruddy and blue-eyed, his blondish hair cut short in an effort to control its savage curl. He crouches next to me, looks at me curiously. "Are you all right, miss?" he says.

He smells of shaving cream and sweat and fresh air.

I stare stupidly at him for a few seconds before answering. "I'm fine," I answer. "Fine." As he stands, I hear the change in his pockets jingle.

"Can I help you up?" he says.

"No, thanks," I say. "Really." I stand then, my feet and ankles tingling, making me think I must have squatted for quite a while. Like goddamn Henny Penny. Afraid the sky is falling. Or, more to the point, a rocket. I feel my face flush. It's not the first time I've dived for cover, but it's the first time I've had a witness, at least a witness who came forward.

Once on my feet, I dig in my pockets for my keys.

The man stoops to pick up my shoulder bag, gathering the things that have fallen out. When he hands the bag to me he says, "Are you sure you're all right?"

"Yes, I'm okay," I say. I think better of telling him, of saying, It was the sonic boom is all.

I go around to the trunk of the Peugeot and slide the key in the lock. I put one bag in and then the other. The man persists, looking at me as if I were demented, someone who forgot to take her Thorazine. "I'm okay," I insist. "I promise." I go around to the driver's side, open the door, slide behind the wheel.

I drive toward the exit, willing myself to focus, to pay attention to the road. I feel the heat of humiliation flare up, scalding the skin of my neck and face. And I rationalize: What are the chances you'll ever see him again? I pass Gloria, who has escorted an old woman to her car and is hefting a bag of dog food into a beige Buick, her glowing white arms magically disappearing into the shadow of the trunk.

Once home, I put the groceries away and head upstairs.

The room is cool and dim. I sit on the floor at the foot of the bed, pull my knees up. I wish it were dark.

Not long after coming home from Vietnam, I forced myself to deal with my ghosts in a conventional way: I went to a shrink—a guy not much older than me. He'd done his residency at McLean in Belmont, Massachusetts, and then moved north to Portland. He lived on Peaks Island. I asked him if he intended to be the first "head man" to force his patients to hop a ferry.

"Only the ones still out on the street," he kidded.

Before finally getting down to the nitty-gritty, we talked about our *professional* lives, swapping hideous med-school stories.

"Amazing anyone survives it," he'd said.

And that was my cue to get on with it.

After I'd described my little episodes, he sat back in his chair, steepled his fingertips, and thought for a moment. "How would you feel about doing a short stint at Maine Med? Eli Lilly's got a new drug, just off trials," he said. "It looks promising. But we'd need to monitor you."

I noticed he didn't say *psychotropic* drug. He didn't want to spook me. Doctors are notoriously skittish about being hospitalized.

"I don't know," I said. "I figured I could be an *out*patient. I saw enough psych casualties in Vietnam to last me a lifetime. I don't want to become one."

"And won't become one, Lily," he said. "You already got through the worst of it. You served your tour. No time off for antics, right? Not one psychotic break. You are not a psych casualty. You're just trying to deal with the aftereffects now, and that's healthy. We'll do some talking and figure out a cocktail."

I put if off for a while, but finally, to appease Ben and my mother, I went to haunt the halls with other "crazies" and grudgingly swallowed capsules the color of paper shamrocks, but not before getting the lowdown on them: side effects, contraindications, and the like. After two days on the stuff my viscera quivered uncontrollably, and as if that weren't enough, my mouth went dry, so that I could barely talk, my lips sticking to my teeth.

I signed myself out on the third day, preferring to deal with my ghosts cold turkey. So sometimes I have these flashbacks when I think I hear *incoming,* adrenaline sending me scrabbling: the first time in a mall parking lot under a VW bus. Only after I got home did I notice my knees, abraded and bloody, peppered with gravel. And I deal with the aftereffects of seeing ghosts by finding sanctuary in darkness. In summer I take walks at night, or weed the perennial garden in full moonlight, feeling for plantain, stalks of tightly beaded buds, easing them out rootlet by rootlet until they give way, as if they were being born of their own free will.

I wake up to hives: delicate chains of small red weals traversing my chest and belly, arms and legs. I often break out after I've had some sort of encounter, anything even slightly related to Vietnam.

Stackpole's Pharmacy is quiet. Jaime is enamored with sponge fishes that grow from minnow to piranha proportions when you immerse them in water; he's carefully whirling his finger in the bowl. I'm waiting for the salesgirl to break open a roll of quarters. She's slipped the box of Benadryl capsules into a small white bag and chatted with Jaime and is intently banging the quarters on the edge of the drawer. I check out the costume-jewelry display, rings and locket sets with imitation birthstones: April diamond, September sapphire, July ruby. As I finger one, I hear a vaguely familiar voice and look up to see the pharmacist talking with the man who had come to my rescue as I'd crouched next to the Peugeot, fists balled over ears.

He glances in my direction and I look away, suddenly engrossed in watching the salesgirl as she dumps the clinking quarters into their own compartment of the cash drawer. After he's left, she counts change out into my hand and tells me to have a nice day.

"Thanks," I say, "you too."

After I tuck the bag into my pocket, I take Jaime's hand, and we peruse the magazines till I've given the guy enough time to have pulled out of the parking lot.

The sky's gone gray while we've dallied in Stackpole's; there's a narrow blue band along the horizon, the last vestiges of fair weather. Jaime runs ahead of me, calling, "I'll beat you, Mum." His short legs are like pistons. He makes the car, turns, and grins at me.

I pull a face at him and feel in my pockets for my keys, only to discover they've fallen through a hole and are hung up between the shell of the coat and the lining. "Mum's lost her keys," I say, pointing out the lump at the hemline. Jaime crouches and tentatively fingers the jumble of keys, then looks up at me quite seriously and says. "Can you get them out?"

"You watch," I say. I plunk my shoulder bag on the car roof, take my coat, and lay it over the hood of the Peugeot, then ease the keys up between coat and lining, finally lifting them through the hole with my other hand. I pull the threads off, unlock the doors, and belt Jaime into his seat. But I'm not quite quick enough. I see my chivalrous friend in my peripheral vision as I open the driver's-side door. There's no point trying to pretend he's not there.

I speak first: "Hello," I say, thinking, What the hell. You don't have to be polite; he probably doesn't even remember you, and even if he does, so what?

He juggles the bags in his arms, one with a box of aluminum foil sticking out and the other a small bag twisted at the top, something from the liquor store. "Why, hello," he says. "You made it home all right? The other day?"

"I did," I say, feeling my face burn.

He seems acutely aware of my discomfort, so he says, "Glad

to hear it," and heads for his truck, where a dog sits behind the wheel, watching pensively.

I grab my coat, slide into the driver's seat, and start the car. I have to pass him, so I wave again. He waves back. And Jaime says, "Who's that, Mum?"

"Just a man who helped me once," I say.

"He's tall," Jaime says.

I concentrate on getting out of the parking lot, when I remember my bag on the roof of the car. I pull into a space, put the car in park, open the door, put one leg out, and stand—no bag. And here he is again, pulling in behind me, holding up my forlorn-looking slack shoulder bag.

He gets out of the truck, says, "It slid off when you accelerated." He hands it to me.

"Really," I say, "I'm not quite as Looney Toon as I appear." He smiles, as you would if you were indulging someone who was basically certifiable. I feel the hives on my belly and chest and ache to scratch them, and I have a peculiar urge to contradict what I've just said, throw my hands up and say, What the hell, I confess, I am Looney Toon. I see, in the most pedestrian places, a Montagnard girl who died eleven years ago in the Central Highlands of Vietnam.

Instead I say, "Well, thanks again."

Ever polite, he says, "You're welcome."

I slide behind the wheel, adjust my rearview mirror, watch him step up into the cab of the truck, the dog waiting patiently, like a good wife.

Rachel pours the beer too fast, sips at the thick fleece of bubbles that threatens to spill over. She would prefer Chablis, but has acquiesced. We split a can of Miller Lite. We are strange bedfellows: women brought together by their children and the fact they've married into the same family. The taste of cold beer reminds me of Vietnam: flying into Tan Son Nhat, steam rising from the tarmac, monsoon-wet but definitely not cool. I remember watching a cargo plane, looking like a full-bellied dinosaur, unloading, among other things, pallets of beer.

"Maybe Jaime's color-blind," Rachel says, referring to Jaime's ensemble, brown cord bib overalls and a turtleneck that is especially busy: stripes, broad and narrow, of red and green and a diamond pattern of navy in between.

"I don't interfere with his choices," I say. "He'll be perusing *GQ* soon enough."

Rachel swirls the beer in her glass. "Seriously," she says. "How is he going to develop good taste?"

"Rachel," I say, "he'll figure it out, and if he doesn't, let's hope he marries a woman like you." She looks preoccupied; she's thinking about it: Have I or have I not insulted her? Before she can figure it out, I say, "Why don't you leave Nina? I'll make them pancakes for breakfast. They can watch *Sesame Street* together."

"It would be nice to sleep in," she says, already the question of insult forgotten.

"She can wear a pair of Jaime's pajamas," I say.

She agrees, though I know she's uncomfortable. Nina will have to wear Jaime's clothes, boy's clothes.

Nina sits on the floor, systematically packing the flatbed of a Tonka truck with dinosaurs of varying shape and size. She is dressed in pale pink overalls, the bib trimmed in cotton eyelet lace, which matches the cuffs of the shirt she wears underneath. The plastic buttons that fasten straps to bib are shaped like rosebuds. Her pale wispy hair floats around her face like dandelion fluff, the French braids her mother has fashioned proving ineffective as a method of control. Everything coordinates. That is why Rachel winces at the thought of Nina being another Jaime.

Rachel leans forward in her chair, tentatively asks Nina: "Would you like to sleep over with Jaime?"

Nina clamps her hands over her mouth and giggles.

"Yay!" Jaime cries.

"That must mean yes," Rachel says.

I watch the moon through the upstairs bathroom window. Jaime has pulled his stool up to the sink and is washing his hands. He's fastidious about keeping his hands clean, though that fastidiousness applies to almost nothing else in his life.

Nina is engrossed in lining up Matchbox cars parallel to the threshold.

"We'll go for a moonlight walk as soon as you're finished," I say to Jaime.

"Be done in a shake of a lamb's tail," he says, mimicking me, using an expression I often use with him.

Everything is ghostly in the moonlight, the tall grasses bordering the lawn, the path we walk to the cemetery. I breathe deeply; the air is wintry, heavy with molecules of frost.

When we reach the low granite wall that surrounds the Woodman family plot, Jaime runs a mittened hand over its surface, gone platinum with rime. I open the wrought-iron gate. The Woodman monument, an obelisk needling the night, holds sway over the lesser stones that surround it. I sit on its base. Jaime climbs into my lap; Nina crawls up next to me. We look out over the fields to the sea. Moonlight creates a glittering path that reaches past Browns Light to Brices Head. Jaime nestles into me and slips his thumb into his mouth. Nina leans across and whispers, "It's kind of pretty."

After a few minutes, when the cold has seeped from granite into bone, I arouse Jaime, who is still gazing at the water. I say, "Time to go for a walk."

They run ahead of me and gyrate at the gate as I make my way between the graves. "Hold your horses," I say. As soon as I open the gate for them they're gone, Jaime leading. He knows the way by heart, his ability to navigate at night amazing. He is as much nocturnal as diurnal. Nina, not accustomed to navigating in the dark, depending entirely on her eyes, trips over hummocks in the field. "Wait for me," I call. Jaime is impatient, turns, runs back to his cousin, takes her hand, guides her over convolutions where the field was once plowed and planted. I run to catch up, feeling the humps before I come to them. I've developed a kind of sonar: I know from the sound of the earth under my feet when to sidestep the tip of a boulder making its way up through what was once cropland and now a meadow alive in the summer with heliotrope, goldenrod, and Queen Anne's lace.

"Here," I say when I catch up to them. "Take my hands." They grab on and fairly haul me forward. The meadow falls away behind us, and in front of us an outcropping of ledge rises.

"Faster, Mum," Jaime says, "faster."

"No, Jaime, we're almost there." I say this for Nina's sake. She trips over rocks sticking up out of the hardpan of the path and I say, "Sorry, Nin, sorry."

We stop within about ten feet of where the ledge drops off. Still holding hands, we stare at the moon, as round and pale as a baby's belly, its shimmering light refracting on rough chop. And as I watch the sparkle brighten, honed sharp by an agitating sea, I am struck by the warmth of the small fingers holding mine. And grateful, finally, for the simple trust they convey.

CHAPTER 3

Christmas was small. My mother flew to Seattle to be with my brother, Mark, and his family, since she had been with us for Thanksgiving. I haven't seen Mark much in the last ten years and I miss him. A week after I got home from Vietnam, my family took me out to a neighborhood restaurant, my mother, brother, a favorite aunt, and my cousin, Walt, who wanted to hear some war stories and kept pestering until I told them about my first *push*, how a dying grunt stunned me by believing that his exposed intestines were a nest of snakes. As I told the story I heard my voice go hollow and sort of slide away from me. That seemed to frighten my family more than what I had said. Walt abruptly changed the subject and practically hauled me out of my seat so I could "get a gander" at the new waitress, a Kim Novak lookalike, who just happened to be passing by the window on her way in to work. Mark rescued me, took me to the bar to have a "toddy." "It's okay," he said. "You don't have to talk about it if you don't want to."

I stayed with my brother for a few weeks that summer, baked more Irish soda bread than we could eat in the tiny galley kitchen attached like an afterthought to the one-bedroom walk-up. He regularly took loaves to the record store where he was assistant manager and resident expert on Pink Floyd; he gave the bread to the clerks and to special customers.

In the evening, instead of a conventional meal, I fixed him plates of hors d'oeuvres: finger sandwiches: cream cheese and olive; egg salad sprinkled with paprika; paper-thin slices of Danish ham pinwheeled in white bread I'd flattened with a rolling pin. Somehow it made the act of eating special. A way of celebrating simply being alive. My brother ate with exuberance, flattering me, entering into my need for ritual.

So Christmas was Christmas at Pointe Blue. We spent Christmas Eve at Ben's brother Philip's house, where Rachel did her grand hostess thing, cooked and served an elaborate dinner straight out of *Bon Appetit*: braised veal shanks, peas with pancetta, cheese timbales with eggs and spinach, and chocolate caramel torte. Jaime was cranky, laying his head in my lap between bouts of fussiness. We left the party early as Rachel, with her friends acting as ladies-in-waiting, brought out the torte, the silver dessert forks, and Neapolitan plates newly charged on the company Visa.

I knew it was an ear infection, the same old thing. I called Ed Miller, the pharmacist, at home. Apologized for interrupting his Christmas Eve and asked if he'd mix up a bottle of amoxicillin for Jaime.

"No problem," he said. "Take two minutes. I'll call Irving tomorrow for a scrip."

"Ben'll pick it up," I said. "And thanks. I owe you."

"Glad to do it," he said. "Tell Ben to come to the house."

I was grateful. If Ed hadn't lived next door to the pharmacy and been so accommodating, we would have had to take Jaime to the ER in Brunswick. To meet Dr. Irving, or whoever happened to be the ENT man on call. And I was only too happy to avoid the hospital.

By Christmas night Jaime was appreciably better.

Now I sit in the third-floor bedroom, rocking in the dark, stopping to look out over the back garden covered with more snow than we've had since 1957. Moonlight, flooding through the branches of oak trees still clutching snatches of leaves, throws cerulean shadows of fantastic proportion. I'm trying to figure out Rachel's rationale. She complained to her husband, Philip, who passed the complaint on to Ben: "They're concerned about your idea of child's play," he'd said, "the fact that you took the kids for a walk in the dark to the cemetery. They were worried about the sunken graves, afraid the ground might give way."

I'd sat forward in my chair, amazed at what I thought laughable. "Leave it to Rachel; she's always an alarmist," I said. "Do you think I'm a complete idiot? That I'd not watch them? What did she do anyway? Interrogate Nina? It was a beautiful evening. We took a moonlight walk. What is this? Child rearing according to Rachel Townsend?"

He tried to make small of it: "Just humor them," he said. "Don't take it personally."

I closed the book I was reading, slid it across the trunk that served as a table. "You're supposed to defend me, by the way," I said. "You know how anal Rachel is. Why are *you* interrogating me?"

He sat forward in his chair. "Lily," he said, "sometimes you have to think about how other people perceive things. Rachel wasn't necessarily criticizing. She was mystified, that's all. You've got to admit that it's a little eccentric, taking the kids for a walk in a dark cemetery."

"Oh, come on," I said, "you don't really think that, do you?"

He got up then. Came over to where I sat in the wingback. Squatted in front of me, one hand on my knee. "No one's getting wound up," he said. "And I'm used to your eccentricities." He smiled then, holding my eyes with his as if we were conspiring, keeping it a secret, my so-called idiosyncratic behavior. He waggled my knee a little. "You know how Rachel is. Anal. Your word. Just keep that in mind when you have Nina. And for the record, I told Philip he and Rachel were overreacting."

I shifted my knees, causing him to lose his balance.

He stood. "Like I said, don't take it personally."

"I think you should have defended me just a tiny bit more vigorously," I said, "and not come home to lecture me."

So now I sit in the dark still feeling irritated, though that conversation took place almost a week ago. I look out on the snow and decide that I should, in fact, confront Rachel. Before I leave the room, I switch on a lamp; a V of light softly washes the wallpaper. When I look into the dresser mirror, I see a younger version of my mother: dark-lashed wide eyes; full mouth, cleft in my chin, something I've always disliked; dark wavy hair that accentuates the natural arch of my eyebrows, the best of my mother. And an inclination to look straight on, only the expression is different, an expression my mother never has had.

I wake breathless, my hands clenched in fists. Ben, a blanketed cocoon beside me, does not stir. I throw the covers back, slip out of bed, and navigate the narrow pathway to the door.

The bathroom light is on. Jaime must have gotten up. I see the raised toilet seat before I switch the light off. In the dark, I ease the seat down, then the cover. I sit. The coolness of the wood floor seeps into the soles of my feet. I can see the star-crazed sky through the upper panes of the window.

I'd dreamed of Vietnam, of its mind-dulling heat. I felt it penetrating my skin, loosening my muscle, simmering the marrow of my bones. I walked through elephant grass that towered over my head. I followed a grunt. The skin of his neck was dark and leathery and beaded with sweat that ran in rivulets down his back. The fetor of rotting vegetation hung on the hot air.

Blades of the saw-toothed grass tore at my clothes and I looked down at my fatigues ripped and bloody, clinging to the slickness of my skin. I reached out to touch the grunt's back. I saw the barrel of his rifle as he turned, saw how he clutched it, held it so tightly that his knuckles showed white through weathered skin.

Oh Jesus, I said when I saw his face. Oh Jesus. I could see into the empty socket of his left eye, see ligament and muscle and clots of blood gone black. His other eye stared at me, the dark pupil dilated. His skin turned gray-blue under the hideously dark tan. He disappeared then, disappeared into thin air.

I squatted, lay my palm on the flattened grass where he had stood, and heard them coming; heard their machetes slashing the grass; smelled it bleeding, raw and green. I turned to see them before they were on me. I remember thinking how slight they were, how thin and small-boned. And then they were over me, and when they raised their machetes, I saw the hard knotting of muscle bulge under the skin of their arms. And I closed my eyes and woke up.

I push my hair back, wet strands sticking to my face. I stand, pull my nightgown over my head, let it drop to the floor. My skin radiates heat. It is stultifying. I move to the window, fiddle with the lock at the top till it releases, then push the sash up with too much force so that it bangs and rattles in the frame. Cool air lifts the curtains. I feel the shock of it on my wet skin. Then the relief.

Four months after I arrived in Pleiku, I was sent to the 1st Australian Field Hospital, southeast of Saigon on the South China Sea. I was sent to observe a surgical procedure developed by the Aussies to prevent nicking of the hepatic artery during liver surgery. Close to the 1st Australian, the village of Vũng Tàu was renowned for its long stretches of sand fine as sieved sugar. The town was rife with colonnaded pagodas and outdoor markets where you could buy shrimp and delicate silver-scaled fish. Typically, crumbling colonial villas converted to hotels stole some of the best views of the sea.

I met Ian on the beach at Tam Duong Cove. I was doing the

tourist thing with Seb Hawkins, the talented surgeon whom I'd watched repair a liver, one that we'd waited for for nearly a week; the patient, a Vietnamese farmer, the victim of a mine, was more worried about his water buffalo than himself. The surgery was successful and the buffalo too had survived.

Seb recognized Ian right off. He was sitting in a chair of faded striped canvas, the awning over his head billowing in the breeze, a can of beer screwed into the sand next to him, a broken-spined paperback splayed open in his lap. Engrossed in his book, he didn't notice us at first.

Seb stopped in front of his chair and grinned. "G'day, mate, I thought you'd be out there under triple canopy by now," he said, "covering another mad Yank recon mission."

Ian stood, smiled broadly, and clapped Seb on the shoulder. "Well, well, look what the tide's washed up," he said. "If you must know, I'm taking a little R and R before heading up to Đắc Tô. Catching a ride with an American wildman who flies a Huey for the First Cav. A reliable bloke, despite that. And you, Sebastian. Why aren't you hard at work?"

"Quiet at the hospital just now. Must be the fact, Ian, that you're not out there nosing around, riling up the VC."

"Right," Ian said. A gentleman, he then turned to me. "Ian Morris," he said, extending his hand.

"Oh yes, sorry, introductions all around." After Seb made the introductions, we talked a bit, I answering Ian's obligatory questions: Where are you from? Where did you study? How'd you end up in Nam, of all places? He was tall and sinewy, a man who seemed comfortable enough, though there was a kind of nervous energy about him. It felt familiar to me, almost the same behavior I'd witnessed in the grunts, a kind of edginess that said they were tired of waiting for the next firefight, that they just wanted to get it over with, as if the possibility of dying were better than the sheer boredom of waiting.

Engaging in polite conversation, I asked how they had met.

"At school," Ian answered, "in Brisbane, and that's a story I can't tell in the company of a lady, I'm afraid."

While Seb relayed his own refined version of their meeting, I was free to take Ian in. His dark hair, curling over the collar of his white shirt, deepened the color of his eyes, an amalgam of hazel and blue. His Roman nose saved him from being conventionally handsome, though he was striking nonetheless.

When they began their stories of debauchery in Brizzie, I excused myself. "I'm going down by the water," I said, "out of earshot, so you two don't have to edit."

I walked to the edge of the water and sat on the sand to watch children clambering over fishing boats tied in a clutch. Their laughter floated across the water like music. I squinted to see them better, but the sun, vertical at noon, fractured the surface of the sea, a billion facets of flawless aquamarine, blinding me momentarily. I shaded my eyes with my hand and turned to look obliquely at the boats. The incoming tide sloshed against the gunnels, making the children's game, a kind of boat tag, more challenging.

I got lost in my reverie and didn't hear Seb come up behind me. "Come on, then." He held out his hand to help me up. "Hope we didn't chase you off with our stories. Brizzie's infinitely more interesting when you're away from it."

"I was enjoying the children," I told him.

He watched them. "They renew your faith in humanity," he said, "don't they, now."

Ian joined us then, book and beer in hand. He walked us back down the beach to the jeep and saw us off before heading back to his chair.

I didn't see him again until after my stint at the 1st Australian. I had a few days of R&R in Saigon before flying on to Pleiku. I'd planned to have dinner at the Caravelle with a friend who worked for an NGO based in Cholon. When she canceled I decided to go anyway for an early dinner and an early night.

The Caravelle Hotel was the tallest building in the city, at the time. It was the absolute *ne plus ultra* of contemporary Saigonese hotels, a measure of modernism in the midst of French Colonial neoclassicism: shaded porticos, Palladian arches, Corinthian columns, louvered doors opening out onto elaborate wrought-iron balconies, and open verandas. Elegance still apparent amid faded saffron stucco and broken roof tile and rusted metalwork.

I saw Ian immediately. He was off by himself, removed from the guffawing inebriates loosely knotted, drinks clutched in their hands; they'd apparently seen it all before: war from the rooftops, a DC-3 dropping chandelier flares beyond the river, and then explosions in the distance. Curious veins of light twitched like volcanic lightning against the dark wall of the sky before being obliterated by a white flash.

I went to stand at the balustrade a few feet from Ian, who was still unaware of me, absorbed it seemed in a world of his own. And almost at once, I felt a tremor. As if a tractor trailer had passed close to the building. But there was no truck. Rather, a bomb detonating. Some people on the rooftop laughed, finding a thrill in this toy war removed from the city, Saigon, in all its old European decadence and decay.

The surrealism of the moment made me feel detached, the sensation heightened by the wet gauziness of humidity. I turned away from the fireworks and went back to my table. The waiter, a wizened man who looked seventy but was probably forty, approached. "Is madam ill, please?" he asked, his English accented in Vietnamese French. I told him I was okay, and he bowed and left me, a proud man in an immaculate though threadbare tux. I patted my face with a napkin and moved my chair slightly away from the table, the cloth of my shift like a wet shroud clinging to my body. I closed my eyes, wishing I were somewhere else, away from the suffocating humidity, the stench of the streets, the schizophrenia of a Westerner living in the East.

Before I could muster the energy to pay my check and head back to my hotel, Ian approached the table. "Lily, is that you?" he said. "You look a bit green around the gills. Are you all right?"

I tried to compose myself. "Yes," I said. "It's Lily, and it's just the heat. I'm okay." I resisted responding to his concern—I didn't want to look like a female about to swoon.

He persevered: "I'm heading back to my office, near the other end of Tu Do," he said. "Can I give you a lift?"

"I don't want to impose," I said, "and it's only across the square." In reality, I preferred a ride. I didn't want to have to deal with wading into the traffic.

"No worries," he said. "I'll be glad to drive you."

The exhaust produced by legions of motorbikes, Lambrettas, and vintage oil-burning Citroëns hung like a veil over the city. It seemed to trap the humidity, exacerbating its effects. The streets were jammed with people; all seemed to be talking animatedly, the rhythm of the language dissonant to my ear, the din of engines above the voices intensifying the sense of dissociation. I climbed into Ian's Peugeot, wedging my feet between two boxes of manila files.

"Let me move those," he said, "so you can be more comfortable." I tried to tell him that it was okay, that there was room for my feet, but he insisted and came around to my side of the car, and in the process of lifting the boxes he grazed my bare calf with his knuckles. I had a visceral response to the touch, as if I'd been stung, the only distinct feeling I'd had in the past two hours. After he wrestled the boxes into the back, he came around to the driver's side and slid behind the wheel.

"I'm at the Continental," I said.

"I know," he said. "I'm staying there too. I saw you at breakfast in the courtyard this morning. You were reading and looked as if you didn't want to be interrupted."

"Must have been studying," I said, "a new surgical technique you Aussies developed. Sorry I didn't see you."

He pulled out into traffic. "No worries," he said. "Just hold on to your hat."

And I was quiet then. All I wanted was ablution in tepid water, to immerse myself in the claw-foot tub that dominated my elaborately tiled bathroom. Close to curfew, it was a relief to be driven by a Westerner. It could be a harrowing experience, driving in Saigon. As it turned out, Ian did a fine job of navigating the short but chaotic distance to the hotel, swerving to avoid a young man on a motorbike and then not ten seconds later going up over a curb to avert a head-on with a Mini Minor, behind the wheel of which was a Vietnamese driver insanely intent on getting his passenger, a Caucasian male, to wherever he was going. I saw the expression on the face of said passenger as the vehicle careened past: A sort of cartoon terror widened his eyes, Wile E. Coyote just before he hits the wall, the Road Runner looking on. This event matched so perfectly the surrealism of the evening that it momentarily suspended my lethargy: "Good work," I said, commending Ian on his defensive driving.

He smiled. "No worse than Brizzie," he said.

The fact that he was Australian accounted for his demeanor, a kind of relaxed manner made more appealing by the refusal to take himself seriously. No American arrogance. A relief.

Earlier in the day, I'd happened to pass his office. Seb had told me that Ian worked for Reuters. I'd strolled through a park of tamarinds and flame trees, and frangipani in blossom, lovely sweet-smelling flowers, all creamy petals with soft yellow throats. The news agency, across from the park, was housed in an unpretentious building squatting close to the end of the street. A modest plaque directed the visitor: *Thông Tấn Xa Reuters London.* I remember noticing the English lettering, undistinguished compared to the beautifully graceful Vietnamese calligraphy.

Ian pulled in front of the Continental. I got out. He cut the engine and got out too.

"I'll see you in," he said.

Once in the lobby, he said good-bye and left me at the foot of the staircase, a nineteenth-century work of art in mahogany.

The tub more than accommodated me. Water, smelling of monsoon rain, to my chin. But relief was not to be had, my body seeming to act as a heating coil, warming the tepid water and making the tendrils of hair around my face curl and drip with perspiration. I climbed out of the tub, dried myself, if it could be called drying, and lay on damp sheets under a slowly rotating ceiling fan.

I looked for Ian at breakfast in the courtyard the next morning but he didn't appear. After a third cup of coffee, I went upstairs to change into shorts. The concierge had arranged for me to rent a bicycle. I cycled around the city, an experience only slightly less terrifying than driving. By eleven o'clock, I was ready for a break. I needed the comfort of noodle soup.

I sipped fragrant broth in front of a stall I'd seen on my first turn around the city, the bike parked close, the metal of the rear fender still radiating heat, though it had been out of the sun for some minutes. In the crowd of Vietnamese beyond the stall, I caught sight of Ian, mainly because he was head and shoulders above everyone else. I hesitated a moment, wondering if I should let him go by, but he spotted me before I could make a decision.

"I thought you'd gone," I called out as he made his way through the throng that had congregated.

"Not for another two days," he said. "I just stepped out for some lunch. May I join you?"

"Yes, of course," I said, glad then that he'd seen me, and, frankly, baffled at my earlier reticence.

He impressed me by ordering in Vietnamese. The cook's

children hid behind her, tangling themselves in the loose drap-
ery of her trousers, peeking out to grin at Ian before their
mother disentangled herself and sent them giggling to the
back of the stall. They were lovely, tiny bare-bottomed toddlers with dark eyes and mouths like succulent red fruit. The
cook handed Ian his soup and he smiled and spoke again in
Vietnamese. She responded by demurely covering her mouth
as she laughed.

He stood next to me, his soup steaming.

"What did you say to her," I asked, "that made her blush?"

"I thanked her and told her she had lovely little girls,"
he said.

And the girls must have heard him, because they reap-
peared and stood before him smiling shyly in the manner of
their mother. He asked me to hold his soup while he played a
trick with them, the magic of a quarter appearing from behind
a diminutive ear. They ran to their mother after, squealing
with delight, coins clutched in their tiny fists. And I was
smitten.

When I got back to the Continental that afternoon, there
was a message from Ian. Would I like to meet him for dinner?
At a sit-down place, this time. It never entered my mind not to
accept, though I instinctively knew that he was dangerous, in
the way that intensely alive people sometimes are. What the
hell, I remember thinking. I was heading back to Pleiku, after
all. Why not spend the evening with Ian?

Just the thought of good old Rocket City and the next push
set the adrenaline surging. I'd come a long way from my first
days at the 71st EVAC; I'd put in a couple hundred chest tubes
since then; done countless trachs and too many amputations
when the bone man was up to his neck in kids with legs and
arms hanging by a little connective tissue or a bit of skin; and
bellies—I was into bellies up to my elbows. Ian Morris was a
piece of cake.

On my way to meet him, I passed a group of schoolgirls

dressed in uniform: pleated skirt, round-collared blouse, and socks neatly cuffed below the knee. The girl in front, taller than the others, exuded confidence, her sleek hair sliding over the yoke of her white blouse like India ink spilling on white paper. They were children of the Vietnamese elite, no doubt, speaking French.

Ian had reserved a table at L'Amiral on Tu Do Street, around the corner from Reuters. Our waiter, a delicate soul with dark, swept-back hair, was of the tradition of all good waitstaff: unobtrusive and gracious. We ate, sheltered by a lush potted fern, home to an exquisitely spotted lizard that gave off an interesting scent reminding me a little of raw rhubarb. Ian ordered a bottle of Pouilly-Fuissé and escargots sautéed in butter and garlic. The *pièce de résistance* was honeyed rack of lamb and glazed carrots, followed by fruit and cheese, espresso and cognac.

Ian, suave and erudite, leaned across the table and said, "I want you to know that this is an aberration: We Aussies really are as rough a bunch as you ever want to know. And I'll tell you now, I'd give this up in a minute for a few rissoles and snags on the barbie at Coolum."

Rissoles, as it turned out, are glorified hamburgers, made with onion and garlic and chutney; snags are sausages, and Coolum is a seaside town a little north of Brisbane where Ian grew up. We talked about home, continuing our conversation after dinner in the bar at the Continental, he waxing poetic about fishing for mud crab, I about sleeping in a cold room under a pile of blankets. But finally the talk settled around food, all the things we missed.

"Lobster rolls," I said, feeling a sudden flood of saliva under my tongue. I explained how a real Maine lobster roll had to be made with a soft hot-dog bun, buttered and lightly toasted, the lobster meat fresh, not frozen, and not too much mayonnaise, and no celery.

And to really up the ante, I went on to describe the almost

mythical crab cakes of my childhood. "A pound of freshly picked white meat," I said, "mixed with grated bread crumbs made from freshly baked bread, preferably from Auntie Leonie's on Maple Street. Add a little mayonnaise, a teaspoon of Old Bay seasoning, and a handful of finely chopped sweet red pepper and sweet onion." The secret, I told him, was to fold in half the crumbs and chill the mixture for a couple of hours. "And then you make the patties, being ever so gentle, dredging them in the leftover crumbs," I said, "and you sauté them in butter till they've formed a golden and slightly crispy crust."

Ian smiled at the obvious pleasure I took at describing these gastronomic goodies, but before he could respond, I remembered the tartar sauce. Homemade with sweet pickle relish, I told him, and a *good* brand of mayonnaise.

Because the bar became increasingly noisy, making it necessary to shout above the din, we went upstairs to sit on my balcony. We carried on half the night, telling stories about being snotty-nosed kids, Ian always seeming to one-up me. I described the trials of sledding in the subarctic cold of mid-coast Maine. "We'd pile onto the toboggan," I said, "my brother and the neighboring kids, all boys, and because I was the smallest, I was expected to stuff myself in on the very end. And about halfway down, I'd fall off and have to walk, in snow to my waist, back to the top of the hill, where I'd wait with ice-encrusted mittens and boots for the boys to drag the toboggan up, and when they made it to the top we'd do it all over again with the same results." I shook my head, finding it hard to believe how incredibly obtuse I'd been. "Either I was a goddamn determined child," I said, "or else just plain stupid."

"I can relate to running with a bunch of boys," Ian said. "My older brothers and I'd steal boxes from the back of Mc-Connaughy's Market, and the six of us would trudge up a grassy hill above Coolum Beach, alongside the track we'd made from sliding, the boxes balanced on our heads. At the top of the hill we'd flatten the cardboard and pile onto one piece as many of us as we could, because the more of you there were, the faster you'd go.

"And sometimes we'd scavenge a piece of roof iron and borrow a huge rectangular bricklayer's sponge from our dad to soften the impact on our bums, and we'd fly over the track, mined with rocks and clumps of blade grass."

He mused for a moment, fingers clasped loosely behind his head, the memories obviously fond. "I still carry the scars," he said, "in places I'm too modest to name."

And when I told him about catching pickerel on Webber Pond with my friend Theresa Beatty, he told me about spear-fishing barracuda on the Barrier Reef with his uncle Colin.

I was enjoying myself thoroughly until we heard the crackle of gunfire in the distance, not an unusual occurrence after curfew, really. I got up from my chair and went to lean against the wrought-iron railing. In the darkness below, a woman called out, "Wait for me, dammit!" And then someone laughed.

I sipped my water, tinged with scotch. "A depressant, this," I said, holding up the nearly empty glass.

Ian came to stand next to me, gently took the glass from me, and set it down. "It does turn on you," he said, "some-times."

On an impulse, I took his hand and led him into the room. "Could you just hold me, please," I said.

We lay down on the bed, and he did, hold me. And we slept like that, waking, finally, at dawn. It was so natural making love then, no talk, everything muted by sleep, the sanctity of touch before the mind had started its furtive questioning about what is right and what is wrong.

I cringe to think of how naive I still was then. That would change before I left Vietnam.

CHAPTER 4

Ben reaches out, touches my shoulder. "Hives again?" he says.

"Again," I say.

"How come?"

"Who knows?" I say. I turn over, pull the covers up over my shoulders.

He runs his hand up under my nightgown.

"The Benadryl's made me sleepy," I say. He presses up against me.

As I drowse, he strokes my back, my legs. He's so goddamn persistent. I finally give way, knowing the routine, that he'll act wounded and be ever so polite, but cool, for days if I don't submit.

In a timely manner Jaime calls from his bedroom. I roll over on my back. "I'll go," Ben says. I watch as he struggles into his robe, obscuring his erection under the heavy terry cloth. I doze off and wake with a start when he comes back to bed. He disposes of his robe and curls up around me and before continuing says, "He's got to be your child: the only kid I know who asks to have his night-light turned off."

Ben is comatose in the time it takes me to pee after. And

already snoring. I'm grateful for the darkness of the hall. The back stairway, captain's stairs, seems to fold out like a paper fan. I take them quickly, keeping to the wider ends of the treads. It is cold in the third-floor guest room. But blissfully quiet. It takes all my strength to fully open the radiator valve. There is no moon and very little snow left to reflect light.

The sheets are cold. I pull my knees up and tuck my feet into the folds of my flannel nightgown. I can see a spattering of stars through the tops of the windows, where the lace panels part. They shimmer like glitter, the silver stuff Jaime and I sprinkled over black construction paper not long ago: a night sky over snowdrifts cut from sheets of pale blue stationery. It hangs on Jaime's wall, and in the glow of the night-light the stars glimmer and the drifts look moonstruck. I go to sleep thinking about Ben, that he is a good father, and a decent man, and that I should try to love him beyond those things. But I am beginning to disconnect when he touches me, to merely bear it, repulsed by the wetness after, by the smells of his body.

I wake to nonsensical prattle, Jaime on the end of the bed, a red Tyrannosaurus rex in one hand, a purple triceratops in the other. He looks at me and grins, and walks the two creatures up along a fold in the spread.

"So, child," I say, "what brings you up here so early?"

"Daddy said to wake you up."

I throw the blankets back. It's like a sauna in the room. The radiator clanks and hisses as it has done all night. The hair at the back of my neck is wet and my skin is parboiled from simmering all night under a bedspread, a wool blanket, and a top sheet.

"Excuse Mummy," I say as I climb out of bed, trying not to disturb the fragile highways of tufted chenille the dinosaurs are traveling on.

I close the radiator valve, unclip the barrette hanging loose in my hair and stuff it into my nightgown pocket. Jaime is on his belly, intent on creating dialogue between the two dinos. "Hate to interrupt," I say, "but I'm dying for a glass of orange juice and a cup of coffee. How about you?"

Jaime slides off the bed. "I had cereal and orange juice," he says, "and a muffin, but no coffee." I smile, shake my head, and ruffle his hair, but he's still preoccupied with his dinos and without looking up gently hands me a turquoise T. rex. "Here, Mum. This guy needs a little time-out," he says, using an expression he picked up from Rachel.

I look closely at the plastic creature; his open mouth is chock-full of nasty-looking teeth. "How about I put him in my pocket," I say.

Jaime nods. "Good idea, Mum," he says. "It's dark in your pocket, right?"

"Absolutely," I say, "absolutely."

I smell burned coffee long before I hit the kitchen. Ben's pouring himself a cup of what looks like sludge. "Finish it," I say. "I'll make a fresh pot."

"Sleep well?" he says.

"Once I got out of earshot of your snoring," I say.

"Figured that," he says, "when I woke up alone." He shuffles through sale flyers, preoccupied.

I pour myself a glass of juice and sit at the table, across from him. "Jaime has an appointment with the ENT guy on Wednesday," I say.

He looks up from a True Value Hardware flyer.

Before he can ask why, I say, "Tubes. Remember? His ears."

He goes back to his flyer and without looking up says, "He hasn't had an ear infection in a while, has he?"

"Only two," I say. "The reason I bring it up is there's a conflict. Didn't you tell me the plumbing and heating guy was coming Wednesday afternoon?"

"I'll give him a call," he says. "I'm sure he doesn't need you to be here." After a moment he slides the flyer between the pages of the magazine section and says, "Maybe you should see someone about the hives. And the nightmares."

"Ben, you know I've gone that route. I don't have much faith in shrinks or drugs. I've seen too much. I've been on the other side of it. Seen them in action, the Freudians, the Jungians, and the Gestalt guys. It would scare you, believe me.

"And as for the hives, Benadryl's fine. And you'll just have to accept me and my eccentric—your word—behavior."

He chooses not to respond to my declaration. Goes on to shuffle through flyers spread out on the table. I push my chair back and stand, put my juice glass in the sink, and realize, with some sadness, that I simply can't talk myself into loving him the way I should.

I'd dropped Jaime off to play with Nina, biting my tongue when I saw Rachel, figuring there was probably no point in confronting her. I kissed Jaime and Nina good-bye. Gave Rachel the treat I had brought for them: peanut butter cookies, homemade, crisscrossed with a fork, each the circumference of a saucer.

Now I wait, idly watching out the bedroom window for the plumber who had agreed to come earlier. I scratch my chest and wonder if I should take another Benadryl. Just as I decide I'll take another dose, I see a van. The driver carefully negotiates the narrow turnaround at the head of the driveway, taking care not to drive over the lawn, which floats in a pool of melted snow, the Kentucky blue looking more like pond weed than grass, a January thaw in progress. A minute passes before the man steps out of the van. I move away from the window and wait for the bell to ring.

When I open the door, I see by the way he smiles that he recognizes me, and I certainly recognize him.

Before I can respond, he says, "Hi, Mrs. Townsend? I'm Kevin Callahan. I'm here to look at your furnace."

"Come in, Mr. Callahan," I say, figuring if I don't allude to our previous meetings, he'll go along with me. And he does. "Let me show you the way to the cellar." He follows me out of the front hall, through the living room and dining room into the kitchen. I feel his curiosity, but know instinctively that he won't mention the parking-lot incident unless I do.

I open the cellar door, stand back, say, "The lights are on."

He moves past me, and before disappearing down the stairs he says, "Thanks."

I close the door behind him and glance at the floor, a brick-colored inlay. I see a sticky spot in front of the refrigerator and a spattering of milk. I stand, back to the cellar door, and scratch like hell, belly and chest.

The Benadryl capsule goes down hard. I take another sip of water and think about Kevin Callahan's face: an intensity in his eyes that's unsettling. Of course, maybe it's unsettling to me because we share the knowledge of my aberrant behavior, my little dive for cover.

After a few minutes, I decide to go down to see what he's found, knowing perfectly well that I'll see little; never properly wired for electric lighting, the cellar is virtually nineteenth-century except for the enormous bullet-shaped furnace, circa 1955, and a maze of pipes overhead.

I make my way down the stairs, feeling the warp of the wood through the soles of my shoes. I inhale the must exuding from the vast stretch of ground that acts as floor. There is only one bare bulb at the bottom of the stairs throwing a cone of feeble light, leaving most of the first chamber in darkness. I move quickly out of light into semidarkness, passing wooden shelves of jarred tomatoes, spaghetti sauce, green-tomato pickles, and tomato relish, canned goods I put up two summers ago. I walk under a brick archway into the second chamber, which is totally dark except for a beacon of light coming from the fourth chamber where Callahan is.

The third chamber was used to store coal. There's still

about a quarter ton left in the coal bin that extends some ten feet out from the granite foundation. The coal chute, still in place, creates a strange sense of expectancy, as if any minute a wagonload of bituminous will come rolling down.

I stop just beyond the chute, feeling both a sort of shame and irritation. Of all the people. Why him in my cellar? I watch him. He uses a high-wattage flashlight to augment the lighting: two porcelain fixtures fastened to stringers running horizontally overhead, one barely illuminating the furnace, the other paradoxically casting its light on a cellar window choked with a thick snarl of bridal wreath.

A strange tension makes the muscles in my calves contract. As I watch, unseen in the darkness, he goes about his work, following pipes overhead with the beam of his flashlight, stopping intermittently, reaching up to touch joints. Feeling for what? Corrosion? Moisture? Sometimes he disappears from view and then comes back to what he's checked before. At the farther wall, he peers up at a tangle of pipes, each diverging in a different direction. He checks their fittings, then squats to feel the floor directly beneath them. When he stands, I hear his knees crack. Ridiculously, I feel embarrassed at the sound.

For some reason he turns from what he's doing and stares into the void at me. I know he can't possibly see me but it spooks me just the same. It's as if he's become suddenly aware of my presence. I turn and prowl, sure-footed and silent, passing back under the arches, leaving behind green-tomato relish and spaghetti sauce, waiting on wooden shelves in the dark like offerings to the dead, exotic fruits that must be eaten before they pass to the other side.

I take care to close the cellar door as quietly as possible. Gray light falls dull and leaden through the windows, the day gone overcast. I put the kettle on for tea, take my shoes off, place them neatly in front of the radiator, a silvered monstrosity embossed with delicate filigree. I sit at the table waiting for the kettle to boil. But even when it steams furiously, I wait for it to whistle before I get up to slide it from the burner.

My sock sticks to the spot on the floor in front of the refrigerator as I shift juice containers and condiments around, looking for the milk. I find it behind a jar of pickles and shake it as I step away, and as I do, my left sock is literally snatched from my foot, so powerfully gluey is the spot on the floor. I go to the table and pour milk into my tea, and before I can put the carton back, retrieve my sock, and wipe up the sticky spot, Callahan appears, startling me. "Oh," I say, "you scared me. I didn't hear you come up the stairs."

"Mind if I wash my hands?" he says.

"No, go right ahead," I say.

While I watch him from behind as he uses the sink, I slip off my other sock. He reaches for the paper toweling set on a wooden dowel nearby and methodically dries his hands before turning to ask where he should dispose of the damp toweling he's wadded into a ball. Under the sink, I tell him. I hadn't realized how tall he was, six-five or six-six maybe. I should have known, remembering how he had to hunch in the cellar.

Christ, just get on with it and go, I think.

When he turns, he glances at my bare feet, and he can't help but see a sock puddled in front of the refrigerator as if I'd just jumped out of it. I look at its mate in my hand and feel like telling him that it's rude to stare.

He lifts his eyes to my face then and says, "It doesn't look as bad as I anticipated. Someone did an ingenious job, really. It's functioned well for some thirty years. We should replace the lead with copper, and of course there are a few more-complicated problems."

He taps the shaft of his flashlight on his palm as he talks and I am struck by the size of his hands, the breadth of his palms almost twice the size of mine; his fingers, which I remember noticing as I cowered next to the Peugeot, are long and powerful-looking; his nails, cut short, are naturally

almond-shaped, beautiful hands really. They seem incongruous. Strangely missing the dings, the popped joints of fingers
routinely engaged in physical labor. I feel myself flush with
this ridiculous observation. "You really should be talking to
my husband about this," I say, cutting him off.

He does not seem to be taken aback by my rudeness, in fact
takes it in stride. "No problem," he says. "I'll work up an esti-
mate and get in touch with Mr. Townsend."

He goes out the back door. I go upstairs and watch from the
bedroom window as he slides in behind the wheel of the van
and reaches out to close the heavy panel door in one motion as
if it were light as papier-mâché. He starts the motor and maneuvers the hulking vehicle with precision. Not once does he
back over the flooded lawn. Practically an impossibility. Even
Ben in his fastidiousness can't seem to back the Mercedes
down the narrow drive without leaving tracks that look, in the
spring, like they were left by tank treads. I slip to the side window so I can see the van to the end of the driveway. He stops to
check for traffic. Before he backs out he seems to look up at the
window. I jump back, then hear the van accelerate. He's gone.
I spy myself in the full-length mirror attached to the closet
door. As if I don't look ridiculous, face blazing, bare feet the
color of milk, chipped toenail polish, Brandied Plum, creating
a vivid contrast: oddly vampirish.

I turn my back to the mirror. He won't say anything to Ben.
No: Oh, by the way, I helped your wife out from under her car
a few weeks ago. He's indifferent. No problem that his client's
wife is a nutcase.

Jaime and I peruse the toy aisle of Woolworth's. He's still a
little cranky, though it's been almost an hour since we left the
office of the ENT man. He's not fond of doctors. He associates
them with pain. Who can blame him? Anyway, no decision
was made about tubes. We'll have to go again in another week.
Hopefully, things will be more definitive then.

The blaze of fluorescence pulsing overhead reminds me of Pleiku, the Quonset huts, how trays of lights suspended from the ceiling blanched color, made the rows of sheeted beds seem to almost disappear into a sort of whiteout.

Jaime inspects a metallic-green coupe, fingering the curve of its hood through the bubble of plastic that fastens it to a rectangle of cardboard. Without looking up, he says, "How about this, Mum?"

"Looks fine to me," I say. I touch his hair and feel the down of it slide through my fingers. It has gone platinum in the fluorescent glare, has been bleached of its natural dark honey color. I take his hand in mine. "Mum's head's beginning to ache," I say. "Let's get this paid for."

The black-walnut paneling and stained-glass windows of the library are comforting after the surrealism of Woolworth's. Jaime sits next to me at a reading table, perusing *The Pictorial Encyclopedia of Dinosaurs*. A lozenge of light, falling from beneath the green glass shade of a reading lamp, illuminates the pages of his book. I look up from *Renovator's Guide,* the book I'm studying, put a pencil in the "Rescuing Walls" chapter, and gaze at the window closest, an oval of stained glass, deep-colored fruits and flowers: aubergine grapes, voluptuous roses; pomegranates bursting with jeweled seed, reminding me of Persephone, and the kingdom of darkness.

Jaime is under the kitchen table making a nest for his dinosaurs. I lay the last chicken breast into the soy marinade, cover the dish, slide it into the refrigerator, and wash my hands. Dusk falls in pink shafts across the table and bathes the cabinets beyond. In the time it takes me to rinse lettuce and tear it into pieces, the light is gone.

Jaime does the T. rex growl. Each dino has its own sound. I've learned them all. "Why don't you give Rex a rest," I say. "Let Brontosaurus off the hook."

"Brontosaurus took Rex's hiding place," Jaime says. He growls then in the most bloodthirsty tone he can manage.

I stand at the window and look out on the frozen lawn and the last ache of light as it sinks under the horizon. Jaime has not relented and in fact has added Brontosaurus's most pitiful keening, and at that moment I am caught by car lights, long beams playing up the driveway. I flip the light on over the sink.

But it's not Ben. It's Callahan. When I open the door, he smiles, says, "Sorry to bother you. Figured out a custom fitting." He holds a curve of copper that looks less than utilitarian, more like sculpture. "I'd like to go check it out, if you don't mind."

"Be my guest," I say, feeling a little distracted and not quite comfortable with his appearing unannounced.

Jaime stuffs dinos into his pockets, forcing his already low-riding jeans down lower on his hips. "Can I go watch, Mum?"

"Okay with me," Callahan says.

"Thanks," I say, "but Jaime has to pick up before dinner."

"I'll pick up after," Jaime says, interrupting me.

"Not this time, Jaime," I say. "Maybe another time you can watch Mr. Callahan."

"Maybe tomorrow," Callahan says.

Jaime, his bottom lip pouting, stuffs his hands deeper into his pockets, unintentionally exposing his belly.

"Sorry," I say, "that's the way it goes."

He's off then, scuttling under the table to collect the rest of his dinos and their nests, a basket lined with the outer leaves of romaine lettuce and a leggy oxalis plant in a small clay pot. Callahan disappears down the cellar stairs, but not before pinning me with his eyes. No doubt he thinks I'm a shrew. Stick to pipes, I feel like saying.

Rachel picked Jaime up at nine. He and Nina are part of a new "play" group. The suburban sprawl in Pointe Blue,

encroaching on pastureland, has produced numerous three-
and four-year-olds, and eight of them are part of the group.
Most of them are dressed like Nina: matching ensembles right
down to their shoelaces. Jaime went in faded denim overalls
and a red turtleneck too short in the sleeves. He dressed himself. Rachel doesn't approve. She was lucky this morning.
Jaime looked uncharacteristically benign, except for his socks,
one green with black stripes and one white with red stripes.
Rachel eyed them long enough for me to notice, but to her
credit she said nothing, which must have killed her. I see
strains of eccentricity in Nina too. But her mother has the last
word, so everything is in shades of pink or lavender-blue. I
once caught Nina flushing her hair ribbons down the toilet.
White grosgrain embossed with pink satin rosebuds. Rachel
nearly went berserk: "Where could they have got to?" she said
when she picked Nina up. "We must have lost them at the
playground," I hedged, refusing to give Nina away.

I don't expect them back till two. I have a kind of revelatory
project: stripping the woodwork in the third-floor bathroom, a
former sewing room converted by the family who owned the
house before us. I'd spread paint remover over the door casement before Jaime woke, so it should be ready to scrape.

Multicolored snakes of old paint roil and writhe the length
of the casing. I vivisect them with a putty knife and scrape
them into a metal coffee can. About a half hour into the project, I hear Callahan call. I lay the putty knife on newspaper I've
spread over the floor, go into the hall, take the captain's stairs.

He's standing on the first-floor landing. "Sorry to bother
you," he says. "I just wanted you to know that I'll have to cut
the hot water for an hour or so."

"Thanks," I say. "I'm stripping woodwork. Don't need hot
water for that."

When he turns to head downstairs, I notice his sweater is
made of navy wool, obviously hand-knit. The kind of sweater
a wife or mother makes you.

When the casement's finished, and I have a can full of paint shavings, I realize that my fingers are stiff and cold. I take off my rubber gloves, flex my fingers, and turn on the hot-water faucet before I remember there's no hot water. I figure it must be lunchtime and Callahan will have left, but as I walk through the living room, I see his van is still in the driveway.

I move quickly around the kitchen, putting the kettle on and turning all four burners up. I wait for a few seconds before holding my hands over the pinging orange elements. When my fingers have warmed a bit, I switch the burners off and get a mug from the cupboard and a tea bag from the canister. As I pour the boiling water, I hear the furnace kick in. And then I hear Callahan on the stairs. Shit. I really don't want to have to make small talk. I snatch up the mug and manage to spill the tea down the front of my sweatshirt. "Goddammit!" I yank the shirt out to keep from burning my skin and set the mug down and grab the dishcloth.

Callahan appears. Glances at the dark stain I've only made worse with the dishcloth and says, "Give it about fifteen minutes and you should have hot water." I don't answer and he deliberately keeps his eyes fastened on my face. "I'll be back shortly," he says.

I sit at the table after he's left, knowing full well why he makes me uncomfortable. He's seen me when I was right back there, rockets whistling overhead, down on my knees in the OR trying to get a chest tube in, someone holding a flashlight, someone else using a manual pump, the axillary power fucked.

I'll avoid Mr. Callahan. Keep right the hell out of his way.

CHAPTER 5

It's Saturday. I've gotten through endless hours of daylight, it seems. I think about going to the third floor, but of course I can't—Ben's in and out. I go on autopilot. Do all the laundry, even the sheets, though I've done them once already this week.

At six, while Ben is watching the news, Jaime asleep in his lap, I take myself into the first-floor bathroom, switch off the flickering fluorescent tubes next to the mirror, and move like a mime in the dark, caressing the rolled lip of the tub, the shell of the sink, working my fingers down to the glass knobs on the cabinet doors. I turn my back to the sink, slide down, and sit cross-legged. I push hard against the knobs affixed to the cabinet doors. I feel them digging in and digging in until they are like thumbs hooked under my ribs.

I press the pads of my fingers against my closed eyelids and in the dark I see red. Like the face that wasn't a face: no nose, lower jaw blown away, eyes gouged out by shrapnel from a Bouncing Betty. The face that could not see or speak. The tongue swollen, a fist of meat, sliding back into the shallows of its throat, so that when it moaned the sound was inhuman. And it would not die; its fingers traveled over my skin, holding on, reading me, the rise of my knuckles, the circuitry of my veins;

it grasped my arms just above my wrists, fingers digging in and digging in until the nails broke the skin, leaving crescents of blood. And when I extracted myself, its arms flailed the air.

He'd been a Romeo, a radioman; he had humped the radio, and a battery weighing as much as a two-year-old. We had re-strained him with soft shackles of gauze tied to the stretcher rails and I injected morphine. Five times the normal dose. I sat on the side of the bed. Held one of his hands. Held it till I felt the fingers loosen.

I stand with some effort, my knees stiff. I can still feel where the knobs pushed into the ladder of my ribs, where to-morrow there will be bruises: twin wheels of blue. I pull the shower curtain back, step into the tub, and slide down into the enamel womb.

And I think of Bao-Long, as I sometimes do, to consciously evoke the last evening we spent with him and his family. Half Vietnamese, half Chinese, Bao-Long was a Reuters correspon-dent who wrote fluently in English but spoke it shyly, smiling broadly at his own sometimes distinctive pronunciations, re-deeming himself with impeccable French, which, unfortu-nately, was nearly lost on me. Always the joker, he would smile and shrug, making light of my ignorance. "Not of importance, Dr. Lily," he would say. "The French out of favor in Vietnam, anyway."

He lived in Saigon with his family: his wife, Lananh, his lit-tle daughter, Mai, and his widowed father. The family home, a walled villa on Công Lý Street, was in slow decline—though, strangely, in the presence of Bao-Long's wife, the genteel shab-biness had a soothing effect. Lananh, a beautiful Vietnamese woman, carried herself elegantly despite a distinct limp. She had suffered a bout of polio in childhood and compensated for the disfigurement with a natural grace. She was not afraid to speak frankly, though always in a voice that was the essence of calm. She did not embody the inscrutable, almost pathologically shy woman that I had stupidly suspected many Vietnamese women were. She and Bao-Long had treated Ian as part of their family for the year that he had been in Saigon. And, by extension, I too was welcomed.

After Ian came back from Khe Sanh, where he had lived with the Marines in the rat holes of their bunkers, trapped by almost constant incoming, he had described some of the grunts to me: the thousand-yard stare that I already knew too well; the grunt who played the quintessential clown, high on false cheer and bravado; the chain-smoker; the storyteller; the fast-talking bullshitter, oblivious to the fact that in his almost maniacal need to jabber, he was indiscriminately spraying his bunker mates with spit. "I tell you," Ian said, "watching those guys deal with the endless barrage of rockets was a humbling experience. Explosions so violent that your brain lurched in its skull. But those guys hardly flinched, just kept doing what they were doing, playing blackjack, talking shit, writing letters to women who'd stopped writing to them. That's what kept me from jumping out of my skin," he said, "their uncanny ability to keep it together, to keep from going completely mad in the absurdity of it all." Even the filth of the hole hadn't seemed to bother them: the rats; the sandbags fitted and piled, looking like the haunches of hogs; no one even thinking about sticking their head up, to say nothing of using the latrines, some of which had been "blown to shit."

Ian grew progressively withdrawn after he came back from Khe Sanh. He began drinking in mid-afternoon and couldn't sleep without smoking a joint. He'd vanish for hours, sometimes overnight, then suddenly reappear, smiling in a way that made him look soppy and boyish, that made me forgive him for making me feel yet more anguish, as if I hadn't had enough in Pleiku with the nearly constant pushes, a continuous stream of mutilated grunts. "Jesus, Lily," he'd said, when I questioned him, "I needed to drop out for a while, that's all. And of all people I expect you'd understand."

And with the tension acting as an aphrodisiac, we'd make

love, and I'd come hard, once inadvertently biting my tongue, and it would be okay for a while, and then he'd go right back to it, the brooding, the double shots of Dewar's and the dope, premium Thai. I suspected that what he really needed was to be back out there, humping the Highlands with some recon patrol. Being close to the possibility of death made him feel purely *alive*. What he really wanted was to swing back and forth over the abyss.

When I was at my wits' end, knowing I would soon return to Pleiku and not knowing how to deal with Ian's behavior, I went to see Lananh.

I followed the young Vietnamese woman who was Mai's nanny up the spiral staircase that graced the open foyer with the elegance of a colossal nautilus. Obviously unused to acting as greeter, the young woman smiled shyly as she left me at the entrance of a high-ceilinged room largely empty except for two long, lacquered benches upholstered in a deep-rose silk. Tall louvered doors, opened wide to the breeze, flanked either side of the immense Palladian window that overlooked the courtyard. I heard Lananh on the balcony, reading to Mai. It seemed so intimate, Lananh's voice, reading to her child in French, the urgency of her tone telling me that it was an adventure story. I hesitated a moment, listening before I called hello. When Mai saw me she scrambled out of her mother's lap and first bowed quite formally, then took my hand, giggling and asking, "Please, Miss Lily, you tell me where is Ian?"

"Your friend Ian's away for a bit, Mai," I said. "But I've got a little gift we bought for you." I lifted her chin and looked at her very seriously. "Something you'll really like." While she twirled and clapped, I reached into my bag and brought forth a jar of bubbles. It never ceased to amaze me what you could find at the PX.

I unscrewed the lid and said, "Let me show you a trick, Mai." I dipped the wand into the solution, took it out, and blew gently, generating a spray of tiny opalescent bubbles.

"Oh please, Miss Lily," Mai begged, "let me."

I dipped the wand again and, holding it up for her, I said, "Now blow very gently." She tried a few times but was unsuccessful, the thin lens of the soap bubble quivering slightly each time and then breaking.

"Mai, you go now and try on your own," Lananh said, sending her off with her nanny to practice the art of bubble-blowing.

I sat on a floor cushion and accepted the delicate porcelain cup Lananh passed to me. I breathed in the fragrant steam and carefully sipped the tea. We talked about the weather, about the silks I had bought at the market, Lananh advising me where I could find a good tailor before she, in her inimitable way, asked me what was wrong.

Was I that transparent? I wondered. I'd tried to act, at first, as if it were a casual visit, not quite sure where to start, how to explain what was going on with Ian. I didn't want to feel as if I were being disloyal. And I didn't want to make Lananh uncomfortable by discussing Ian. But when she asked, I felt compelled to tell her what was on my mind. "It's Ian," I said. "I'm really worried about him. He's nearly always preoccupied, disappearing without a word. And when he finally shows up, he expects me to understand his need to drop out. I'm terrified that he's going to get himself killed. His only solace seems to come from covering the next recon mission, or some firefight on some obscure landing zone. He is utterly fatalistic. I can't even talk to him about it."

Lananh was quiet for a few moments, as if she were listening closely to the leaves overhead, shifting in the breeze. Finally she spoke: "You cannot make Ian hear what you say, Lily," she said, "if he does not want to. It is terrible passion that hold him."

She poured more tea into my cup, then into her own. She sipped and was quiet for a moment, seeming to struggle with what she would say next.

"Bao-Long too see it," she said, "what happen to Ian. He think that sometime he make Ian see reason. But Ian can see it for only short time. The spell too powerful; it make him forget. It is the courage of simple men that keep him attach. He see men willingly die for one another. When he return to Saigon that feeling no longer there. And he cannot see important, a life without this."

And there it was, everything I already knew and hadn't wanted to admit to myself. Lananh only confirmed it. I had seen it happen over and over with the grunts, how they would put their lives on the line to save a buddy, or to bring out the dead. It was a point of honor. They had discovered something bigger than themselves and were willing to sacrifice their lives for it, as, on some level, was Ian, in order to witness their courage and document it in his stories.

"You see, Lily, sometime there is nothing you can do. Only pray."

I looked up at Lananh, at the wisdom of her beautiful face. "I know you are right," I said. "But I just can't feel it."

She put her cup on the lacquer tray. "You must try, Lily, to let him find his own way."

Two days later, Ian and I were to meet Bao-Long in Cholon to shop for Chinese spices and exotic fungi; the family cook, a man well versed in French, Vietnamese, and Chinese cuisine, was to prepare a special bon voyage feast. I would be going back to Pleiku soon, and Bao-Long knew that I especially liked this meal. And, knowing my affinity for Cholon, he wanted to give me one last experience there before I headed back to the Highlands.

Bao-Long was the first Vietnamese person to befriend Ian; they had common ground, both driven reporters with an eye for a good story, both sharing a healthy antagonism for American military strategists, Bao-Long complaining how they'd invaded Cholon, the Chinese district of Saigon, building the ugly BOQs, Bachelor Officers' Quarters, concrete structures resembling giant shoe boxes stood on end.

And as with many people, Bao-Long had a great curiosity regarding Australia. While Mai nestled in his lap sucking her thumb and trying to keep her eyes open, her father would absentmindedly stroke the satiny length of her dark hair and have long conversations with Ian about the evolution of the country; Bao-Long, a student of natural history and anthropology, had vast knowledge of the topography. He was especially interested in the Glass House Mountains that had so impressed Cook. He hoped to travel to Australia someday to see the geological wonders. He amused Ian to no end when he sang "Waltzing Matilda" in his flawless French.

On the evening of our last meal together, after the heat had dissipated and the moon roosted on the horizon like an exotic bird, Bao-Long's vintage Citroën pulled up in front of the Continental. The young driver opened the door for me and I slid in, luxuriating in the comfort of the backseat where I could spread out. Ian was coming from Reuters, so we were traveling separately, meeting Bao-Long at the market.

I loved the Chinese Quarter, Cholon: It was pure distraction, a place where you could lose yourself. A completely chaotic and sensual experience: everywhere luscious color, fuchsia-pink blossoms painted on screens of canary-yellow and chartreuse silk, ready for the Tet New Year, chinaware stalls filled with stacks of rice bowls, towers of diminutive teacups one inside the other, plates hung up by twos tied in Chinese-red ribbon like presents, all embellished in a floral motif in shades of cinnabar and cochineal, red pigments; red signifying good luck. The singsong of Chinese and Vietnamese sounded dissonant in the extraordinary clamor, the steely screech of car brakes worn to the metal, the gentle chortling of chickens oblivious of their fate, the silvery trill of canaries hopping and fluttering in rattan cages, the smarmy pop music of the Four Seasons, the Monkees, Herman's Hermits picked up on transistor radios: U.S. Armed Forces Radio Vietnam. And everywhere smell: the aromatic fragrance of Chinese spices, star aniseed, cumin, Szechuan peppercorn, the piquant bouquet of yu choy, its long green leaves sautéed with dry chilies in sesame oil, and the perfume of flowers, lotus, yellow plum blossom, chrysanthemum, and huge leaves, gently serrated, evocative of jungle, of a steamy fecundity. And, occasionally, a trace of the underbelly: offal of pig, turd of dog, and shit replete with oil of garlic and seed of chili pepper. In a perverse way, the aromatic smells were intensified by the foul odors.

I liked nothing more than to spend time perusing Cholon, in particular the pagodas. Each had its own distinctive splendor: an overhanging red-ribbed roof swagged in cerulean and intricately carved; some multitiered with serendipitously upturned eaves; great spiraling coils of incense suspended from ceilings; smoke, perfumed with jasmine or sandalwood, curling delicately in shafts of sunlight over banners of red silk embossed with Chinese characters; and paper lanterns lacquered, and tasseled, and elaborately painted. I gorged on the extravagance that was Cholon, tasting and smelling and feeling and seeing until I was full with it; I hummed to myself as I squatted Vietnamese-style in front of a stall and sipped tea, an erotic sensation at my core persisting even in the midst of the mobbed marketplace. I'd return to the hotel with elaborately wrapped packages, the last time with a robe, what the Chinese called a happy coat, for Ian, and a kimono for me; it was hand-sewn, the stitches of Lilliputian proportion against the cream-colored silk.

When Bao-Long had offered to send his car to the Continental for me, I had, at first, declined and said, "I don't want you to go to the bother. Really." I hadn't wanted to take advantage of his generous nature, but he had insisted. And I was, finally, grateful for the pleasure of riding in the old but immaculately kept Citroën that had once been an embassy car. Its interior smelled of leather softened by a generation of indulged bureaucrats, hands and legs and shoulders and silk-covered haunches. He had sent orchids for me, and their fragrance fused with the leathery smell of the upholstery, creating a kind of floral musk, like traces of perfume scenting disheveled sheets after an evening of lovemaking.

We were off at a good clip, the streets beginning to clear for the eventual curfew. I studied the driver: his dark hair lustrous, shaved cleanly at the neck; his skin the color of honeyed tea. I felt a curious urge to touch him. But instead I gently thumbed an orchid blossom as bars of light from the street slid over it, illuminating the petals. And then, without compunction, I reached out to lightly touch the young man's neck. The softness of his skin was shocking, the fine bristling of hair creating a prickly sensation under my fingertips that thrilled me, in the way an unexpected sensation can.

I could feel the driver's acute embarrassment, but he did not react, other than to shift slightly in his seat. I withdrew my hand and looked down again at the orchids in my lap; in the neon light of Tu Do Street, they looked otherworldly, their white petals stained scarlet, the delicate freckling around their stamens a deep indigo. I closed my eyes. I did not feel contrite, even though I had ignored what I knew was deeply distasteful to the Vietnamese—the idea of a Vietnamese man and a Caucasian woman together—and though it was never my intention to upset the boy, there was no point in trying to explain my actions. You see, they die, I could have told him, by way of explanation. Many even younger than you. Instead I let silence speak.

The Chinese Quarter seemed forbidding after dark. In the daytime, the sun obliterated shadow, saturating and slowly steaming the marketplace, the ramshackle houses on stilts along the Bến Nghé Canal, and the pagodas, their eaves upturned as if curled by the sultry air. Flamboyant color bloomed. People who waited on you in the market seemed kind, some possessing infinite patience: like the birdman who, with a sort of reverence, took songbirds from tall rattan cages, cupping them tenderly, delivering them to diminutive woven boxes. It was considered a good omen to set a bird free. On that day, I had picked a bright-eyed finch with a tangerine-colored beak, slipped him into the shade of my bag, and carried him through convoluted and crowded lanes to the Phu'o'c An Hội Quán Pagoda. When I'd opened the delicately woven box, in front of the colonnaded temple, the bird disappeared into the hot-blue sky high above the tiered roof. I wondered if I'd given him freedom only to die of starvation. I'd walked back to the market after, to ask the birdman if the finch would survive. "No worry," he said. "Bird catch wild. He know world of tree. Where he get food."

I thought that the unassuming man, who so obviously loved his birds, could also very possibly be Vietcong, someone who attempted nightly to annihilate something: to blow up the BOQs, or the restaurants frequented by Americans, or the embassies, bastions of the West: Britain, France, the United States. I felt a vague sense of unease as we drove slowly now, people having to give way for the Citroën.

The driver pulled up in front of the market where I had indicated. He got out of the car and opened the door for me, avoiding my eyes, bowing as I emerged from the sumptuous interior. "Thank you," I said, suddenly wanting to make clear my motives for what I was sure he thought was indecent behavior. But there seemed no way, so I thanked him again.

Ian was waiting, and after winding my way through a throng of people I joined him. He put an arm around my shoulders. "Traveling in style, I see, while poor Bao-Long had to cycle here so you could enjoy the luxury of a chauffeur-driven limousine."

"You can't shame me," I teased. "Since you were also chauffeured."

Babysan Thanh, as the Reuters crew affectionately called their driver, was a diminutive young man who deeply loved his 1948 Chevrolet and had fitted the brake, clutch, and gas pedals with blocks to facilitate his reach. He was a superb driver and an imaginative mechanic. A devotee of Elvis, he would break out spontaneously with a Vietnamese version of "Love Me Tender" when the desire struck him. Ian had bought a collection of Elvis 45s from a Louisiana grunt looking to raise money for his R&R fun in Thailand, and he presented them to Thanh on behalf of the Reuters staff.

Ian nuzzled my hair. "I didn't specifically request a driver, you know," he said in mock seriousness. "Just a benefit of the job. I'd as soon cycle."

After following narrow crowded twists and turns past purveyors of ginger candies and spices, fragrant teas, and rice noodles, we found Bao-Long deliberating over a basket of fresh fungi. He smiled when he saw us, a beatific smile that transformed the serious man, making him look boyish and vulnerable.

He said, "Here, Dr. Lily, we have exactly what you like." In his palm he gently cupped the mushrooms in question, diminutive and brown-tipped, each no bigger than a thimble.

"Heavenly," I said. I could already taste them sautéed in a spicy brown sauce. In Chinese, Bao-Long directed the man waiting on us. I watched the man wrap the mushrooms. He was dressed in a white short-sleeve shirt and loosely fitting black trousers. He would have been nondescript except for the red and white bandanna jauntily tied around his neck, which may have come from a dead grunt, a kid who had once fancied himself a kind of marginal hippie.

Ian took my hand, and I knew he had seen the bandanna and come to the same conclusion.

Bao-Long and his driver jockeyed his bicycle into the trunk of the Citroën, and we followed in the Reuters "limousine" onto Công Lý Street, a short ride that took considerably longer because of the traffic. Công Lý was a tree-lined boulevard alive with the chirping of geckos, tiny lizards that flourished in

Saigon despite the pall of daytime exhaust. We came upon a once-posh residential area, a mix of private homes and government compounds, and turned onto the broad drive set with beveled stone. The perfume of night-blooming flowers permeated Thanh's Chevrolet, obliterating the smells of various cleaning fluids and polishes he used to keep the interior looking like new.

Lananh and Mai were waiting for us outside the house, Mai gyrating next to her mother, a bubble wand in one hand and a jar of soap solution in the other. "Lily," Lananh said, "welcome." Her dark hair was fastened in a sleek chignon, and she wore a silk *áo đai,* a tunic of indigo flowers on a teal background, and a pair of teal trousers. Her unconscious grace made me feel an awkward presence, tall and alien, of a different place and time. But she took my hand and immediately that feeling left me. "Mai want to show you her soap bubble," she said. "Little girl impatient, as you can see."

"Oh, Mai," I said, "your own bubbles! Good for you."

Lananh let go of my fingers gently and put her hands over her mouth as she laughed at Mai, how with exquisite care, just the right force of breath, she created an iridescent globe that floated in the muted light. The intense seriousness Mai exercised when she blew the bubbles disappeared instantly, her face alive with delight as she watched the bubble tremble, float, and finally break, spraying a fine rain over the stone terrace.

She stirred her wand in the soap solution again, but before she'd raised it to her lips she spied Ian and her father. She giggled again and ran for her father. After a hug and a kiss, she carefully put her wand in the soap solution, set the jar on the terrace, and put her hands out to Ian. Something I'd seen her do every time she saw him. She instinctively knew that he was cool with kids, that in some ways he was still a child himself.

"You want this again, do you, Mai?" He took her hands and she walked lightly with pink-slippered feet up his shins and he flipped her over, a stunt that was repeated at her laughing insistence until her mother intervened, saying that dinner must begin.

Mai allowed Ian to pick her up, her face flushed, a rush of talk alternating between Vietnamese and English. "You do after dinner?" she said in all her sincere childfulness.

Ian laughed. "You've tired me out, Miss Mai. We need to teach your father this trick, don't we?"

"You have longer leg, Mr. Ian Morris," Bao-Long said. "Vietnamese leg too short." He took his girl from Ian's arms then and said to her mother, "We are having Lily's most favorite food and Mai's, yes?"

"Mango ice cream, you must mean." Lananh slipped her arm through mine. As we walked across the terrace, one gecko zipped over the warm stone, disappearing into shadow, only to be pursued by a second one that froze in front of us momentarily, swaying back and forth, in a sort of trance before also vanishing into the dark.

Ian and I went back to the Continental after a fabulous dinner. We napped on the double bed, the bottom sheet cool, tightly tucked, the ceiling fan droning above us, slats of light through louvers bleaching the dark wood floors.

I had a crazy dream that night, so vivid that it stayed with me for days after, a conglomeration of colors, tastes, feelings, a maze through which I drifted to find a long low table of fruits and flowers piled in ceramic platters of aqua and butter-yellow and lime-green. Papayas from which I scooped round black seeds with my fingers, then dug into the orange-pink flesh that tasted both sweet and putrescent. Frangipani blossoms spiraled lazily from the sky; with fingers wet from juice, I picked up a blossom, its petals creamy, graduating from pink to deep red at the center. I set the blossom down with the others strewn over the table, and as I sat there, knees to chest, arms wrapped around them, the flowers morphed into flesh, the petals into the soft lobes of ears, baby toes, and pale pink nipples. I remember a feeling of indifference in the dream, as if this were something quite ordinary.

When I woke I could smell the sour odor of sweat that comes with nightmares, the kind that leaves an oily sheen on the skin, like spilled gasoline on wet pavement. Ian's feet seemed fantastically big jutting out from under the sheet, his second toe freakishly longer than his big toe. I needed to take refuge in his imperfections, exult in anything that could be construed as a possible grotesquery, toes of peculiar shape, callused feet, nails softened by jungle rot, his compulsion to be in the field with the grunts, humping through monsoon rains, making him subject to tropical contagions. I knew it was perilous to love him. He could easily end up in triage, as good as dead, cerebral fluid leaking from his ears. I could feel his urge to get back out there, even as he was recovering from the fevers of dengue that he had picked up in Khe Sanh.

What was the difference? What if I'd fallen for some flyboy in the 1st Cav? The odds for dying that much higher? Well, the fact was that Ian wasn't obliged to put himself at risk, like the men he covered. He chose to take the risk and to keep taking it, even after close calls: the guy in front of him hitting a trip wire; a little friendly fire that blew out his eardrums for a while; a sliver of shrapnel striking just slightly right of his carotid artery.

Saigon, for Ian, was more chaotic than even the worst firefight he'd covered on some godforsaken landing zone that had been named after some general's wife: LZ Shirley, Frances, Linda. After a few days' R&R in the city, the grunts, like Ian, wanted out, back to the jungle. Urban warfare drove them crazy: a beautiful Vietnamese woman tooling around on a Honda, shooting Americans indiscriminately; street kids practicing sleight of hand, liberating you of wallet, pen, sunglasses, camera, with such expertise that you didn't even know the object was gone until you went fishing for it in your pockets; prostitutes freeing you of anything that hadn't been taken.

"Less worry out there," Ian had said. "It's this bloody place that'll get you every time."

I left Saigon first, catching a Huey to Pleiku, the guy covering me—a general surgeon from Terre Haute, Indiana—off to Bangkok for a little dubious R&R. Ian stayed in Saigon a week longer before he was back out in the field, semirecovered from dengue.

Back in Pleiku, I found myself feeling grateful for the eighteen-hour shifts, for fatigue so profound that sleep was black and dreamless, and for the inability to think of anything but the ruin of humanity before me.

CHAPTER 6

I watch Ben sleep and hate him for what I feel. He lies on his back and, as usual, breathes erratically through his mouth, making guttural noises. It's a gruesome sound, reminding me of a death rattle—Cheyne-Stoking like the dozens of grunts I saw in triage, most too badly damaged to survive.

I get up, pull a sweatshirt over my nightgown, and leave the room. It really is uncanny, this ability to maneuver in the dark. I know every tread, how high the risers are, the jog in the front hall, the path through the living room.

Ben has left the light on over the kitchen sink. I switch it off and put the kettle on.

I'd fallen asleep in the tub, behind the violet-sprigged shower curtain. So they had gone on a hunt for me, Ben and Jaime, inside and out, and when they didn't find me, Ben called his brother, Philip. And of course Rachel and Nina came with Philip. Rachel found me after Ben and Philip left to walk down to the headland to look for me. She switched on the flickering fluorescence and, "Just on a whim," she said, pulled the shower curtain back.

After they left, Rachel looking smug, Ben put Jaime to bed.

I sat at the kitchen table and listened to him go on and on: "Jesus," he said, "it's like being married to a vampire."

I didn't respond.

"You've got to deal with this," he said, "get some help. God knows what goes on when I'm not home." He paced from table to counter and back again, his arms folded in front of him. "This can't be good for Jaime."

He stopped pacing for a moment, long enough to ask, "Well, what do you have to say?"

"You have no right to question me. No right. I knew you were watching Jaime. I fell asleep, that's all. Can't you just accept that?"

He stood over me then. "Jesus, Lily, think about it. You go into a dark bathroom, crawl into an empty tub, and go into some kind of funk. You think that's normal? And you've most certainly influenced Jaime. He's just like you: He seems to *prefer* the dark."

I fisted my hands and pushed them deeper into my lap. "Leave Jaime out of it," I said.

"I don't see how we can," he said.

I was losing. I tightened my fists till I felt my nails dig into my palms. "I'll go see someone," I said. "Just leave Jaime out of it. Please."

After I washed my face and brushed my teeth, I checked on Jaime. I lifted his hand to my mouth and kissed it. It smelled of peanut butter and soap.

Ben was on his back staring at the ceiling. I pulled my nightgown over my head, let it drop on the floor, and slid into bed beside him. I didn't reach out to turn off the bedside lamp. And in the light, I acted against everything I felt inside. And as if aroused by the anger and fear that he had felt earlier in the evening, he rhythmically ground himself into me, and when he was almost there I got up on my hands and knees, so he would be quick and I would not have to see his face, the slackness of his mouth and the sudden grimacing when he came.

I smell Ben's sweat; it has dried on my chest and thighs. I am sickened. And afraid. I get up, make my way to the kitchen, walking through the dark house effortlessly, a she-rabbit navigating the labyrinth of its warren. In the kitchen, I slide the whistling teakettle off the burner, and in its red glow I pour boiling water over a tea bag. Red Rose.

Jaime has gone down for a nap, though it's only eleven. He'd gotten up at five, unusually early. Found me wrapped in a blanket sleeping on the living-room sofa. He cuddled with me for a few minutes before deciding he was hungry.

I sipped coffee while he spooned Cheerios in, stopping every so often to chat up the gang of dinos he'd arranged around his bowl. After he finished eating, he looked across the table at me and said, "Are you okay, Mum?" When I said I was fine, he went on to say that he wasn't a bit worried about me last night, that he'd told his father I was just probably looking for the moon as we often did.

It made me realize the effect it had on him. I really had disappeared into some kind of funk. Not that I'd ever admit it to Ben. It was hard enough to admit it to myself. I watched Jaime peruse the back of the cereal box, silently mouthing the words he knew. And I felt my bowels narrowing.

The phone rings and I shake the kettle for water and put it on the burner before I pick up the receiver. It's June, the secretary–bookkeeper–tax-preparer spinster who's worked for Townsend Dry Cleaning for more than thirty years, first for Townsend Senior, now for the "boys," as she calls Ben and Philip.

She doesn't make any pretense: "Ben had me make an appointment for you, Lily," she says. "I talked to Dr. Richards's nurse and he can see you tomorrow at four."

I am taken aback. I cannot believe my husband's audacity *or* June's willingness to do his bidding. "June," I say, "I'd like to speak to Ben, now, please."

"He's out front sorting, Lily." Her voice falters. "But I'll get him."

She carefully sets the receiver down.

She has left the office door open, so I can hear their conversation but not specifically what's being said.

She returns, heavy-footed in her tie brogues. Before picking up the phone, she clears her throat. Then she fumbles with the receiver and says, "Hello, Lily? Ben says he'll call you later. He's tied up right now."

And though I feel badly for June, that shit, my husband, having put her in an untenable position, I say, "Thank you, June. And please, from now on, I'd rather you not make appointments for me. You do understand why, don't you?"

She breathes noisily, making a whiny sound like a scolded dog. "Yes, Lily," she says.

"You're too good to those *boys,* June. They ask too much of you."

"Well, it's hard, Lily," she says. "I've known them since they were babies—"

I stop her there: "June, please. You are not their mother. Don't let them take advantage of you."

She sighs again.

"I'm sorry, June," I say, "I've got to get off now so I can cancel that appointment."

I flip through the phone book. Find Dr. Richards's number. Dial it. The kettle whistles and I stretch the phone cord across the kitchen and take the water off. I get the receptionist. I cancel the appointment, telling her that my husband was mistaken: I do not need to see Dr. Richards.

Collapsed helices of old paint lay on the newspaper like dead snails, their thick shells garish, yellow-aqua-gray-salmon-lavender. I pull my gloves off and drop them on the paper. My heart isn't in it.

It's more like April than February. Rain beats against the

storm windows, the air space between the panes acting as an amplifier, deepening the sound. As I pass through the dining room, I see Callahan just leaving. Heading to Glennda's Café for something with seeds and sprouts?

I don't have much of an appetite. And there's not much to eat: peanut butter and jelly, mac and cheese, a little leftover cold chicken, soft ribs of celery. I'll have to go out for groceries before Jaime gets home from play group. I feel hives on my belly and chest. Like tiny mushrooms, they grew overnight. I lift my shirt and scratch like hell, savoring the momentary relief. After, as they burn and pulse, I sit at the table facing the cellar door, focusing on the porcelain knob.

Callahan has turned out the lights. I don't need them anyway. I float down the stairs and through the darkness past the canned tomato stuffs and the coal bin. In the furnace room a gauze of light, tenuous and gray, falls through the two rectangular windows. Callahan's toolbox, a metal monstrosity, is set near the furnace. I carefully put the cover down, making sure the handle is compressed, and sit on the cold, flat surface.

As my eyes become accustomed to the muted light, I can make out the warm glow of copper traversing overhead caught up and banded like sheaves of pink-gold grain. No problem, I tell myself. Just looking at the work, is all. But I let it rise up in me, not fighting it, a kind of disconnection, my vision going grainy, my body blurring, becoming part of the gloom, its distinction disappearing.

When I became aware of Callahan, I have no idea of how much time has passed. I stand, trying to think of an explanation for why I'm in the dark cellar. And then I think, screw it, I owe this man no explanation; it's my house, after all, I have a perfect right to be here. Even in the dark. In my self-righteousness, I trip over a bound sheaf of piping laying on the floor, pitch forward, and fall, landing hard on my hands and knees, grazing my head on the corner of the cement pad upon which the furnace squats.

I see stars for a moment and then Callahan. He squats next to me. "Mrs. Townsend, are you all right?"

"Yes," I manage to say. "I couldn't find the light is all, and I tripped."

"You're bleeding," he says.

I touch the bump, one hell of a contusion, just above my right eyebrow and feel the blood, oily on my fingers.

"We better get you upstairs," he says. Having become disoriented from the fall, I allow Callahan to help me up and hold my elbow as I make my way across the cellar to the stairs.

Once in the kitchen he becomes nurse. "You got peroxide?"

"No, but there's Betadine in the medicine cabinet," I say, "and gauze pads, I think."

He heads for the bathroom. I take a bag of peas from the freezer in lieu of ice, the trays nearly empty, and wash my hands with dishwashing liquid under hot water, drying them on paper towels.

When Callahan returns, he says, "Got it all here. Tape too."

"Thanks," I say.

He puts the stuff on the table. I open a gauze 4×4 by peeling the paper back. Then I take one corner of the pad and bring the other three corners together, creating a swab. "Can you open that for me," I say, nodding at the Betadine. "And pour a little into the sink to clean the lip of the bottle, please."

He does as I ask, unscrewing the top, putting it down on the counter next to the sink before he pours a little away.

I hold the pad over the sink. "Now, just a bit on this, so that it doesn't spread to my fingertips." Efficiently, he pours just the right amount.

I use the toaster as a mirror and carefully clean the abrasion. After I drop the swab into the sink, I fold the other 4×4 into a compress.

"Could you help me with this, please?"

"Just let me wash my hands," he says.

I hold the gauze in place with two fingers, and I look down

as he works, feeling his fingers carefully smooth the tape. I can smell the lemon dish soap on his hands.

"That'll do it, I think." He stands back to survey his work.

"Thanks for helping," I say. I wrap the bag of frozen peas in a dish towel and press it against the dressing.

"Inventive, that," he says.

"Isn't it?" I say.

"Will you be all right?"

"Sure," I say, "it's just a bump."

Instead of feeling grateful to Callahan, I feel resentful. If he hadn't come back when he did, I wouldn't have been startled and consequently tripped. And even though I know this is a childish reaction, my rancor directed unfairly at Callahan, I persist, because to do otherwise would mean to accept what I'm not ready to.

Ben is angry with me. He's never been exactly comfortable hanging around emergency rooms. "You baffle me," he says. "Since when are you interested in the finer points of plumbing?"

"I was curious, that's all," I say. "And why don't you go out into the waiting room? You're not doing either of us any good."

Dr. Richards finally appears, wearing gray flannel trousers, a white coat, and a tie that resembles one of Jaime's finger paintings: shocks of lime green, yellow, and red. "No problem, Lily," he says. "X-ray looks fine. No fracture."

Before I can answer, he says, "Let's check it out." He gently palpates the mushy lump. I want to slap his hand away, tell him to leave me be. Instead, I lean slightly away from his fingers and he takes the hint.

He sits in the chair at the foot of the table, casually crosses his leg, ankle poised on knee, and says, "Ben tells me you've had some problems sleeping. Nightmares waking you. Thinks you might want to talk to someone about it. Is that so?"

"Ben's overreacting," I say.

" 'Physician, heal thyself,' yes?"

"Something like that."

But he persists. "Let me give you the name of a colleague of mine anyway. Just in case you decide you want to see someone. A guy I ski with."

Wonderful, I want to say as he writes the name on a prescription pad.

"Ned Wyman," he says, "a good man. I'll have my office give him a call, so you won't have a problem getting in if you decide to go."

I made an appointment with Dr. Wyman. Used the kitchen phone while Ben was sitting at the table fixing his glasses, messing with one of those repair kits, infinitesimal screws and all. March 14 at 2:15. No, I'd said when the receptionist asked if it was urgent.

I'd been out much more than usual. Food shopping, doctor's appointments, back to the pediatrician. Jaime's ears were still questionable. Tubes still a distinct possibility. At night I prevailed under a halo of fluorescence in the kitchen, by sixty-watters in the living room, and by electrified gas wall lamps in the upstairs bathroom.

And now, as the sun sets, I watch Callahan do his precise maneuvering and back his van down the driveway. Ben is gone for two days, up north with Philip, the last of the ice-fishing for the season. Under the white fluorescence, I stand at the counter and slice a sweet red pepper. I pull the knife back too far and feel the serrated edge cut into the fleshy pad of my index finger. I wince and draw a breath. Jaime leaves his Fisher-Price Ferris wheel, the seats occupied by dinos instead of people. I grab the dish towel and put pressure on the cut to stop the bleeding.

"You all right, Mum?" he asks.

"I'm okay, toots. Just a little cut." I turn the cold-water faucet on, stick my bleeding finger under the stream, let the water sluice over it. Jaime watches closely. I tweak his nose. "Your mum works better in the dark," I joke. He nods in all seriousness, and then goes back to his dinos to give them the ride of their life.

I wake to the sound of an engine, coughing, hesitating. It's dark. I look at the illuminated clock numbers. 12:15. I get out of bed and look out the window. It's Callahan. What could he want at this time of night? I snatch my flannel jac shirt from the chair and pull it on over my nightgown.

The kitchen floor is icy under my feet. I switch the outside light on. Callahan is on his way up the path. When I hear him open the porch door, I unlock the kitchen door and open it.

"Sorry to wake you," he says. "I tried calling but couldn't get through. Your phone must be off the hook?"

Ben had called earlier in the evening. I'd answered it on the living-room phone and in the middle of the conversation went to check on Jaime and finished the conversation on the kitchen extension. I'd neglected to go back to the living room to hang up the receiver.

"I was reading," he says, "when I realized I'd forgotten to reset the oil-burner switch."

"I have the thermostat on fifty-eight at night," I say, "so I'm used to being a bit chilly." I stand back to let him pass me, and he apologizes again before he disappears down the cellar stairs. I sit at the table, my feet tucked up under my nightgown, wait-ing for the furnace to kick in. When I hear it, I leap off the chair and run on tiptoe to the dining room to turn up the thermostat.

Callahan appears, looking sheepish. "I'm sorry," he says, "I'm usually on top of things."

"It's okay," I say, "though we would have been in a mess if you hadn't remembered. It's supposed to drop to five below tonight."

"It's already below zero," he says. "I can tell by the way my truck's running."

"I could hear the engine hesitating when you drove in," I say. "I'm going to have a glass of milk. Want to join me?"

He takes his hat off, shoves it in his pocket. "No thanks," he says, "but I'll keep you company while you drink it, if you don't mind. Give the truck a chance to run a little longer."

I sit across from him at the table, sipping milk from a jelly-jar glass. "How'd you get into the plumbing business, by the way?" I ask, being polite, wondering what the hell I'm thinking: Do I really want to have a banal conversation at this time of night, especially with a man I already feel uneasy with?

He sits back and runs a hand through hair pressed flat by his hat. "In a kind of roundabout way, I guess," he says. "Eight years ago I was teaching calculus at the Saco extension campus for the university. My wife got pregnant. There were complications. She had to quit her job and lay low. Money was tight so I moonlighted on weekends for a friend, a plumbing and heating contractor. When he decided to sell the business a year or so later, I took a loan out and bought it. I liked working for myself."

"Interesting transition," I say, and mean it. Then, after a little more strained conversation on my part, I decide to be candid. "You do remember the IGA parking lot, don't you?"

He picks up the spoon I've set next to a cereal dish for Jaime. Examines the bowl. "I remembered the moment you opened the door," he says, deliberately setting the spoon back down in its former place. "But I could tell that you didn't want to be reminded, and I figured you had your reasons."

I wait for him to ask my reasons, wishing I'd kept my mouth shut, but he doesn't ask. Instead he says, "I learned a long time ago to let people be. They'll tell you what they want you to know. I try to respect that." Then he cups his hand to his ear and listens. "Well, it sounds like she's running steady now. Better get going. Sorry again that I had to bother you."

After he gets into the truck, I turn off the porch light, feeling both relieved and irritated. I stand at the window and watch his lights disappear down the driveway. What *is* it about someone politely minding his own business that makes you want to confess like some sort of reckless suppliant?

CHAPTER 7

I am beginning to feel anxiety: pressure in my chest, as if an anvil had parted my ribs and risen up through, to set itself squarely on my sternum, a permanent fixture.

I dream. I am trapped. In a grave. Drowning in my own blood. I can see it pumping rhythmically from a gash in my belly. I am acutely aware of my heart beating. I can hear it in my ears. The bass is sonorous. I have no arms. Though I feel intractable pain in fingers I don't possess. Phantom pain. My blood fills the grave. Mixing with red earth. It smells of hot metal.

I see a grunt looking down at me. He clambers along the edge on hands and knees, loosening fine red dust that sifts down, falling on my face. I close my eyes and feel it on my skin like powdered sugar shaken through a sieve. He calls to me. I can barely hear him for the blood in my ears. He wears jungle fatigues. I see this when he leans over and reaches down. A clump of earth gives way under him, plummeting down. I hear it hit and submerge. He comes closer. Dust, the color of old brick, powders his hair. His arms reach. There is dirt in the creases of his knuckles. Finally, the blood covers my face. Everything is red. He tries. I can hear his frantic movement.

Fucking Christ, I'm not going to lose this one. He speaks. I inhale. My own blood. That smells of copper pennies.

I am awake. Sitting up straight. Gagging. I get out of bed. My hair hangs in wet strings. My nightgown is drenched. I snatch at it, trying to pull it over my head. It resists, sticking to my wet skin. When I finally get it off, I hurl it to the floor and head for the bathroom.

In the days that follow, I feel more estranged from the life I live, forcing myself out and about for Jaime's sake, making small talk with the mothers of the children in his play group: Shall we take the kids to the Children's Museum in Portland or to the roller rink? The museum, a *real* cultural event, will most likely win out. Nothing really to be gotten from *roller-skating,* after all. And to complicate things further, last Sunday paper's travel section had a full three-page article on the sacred places of Australia. And whether I wanted to be or not, I was immediately reminded of being in Saigon with Ian for Tet New Year. Standing on Flower Street, adroitly fishing noodles from a cup of *pho,* my adeptness with chopsticks improving, thanks largely to Ian's teaching and his humor and encouragement, saying "Good on you" when I managed to grasp the snaky noodles and get them into my mouth in one shot. After this triumph, sticky rice and prawns were easy.

But that was the beginning of the end for us. The start of the Tet Offensive. That night, waking up to a barrage of gunfire in the distance, Ian got out of bed and pulled his pants on. "I'll be back in a bit," he said. "Just going out to see what's happening." I tried to talk him out of leaving; it was only more of the same, I offered, knowing the argument was weak. A typical Saigon night, I pushed on, probably some besotted grunts on R&R. But there was no conviction behind the words, because I knew that it was not more of the same. You could sense panic in the eruptions of gunfire. There was a feeling of danger, the oppressive humidity seeming to magnify it; everything was eerily quiet except for the sharp crack of M16s.

I gave up. Talking was getting me nowhere. I watched him pull on his shoes. And before he could tie the laces, I got out of bed and stood naked against the door to the room, knowing it was no use, that I was powerless to stop him. He tucked in his shirt and grabbed his rucksack and kissed me on the mouth before easing me aside so that he could open the door. "Stay away from the windows," he said. "I'll be back as quickly as I can."

I sat on the bed and watched the door for a long time after he left, listening to the gunfire, more sustained now, making my throat constrict. I got dressed and headed downstairs, not stopping to lock the door to my room, determined to find out what was happening. I discovered sheer chaos in the lobby, people bleary-eyed, journalists and their cohorts, some still drunk after a night of debauchery in Cholon. And soon there was only me and a few support types, a secretary, some gophers, pale young men, seeming to be hardly out of Journalism 101, their eyes showing fear though they tried to affect nonchalance. They were more pitiful for that.

I left them, children afraid that their mothers would find out they'd wet their beds. At the door I evaded the MP, slipping out onto the street while he tried to reassure a woman dressed in mismatched shirt and slacks that she would be better off in her room rather than trying to find a cab to take her to the airport.

I headed across the park, deciding that I would go to the Reuters office, hoping to find Ian there but knowing the possibility would be slim. Gunfire escalated as I walked; it seemed to come from the vicinity of the embassy.

The park was quiet between the bursts of gunfire, no geckos calling, no chorus of crickets. The air was uncannily still, jacaranda and frangipani trees silhouetted against the moonlit sky looked like elaborate cutouts. Nothing stirred, not a branch or a leaf. The cloying perfume of flowers on the static air somehow incongruous in the dead calm.

I crossed from the park to Tu Do Street, avoiding a military jeep carrying soldiers with the clearly marked *MP* on their helmets. The lights were on at the Reuters office; the steel latticework of the grenade guard rattled as I opened the outside door. I imagined for an instant that I would see Ian at the typewriter or reading whatever had come in over the AP wire. But instead of Ian I found Bao-Long. He looked at me as if I were the wrong person in the right place.

"Have you seen Ian?" I asked. The pleasantries we would have usually indulged in seemed pointless.

"Embassy taken by Vietcong. Ian gone."

I felt my mouth go dry.

"I promise Ian Morris I stay at office until he return," Bao-Long continued. "But I take you back to hotel, Lily, after I finish. You not be out in street. Not safe."

"I couldn't wait at the hotel," I said. "Believe me, I know enough to be careful." I put my hands on my hips, trying to affect a sense of confidence I did not feel.

"Lily, sit in chair, away from door," Bao-Long said. "I finish here."

I sat, feeling sick to my stomach, knowing Ian was close to the fray. I tried to focus on Bao-Long and watched him type with amazing speed, even though he was missing the index finger on his right hand; he'd told us nonchalantly that shrapnel from a bomb had cost him his finger but it was not serious considering he had nine other digits. He was a disciplined journalist; almost nothing would keep him from a story. He and Ian must have felt that someone should stay at the office. Maybe they figured Bao-Long could handle any marauding Vietcong because he was fluent in the language.

After he had filed his story, Bao-Long said it was time to go. He took me by the arm before I could protest, and though we were about the same size, the strength of his determination to deliver me to the Continental was resolute. There was no room for resistance on my part, not verbally and certainly not physically. "No worry, Ian Morris be okay," he said. His certainty gave the impression that he believed that. Ironically, it revealed his concern.

We headed back the way I had come. After we crossed the street to enter the park, we looked behind us and saw black shapes slinking like dogs into the shadows of buildings on Tu Do Street. And then they appeared again, sliding from the darkness, moving with deliberate speed across the street, running low to the ground in our direction. Bao-Long pulled me after him. And in the next instant, he pushed me under the lower branches of a tree and said, "You stay. I talk to them. I come get you after." I squatted under the branches, leaves obscuring my view, sweat rolling down my back and between my breasts and over my face. It stung my eyes and made my skin itch, but I did not move. A kind of qualified fear held me. I stayed like that for some time, listening to gunfire, and there was no relief with the dawn. But not for a second did I doubt Bao-Long would return for me.

Finally, Bao-Long appeared, ducking under the branches and squatting next to me. "Like hell you run," he said to me. "Now!"

It wasn't until we reached the Continental that I noticed his wrist, wrapped in a white handkerchief, blood seeping through. Before I could say anything, he told me, "No worry. I am okay," as if I were a child needing to be protected from the reality of the world. He was insistent: "Now you stay, Lily," he said. "Ian be here directly."

But Ian did not return that morning or the next day, and by then the Tet Offensive was in full swing; the Vietcong had immobilized the entire city.

Bao-Long had asked the South Vietnamese ARVN MP to look out for me (that is, to see that I stayed in the hotel), since his American counterpart was busy trying to keep people calm, and so I accepted that there was nothing I could do but wait. I hung around the lobby waiting in vain for any decisive information. After dark, I stayed out on the balcony—stupidly, I knew—disregarding Ian's warning to keep away from the windows. I smoked and listened to choppers flying over the city, their rotors slicing the soupy air. I knew they were heading to the embassy. I looked out in the direction of the noise, shots being fired in quick succession, followed by return fire. I set my jaw, refusing to give in to fear. By mid-morning the sound of choppers had dissipated, though the gunfire continued to escalate, echoing all over the city, it seemed.

I went inside, closing the louvered doors after me, and lay down on the bed, the sheets clammy from the supersaturated air. Ian's glass sat on the bedside table; it still contained the vestiges of the brackish scotch that he preferred. I turned on my side, got up on one elbow, and picked it up; when I slowly swirled the diluted liquor, I saw movement on the surface, a diminutive blue dragonfly, its diaphanous wings dipping in and out of the liquid. I slipped my finger under it and gently lifted it out. I studied it, watching it try to regain its equilibrium, attempting to lift its wings, first one then the other.

I got up, and with great care I managed to transfer it to a swatch of aquamarine silk that I'd picked up from a tailor for a dress that I'd planned to have made. I set the square of fabric atop the highboy where the fan barely stirred the air. The fragile creature had by then managed to right both wings.

I opened the doors to the balcony and lay down on the bed. And I wondered if I could imagine a way out of this. Something I'd been good at since childhood. And it had served me well, even in Pleiku; when a normal surgical procedure was useless (and because of the extent of trauma they were, more often than not, useless), I'd go in at a different angle or use an instrument unheard-of in abdominal surgery, a homemade threading device, for instance. But in Saigon I had no control over the situation. There were no answers, and when I could think no more, and out of sheer emotional exhaustion, I slept.

It was eerily quiet when I woke. I got up to check on the dragonfly, but it was gone. I convinced myself that it had slipped between the louvers and escaped. I opened the doors to the balcony. The street was empty. The silence was more un-nerving than the gunfire.

I bathed in tepid water. When I came out of the bathroom, I sat on the bed and sipped the scotch from Ian's glass, wanting nothing more than the imagined taste of his mouth.

Ben's clothes smell of wood smoke. He wraps smelt filets in wax paper, then foil. Feeling charitable, I say, "We can have them tonight, if you want."

"That's okay," he says. "I'll sauté them for Jaime and me some evening when you don't feel like cooking. Pick up Chinese for you."

"You're a good guy," I say. "If you give Jaime his bath after dinner, I'll go up and finish stripping the paper. The plaster looks in pretty fair condition so far. I've oiled the woodwork. It's a beautiful color. You ought to go check it out."

"Will do that," Ben says.

After dinner, I head upstairs. I slide a putty knife under a loose strip of paper. It falls away, leaving plaster striated with the grain of old paste. Some spots resist the wide blade. A smaller putty knife would work better. I go downstairs to find one.

Ben is bathing Jaime. I stand in the doorway, waiting for them to finish their conversation before I interrupt to ask if we've got a smaller putty knife. His back is to me, his body blocking my view of our son.

He asks Jaime: "Did you and Mom play in the dark while Dad was gone?"

I feel my neck and face flush. I step away from the doorway.

"Mum cut her finger," Jaime says. "She works better in the dark."

I'm going to bed early, to read, I tell him later. I count on him falling asleep on the couch. Usually nothing wakes him.

Not even the National Anthem or the grainy sound of snow or the pall of gray light.

I hear the shower running downstairs. He'd not fallen asleep tonight. I reach for the bedside lamp. Switch it off. When he comes to bed, he slides in close to me. Curls an arm around my waist. Pulls me close. I breathe slowly. Deeply. Feigning sleep. I wonder how often he interrogates Jaime about me.

I spread peanut butter on a slice of bread. Stop to take a sip of coffee before plopping a mound of grape jelly on the peanut butter. Ben reads the paper. Looks up when I drop the knife in the sink, says, "I'll take Jaime if you want."

"Fine," I say.

I watch him, the way he scans the paper. Paying more attention to the goddamn sale flyers than anything else. You're a prick, I feel like saying, spying on me by interrogating your own kid.

After they leave, I call Dr. Wyman. To see if I can get in sooner. The receptionist says there's nothing open but offers to put me on the cancelation list. I hang up the phone and stare out the kitchen windows. And near the oak trees beyond the driveway, I see something. A child, I think. I cinch the belt of my robe. Knot it. Grab the rubber Wellies standing on newspaper next to the door and pull them on. I move deliberately, closing the doors quietly behind me. Take the steps carefully, then walk across the driveway and over frozen grass that crunches under my boots.

She stands just beyond the trees, her back to me, her small body naked except for a tricornered panty the nurses had fashioned from a towel. The napalm burns covering the skin over the delicate bony wings of her scapulae ooze sanguineous fluid, the smell of flesh seared by jellied petrol unbearably putrid.

Suddenly aware of me, she half-turns. Looks at me for a moment with her dark eyes, but when I attempt to speak, she is gone before I can get the words out. I look after her, know-

ing that I will never be able to leave it behind. Sunsets that ig-
nite the sky. Tracers like falling stars. The blood and shit smell
of death.

I bawl. Just goddamn bawl. Stand with my hands over my
face and bawl, acid tears. Dread building in waves bringing all
the dead back: the girl, the boy from West Virginia, and all the
others whose names I never knew.

And then I hear the sound of a car coming up the drive. I
drag the cuff of my sleeve across my face, swallow and breathe
deeply, wishing I could disappear as handily as the Montagnard child did. It's Callahan. I stand there foolishly. Stock-
still. As if by some miracle he won't see me if I don't move.

He gets out of the van. Calls out, "Mrs. Townsend, what's
the matter?" He strides across the grass, his expression reflecting my absolute lack of composure. He looks at me as you
would look at someone whose sanity is questionable, a look
that makes the muscles of my buttocks draw up tightly.
"What's happened?" he asks.

"I'm okay," I say.

"Frankly, you don't look okay," he says.

I attempt to pull myself together, but his goddamn expression, his obvious concern, undoes me. Tears run anew. I hate
myself for feeling crazy and I hate him for being witness to it.

"Jesus," he says, "has something happened to your boy?
Your husband?"

I shake my head no, and he puts his arms around me, and I
find myself responding instinctively for a moment, resting my
cheek against his chest until I become conscious of my runny
nose, and when I pull away I see a shiny string of snot on the
placket of his shirt.

I feel shame. The hot-faced shame of a child.

"Sorry," I say. "Sorry."

"About what?" he asks. "No need to feel sorry."

I start for the house and he follows me until I say, "Please.
I'll be okay. I just need to be alone."

I lock myself in the upstairs bathroom until I hear his truck start.

Callahan never mentioned the episode, other than to ask, nonchalantly, how I am feeling. Like I'm walking a goddamn tightrope, I feel like saying. But I don't. I try to avoid him. I am giving the performance of my life, acting the part of mother and wife, perusing the aisles of the IGA, sorting laundry, poaching eggs, tenderizing London broil, reading to Jaime. Making myself respond to any overture that Ben makes.

Now as I sit in the shadows of the children's reading room, below stained-glass windows, Jaime in a child's chair at a child's table, scanning the pages of a storybook, I can feel fear, a kind of involuntary expansion: like ice forming internally, threatening to crack. I know that if I screw up, it is Jaime who will be in jeopardy.

More and more I think about the mothers who lost their sons in Vietnam, how they must have lived in terror as they watched the evening news, footage of the aftermath of a fire-fight, grunts hustling the dead out, running low toward the chopper, everyone covered in mud. Some must have avoided the news altogether, afraid they'd see their own sons being carried out, bodies gone slack in the middle, heads slung back, faces crude and Picassoan from the odd perspective of the camera.

"It looks like someone ate something weird," Jaime says, pointing to an ochre stain in the middle of the page he's looking at. I get up from the child's seat I've managed to perch on. To get a closer look.

"Hot dog," I say, "with mustard?"

He giggles and says, "That makes me hungry."

I squat next to him. "Give Mummy a kiss," I say. He holds my face, his small hands warm, smelling of wax crayons. When he kisses me he makes a loud smacking sound.

CHAPTER 8

It's Rachel's birthday. I have suggested we have a small celebration. Here. It is in my best interest. I have to play down the notion that I'm antisocial, odd, a woman whose past experience has irrevocably warped her. Made her somehow unreliable, weird, someone who can't be trusted with children.

I hear Rachel in the living room, laughing. She must be talking to a man. The laughter verges on soprano, the notes held too long. Rachel goes all coy around men. Pulls her fingers through her long hair and makes sexual innuendos if she's had a little to drink.

I carry a tray of liqueurs into the dining room: B&B, Grand Marnier, and Cointreau. Set them on the oak sideboard. Stand at the threshold of the living room. Ask who would like an after-dinner drink.

Three out of eight people decline; two of the three are Rachel and Ben, who seem to be in deep conversation.

Philip looks at them and back at me and throws his hands up. "I'll help you serve," he says.

After we have delivered the delicate long-stemmed glasses, I ask if anyone wants more cake. Rachel has evidently gone to freshen up. Ben is standing by himself next to the fireplace.

He gestures to me, making it clear that he can't eat another crumb.

People are winding down. Four of the guests, friends of Rachel's and Philip's, are tucked side-by-side on the sofa. They look to me like Jaime's Fisher-Price people, sitting socked into the same car atop the Fisher-Price Ferris wheel, their eyes vacant black dots. They have overindulged, too much food and drink, the heat of the fire making them sleepy. One woman stifles a yawn. "We better get going," she says. She stands up, smooths the back of her dress, and picks up her empty glass. Her husband follows suit, as does the couple sitting next to them, which leads to an exodus.

Rachel appears in a timely fashion, to hug and kiss and thank everyone. Ben gets coats from the hall closet and people congregate near the door. Philip and I stand back and watch, and when the last couple are creating a three-way hug with Rachel, I head for the kitchen, and Philip follows me.

"Nice of you to do this," he says.

"Other than planning it," I say, "I can't take a lot of the credit. I prepared the salad and hors d'oeuvres—the entrée and the cake came from Glennda's."

"You're a good joe just the same," he says.

I smile at his use of the word *joe*. I feel like a fraud accepting praise. I did, after all, have an ulterior motive.

I pull out the lower rack of the dishwasher and Philip says, "What can I do to help you?"

"You can put the booze under the cabinet," I say.

He methodically goes about his task, and when he's done I ask him to put water on for tea.

I finish rinsing and stacking the dishes, and when I turn to speak to Philip I see that he has fallen asleep in the chair, his chin resting on his chest, his tea untouched on the table in front of him. He looks childlike, vulnerable, amazingly oblivious. I dry my hands and head for the dining room to collect the dirty table linen.

I don't bother with the light, so neither Ben nor Rachel sees me. They are kissing. Ben has a cordial glass in each hand. Rachel's arms are around his neck. I watch Ben's right arm slip around her waist, the stem of the glass held between his fingers. The back of my neck goes numb and prickly for a moment. I leave the tablecloth and napkins.

Philip is snoring. I take a mug from the cupboard. As I reach for the tea, Rachel comes into the kitchen. "Oh, look at this, would you," she says, "it's *my* birthday and guess who gets pissed?"

I turn to watch her tug her husband's hair and kiss his temple. She goes from one man to the other in a matter of minutes without the slightest hint of guilt.

Philip yawns, blinks. Reaches for her hand. "Sorry," he says.

After they leave, and well after Ben has gone upstairs, I go to bed. But he is not asleep. He moves close and puts a hand on my breast. Too tired, I tell him, too goddamn tired.

I decide to let it go. They were drinking, after all. People do things they would otherwise not do, when they're drinking. I'm more concerned about his interrogation of Jaime.

They've gone off for the afternoon, to a movie. I picture them driving to the theater, Ben talking about the film for a minute before segueing into "What has Mom been doing?"

I sip warm ginger ale and focus on pressing crumbs from a banana–peanut butter sandwich into a plate that depicts a goose in a velvet vest. I avoid gazing out of windows. I don't want to see the small exposed shield of breastbone or the curved bars of her stark white ribs.

It is peaceful down in the furnace room, copper piping overhead glowing like new pennies in the half-light. I sit cross-legged on the dirt floor, feeling the dampness permeate the bones of my pelvis. Just for a few minutes, I promise myself. I'll sit here. Feel safe. All the time knowing that what I'm doing is perilous.

Callahan brought me a book of poetry: *The New England Enlarged Anthology of Robert Frost's Poems,* a hardbound volume, the spine frayed, bottom and top, some of the pages turned over at the corner. He frequents, he says, a used-book shop in Portsmouth. "Thought maybe you'd be interested." He'd nodded at the book in my hands.

I knew right away why he gave it to me. I still felt shame when I remembered him holding me in his arms out in the driveway, my nose running, snot on his shirt. I think he wanted to help me somehow. And let's just say I was not exactly open to frank discussion. So this was his way of doing what he could. I wasn't surprised that he read poetry, though I'm not sure how many poetic plumbing contractors you'd find. But it seemed consistent with his character.

That afternoon, after he'd left for the day, I found myself at the table where the Frost book was perched on top of a batch of catalogs, L.L.Bean, Eddie Bauer, Burpee Seeds, current and not so current. I opened up the book to the middle and began to leaf through, recognizing poems I'd read for a high-school English class: "Mending Wall," "The Wood-Pile," and, of course, "The Road Not Taken."

I paged from the back, reading indiscriminately a stanza here and there, flipping to the front, stopping to read "Home Burial." About the death of a child. The disparate ways that grief holds sway over the woman, the mother, and the man, the father. The woman saying: *What had how long it takes a birch to rot / To do with what was in the darkened parlor.* The image of what was in the darkened parlor chilled me. I closed the book. Put it apart from the catalogs so I'd remember to give it back to Callahan, the unease I already felt around him only intensified by what seemed his too-intimate knowledge of my sense of loss.

Jaime's breath smells fruity with fever. Good old otitis media again, both ears this time. On the heels of the flu. He's had a dose of ampicillin. I can feel it stick between my fingers as I rock him. It is bubble-gum pink and, according to Jaime, nasty-tasting. I use all my powers of persuasion to convince him to take it. His limbs spill over my lap, his head resting in the crook of my arm is heavy, his hair, curling with perspiration, the color of wet straw. I gather him in my arms and feel warm drool drip onto my thigh as I stand. He twitches as I lay him on the cool sheet. I cover him and go back to the chair. Close my eyes and rock.

I watch from the kitchen window as Callahan spreads a blueprint or schematic or whatever over the hood of his truck. He runs a finger over it, stopping to make sure his apprentice, an acne-ridden boy, has gotten it. The boy says something and reddens. Callahan slaps him on the shoulder, apparently affirming his answer.

They come to the back door and knock. I open the door.

The boy blushes and says, "Good morning." When his acne goes, he'll be astoundingly handsome, I think.

Callahan sends him downstairs, telling him he'll be right along. "We'll finish up today," he says to me. "Be back at the end of the month. Can't do the outside connection till then."

"Okay," I say.

He heads for the door and I say, "Oh, by the way, I'm amazed at the water pressure. I didn't expect it. A perk."

"Glad to know it makes you happy," he says, his tone businesslike. He disappears down the stairs, closing the door behind him, leaving me wondering if I'd done something to offend him or if he was just plain distracted by too much work.

It was my turn to have play group. Everything went fine until the last child was picked up by her mother. She forgot her Pooh Bear, so Jaime went tearing after them, bear in hand, then fell on the walk that had become a sluice of spring snow. He cut his chin badly enough to need suturing.

So here we sit in the ER, Jaime in my lap, wincing every time the nurse tries to swab the laceration with Betadine. I feel Jaime's warm head press against my chest; he's trying to escape the sponge saturated in the brown solution. "Okay, sweetie," the nurse says, "let's give you a little break." She disappears behind the curtain, and Jaime snuggles into me. "Well, Jaim'," I say, "if it's not one thing it's another."

The ER visit triggers a rash of nightmares. I dream nightly of Pleiku, of mists that rise, strangely tangible, creating walls that aren't walls. Quite. As they have in the past, the dreams come unbidden. You hunker down and wait them out, getting used to the stink of their aftereffects—bedclothes drenched, hair hanging in salty strings, sweat slathering your inner thighs, running down the bony channel between your breasts. And you reel out of bed and peel off your nightclothes.

Even now, wide awake, as I watch a band of light stretch along the horizon, I cannot wrench myself away from what the dreams bring me. I remember the grunt who'd come in not long after I arrived at the 71st EVAC. "I stopped taking those malaria pills 'cause they gave me the shits," he told me. And maybe because I was new and obviously green, he trusted me and told me a story, one that became more plausible as time went on. He'd been ordered to a listening post, so had hunkered down under the triple canopy, tiers of greenness that made the night absolute. "After a few hours," he said, "I could see in the dark. I could fucking see in the dark, and I watched these weird shapes rise up out of the undergrowth in front of me. They rose up slowly and began to spin. And they became women, gook women." He'd looked at me hard then, daring me not to believe him. "They were dancing. Fucking A, they were dancing. To gook music. I could see their hands floating over their heads. Like little white birds." He stopped to light a cigarette, snapping open his Zippo one-handed. "I could smell the flowers they had in their hair," he said. "But listen to this—and you're not gonna believe me, but I swear to God it's true—a bunch of gooks rose up behind them, and I couldn't smell the flowers anymore. Only that evil-smelling fart-stink of rotting jungle." He looked at the ash growing fat and dusky on his cigarette, looked at it as if it were alive. "Those bastards hung back for a while, and the women moved like they were in a dream. All I could do was watch. And as the music got faster, the women danced faster. And I had this fear in my chest, 'cause I knew something bad was gonna happen. They were in some kind of frenzy, the women. Like the dancing had made them drunk. No, not drunk. Intoxicated. You know. And just when that happened, those fuckers came up on those women and they fucking lopped off their heads. Even as they danced. I heard it. Heard the blades of their machetes slice through the muscle and bone of those long beautiful necks." He was quiet for a moment, his face glistening—malarial night sweat. He flicked the cigarette ash and stared at the floor. "The smell of blood was awful. Warm blood. It made me gag and puke."

I didn't tell him what I thought, that his temp had spiked out there, while he was on that mission, making him delusional. Instead, I told him that I believed him. Because he was convinced that it really happened. There was no point arguing it. He was too sick. "And I'm not going back out there," he said. "If I have to blow a few of my toes off, I will."

By week five at the 71st, I began to believe that maybe that grunt wasn't delusional, that maybe there was something mad about the Highlands. Sometimes I couldn't sleep and I'd get up and stare out into the mist, and if I stood long enough, I'd see things—fleeting things. One night I saw the undulation of stripes low to the ground, and just as I was trying to talk myself out of what I might be imagining, I saw tufted ears and the shadow of a great head. I froze, and the mist reconfigured itself, becoming opaque again, giving cover to whatever skulked within it. Some minutes passed before I was able to shake myself loose from the dread that held me.

I never discounted anything I heard after that. Beyond the 71st, where the smarmy pop of AFRVN played almost continuously, a hauntedness abided.

CHAPTER 9

Dr. Irving saunters into the room, the rattle of the food cart like some derelict train coming down the hall making his soft hello nearly inaudible. Jaime covers his head with the top sheet and giggles. The little boy in the next bed follows suit. Dr. Irving sits on the end of the bed, catches Jaime's left foot, and tickles his toes.

"This guy's ready to go," he says to me. "I checked his ears earlier this morning while you were showering. Things look good. You can take him home anytime."

I feel incredible relief. Three nights of sleeping, or mostly not sleeping, in a lounge chair has nearly driven me round the bend. The pediatric isolation unit across the hall brought back memories of napalmed grunts and Montagnards alike; Crispy Critters, we called them. When I couldn't sleep, I stood in the doorway of Jaime's room and watched the flurry of activity: IV poles wheeled frantically down the hall, bottles of IV solution clanking; covered trays of sterile instruments, nurses gowning-up in the outer chambers of isolation, shaking excess powder off sterile latex gloves before snapping them on.

When I crawled into the lounge chair, and covered myself with a flannel bath blanket, and closed my eyes, I saw them,

Montagnard children, glassy-eyed and shocky. I questioned the existence of a God the first time I saw small fingers burned to bone.

At the first stoplight after the hospital, I feel a chain of hives encircling the base of my throat, draping in strands over my breasts, like the strings of a finely beaded necklace. I'll have to dose myself with Benadryl when I get home. Jaime is already asleep in his car seat. The high adventure of his hospitalization has taken its toll. I turn on the radio, keeping the volume low.

By the time I reach our driveway, the rash has flared beyond the angle of my jaw. As I pull up in front of the barn-turned-garage, I see tire tracks in the wet grass, disappearing around the side of the building. Wondering why Ben would drive around back, I get out of the car, closing the door gently, so as not to wake Jaime.

I follow the tracks through grass so green that it makes me squint. The ground, saturated with rainwater, makes a sucking sound as I walk, pulling at my shoes. I move closer to the foundation to avoid pools of water shot with brilliant green spikes. When I come around the barn, I see Rachel's car parked close to the shingled outbuilding we use as a potting shed. I stupidly stare at the car for a few seconds and then feel oddly distant as if I'm floating high above my body, looking down on myself standing next to the polished Volvo.

Ben didn't expect us home until tomorrow.

I open the driver's-side door of the Volvo and slide in. The gray leather upholstery is uncomfortably cold, chilling me. Rachel's bag is on the passenger seat. Apparently in such a hurry she forgot it. I pick it up as if it were something alien, the buttery-soft kidskin obscene, the hide of a freshly slaughtered calf. Then I tip it upside down, the contents tumbling to the floor: wallet, checkbook, compact, embossed leather address book. And I lay on the horn, just lay on it. Seconds pass, the sound deafening, reminding me of air-raid warnings, of how we'd climbed under our desks in grade school, the smell of floor wax and mucilage pervasive.

I jump when he opens the door, but I do not ease up on the horn. He reaches in, pulls my hand away from the wheel, and holds it firmly in his. I don't resist, only use my right hand to depress the horn once more.

After he has seized both my hands and the quiet is startling, he speaks: "It's not what you think."

He blinks. And gazes over my right shoulder, apparently finding it difficult to look at me. "She just came to talk," he says.

His shirt is misbuttoned. I try to wrestle free, but he holds my wrists so tightly that I feel the tingle of impaired circulation. "You're hurting me," I say.

"Don't jump to conclusions," he says.

I don't answer him. He lets go of my hands and moves away from the door. I rub my wrists and then, with perfect grace, I get out of the car.

He steps back.

And I step forward. And slap his face. The print of my hand is beefy-red on his cheek. His eyes water.

I strike the trunk of the Volvo with my fist and remember Jaime.

I have slept in the third-floor bedroom for over a week. I can hardly bear to look at Ben. I go to bed early, after putting Jaime down. Sometimes I smoke in the dark, the windows open wide. After I'd slapped his face, and bruised the heel of my hand hitting Rachel's Volvo, I'd headed for town, Jaime, amazingly, still asleep. I got gas at the Mobil station and bought a pack of Tareytons, then drove around aimlessly till he woke up.

During the day, when Jaime is napping, I venture to the dark cellar, where I sit on an old crate and smoke. Trying to figure it out. I don't fear losing Ben. If I'm honest with myself,

I have to acknowledge that I only gravitated to him after the war because he was safe, a known. With him I didn't have to explain anything. And because he loved me, I knew he'd be patient. And I guess he was, for longer than I should have expected.

No, I don't fear losing Ben. I fear losing Jaime.

I look up at the sheaves of copper piping overhead and watch plumes of smoke float like mist in shafts of weak light. When I close my eyes, I see Pleiku, sun burning through noon fog, revealing all manner of green, shades soft and deep. Greens so sublime it would break your heart.

I watch from the front hall as Callahan's van climbs the driveway and eases into the space next to the Peugeot. Fuck. He knocks at the back door and for a moment I think I'll not answer. I don't want to see anyone, and that includes the plumbing contractor.

As I pass through the dining room, I catch a glimpse of myself in the mirror above the sideboard. Dull lank hair. Bangs a greasy fringe separated in the middle by a cowlick, obvious only when I haven't shampooed for a few days. And God, my face, pale as raw pie dough.

Callahan knocks again just as I come into the kitchen. When I open the door, I can see that he tries not to react to my appearance.

"Sorry to bother you," he says, "but I didn't want to just walk in. I called last night to let you know I'd be coming, but there was no answer. Figured you were out for the evening."

No such luck, I want say. But, of course, I don't. His eyes are weirdly penetrating. They're almost too blue, a kind of freak mutation. I want to tell him to save his scrutiny for the finer points of plumbing and lay off staring at me. But instead I say, "It's okay, but from now on you don't need to knock. Just let yourself in."

I move aside so he can pass.

He opens the cellar door, but before heading down the stairs he says, "Oh, by the way, how's your boy? Your husband told me he was in the hospital."

"Minor surgery," I say. "Tubes. His ears. He's doing fine."

"Good," he says, "good."

And before he tries to engage me further, I excuse myself and head upstairs.

There's little talk at dinner. Ben speaks perfunctorily. Is cool in tone and demeanor. Which mystifies me. You would think he'd be contrite. After all, he's the adulterer.

I begin to clear the table. Ben stands, takes his plate to the sink, and on the way out of the room ruffles Jaime's hair. Good, I say to myself, who needs you?

Jaime comes to the sink, the bread basket a handy carryall for his dinosaurs. "They need a bath," he says. So I pull a chair up and let him have first dibs at the thick meringue of foam.

After the dishes are done, I take him upstairs for a bath. The water pressure astounds me after living with dribbling faucets all these years. I sit on the windowsill and flip through Jaime's book while he maneuvers an empty shampoo bottle as if it were a Polaris submarine. I've taken another Benadryl, the hives persisting, so I feel dry-mouthed and drowsy. I straighten up, push my hair back, and say, "Here we are: Toad's adventures, where we left off. Shall I read a bit?"

"That'd be good, Mum," Jaime says, letting the shampoo bottle that he's holding under the surface pop up. "But can I see the pictures too?"

I leave the sill and sit on my knees next to the tub, open the book wide so he can see the drawing of Toad disguised as a washer-woman, wearing hat and dress, shoes and shawl, standing on the grassy bank of a canal, having a conversation with a barge-woman.

"Toad's still trying to get home," I say. "Trying to hitch a ride."

"He makes an ugggly woman, doesn't he, Mum?" Jaime observes.

"He's quite desperate, I'd say, and, yes, he's no beauty. Are you ready?"

Jaime nods enthusiastically. I read then, in my most authentic barge-woman voice: " *'What a bit of luck,' observed the barge-woman.*

" *'Why, what do you mean?' asked Toad nervously."* And for some reason I make Toad a contralto.

" *'Well,' the barge-woman says, 'there's a heap of things of mine that you'll find in a corner of the cabin. If you'll just put them through the washtub as we go along, it'll be a real help to me.' "*

Jaime laughs at Toad's face, the look of distress at the prospect of having to deal with the barge-woman's laundry.

"Looks like your mum, doesn't he?" I say. "When she has to wash your stinky socks."

At this Jaime plugs his nose and submerges.

And of the two of us, I don't know who enjoys the irreverent Toad more.

I hear Ben on the stairs. I reach to turn on the bedside lamp, then carefully stub out my Tareyton in a scallop shell I use as an ashtray.

He knocks.

"It's open," I say.

He comes in and stands just beyond the threshold, squinting theatrically as curling tendrils of smoke drift past him into the well of the hall.

I preempt him. "I don't need a lecture," I say, "particularly about smoking."

He slides his hands into his pockets. "Believe me," he says, "I have no intention of lecturing you about smoking. We have more important things to talk about."

I push myself up in bed, sit straight-backed against the headboard, and fold my arms across my chest.

He takes his hands from his pockets and absently adjusts the tab of his belt, sliding it under a loop. "I've decided to move out," he says. "You obviously don't want me here."

"Don't try to make this my fault," I say. "I was in the hospital with Jaime. You were the one here, screwing Rachel."

He blinks rapidly, rubs his hands together. "You better think again," he says, "if you figure you have no responsibility in this. Whatever went on over there did a real number on you, Lily. Oh, you go through the motions all right, but you know what? You're not really here. It's like living with an automaton. You cook, you clean. You spread your legs and act accordingly. But you're not here.

"I used to think given time you'd get over it. But it's only gotten worse, the nightmares, the reclusiveness, the way you shut yourself up in the dark."

He's quiet then, his jaw muscles quivering, his throat making a distinct clicking sound. I feel a numbness creep up the back of my neck and under the skin of my scalp.

"And you know what scares me most, Lily?" he says. "How you've affected Jaime. He hears you prowling around after you've had one of your nightmares and gets up to see if you're all right and you don't even know that he's there. You're still listening for the sound of a rocket, or taking care of some poor bastard who got caught outside the wire.

"And that little boy's frightened for you."

I tuck my fists under my arms and deny to myself that there's any truth in what he says. Any.

He looks at me and it's clear what he's thinking, that I'm an object of pity. Damaged goods.

"The sad thing," he says, "is that Jaime's more a parent to you than you are to him."

You sonofabitch, you goddamn sonofabitch, I think, telling myself not to react, not to let him have the satisfaction of goading me into a response. But my heart pounds in my ears, and it's only when he comes closer to make a point that I can hear through the din of rushing blood: "And while we're being perfectly honest, and because there's no point in trying to pretend anymore, I should say that Rachel's the best thing that's happened to me in years. I'm only sorry I have to hurt my brother."

He looks at me then as if he's waiting for me to concur, and I cannot believe his gall. My rage crackles in my temples like static, and finally I launch myself off the bed and fly at him. "Get out, you bastard!" I scream. "Get out!" And I shove him, and batter him with my fists, my knuckles thumping the hard bone of his sternum. My fury momentarily disorienting him, he throws his arms up to shield himself and stumbles backward. When he regains his balance he grabs my arms and shoves me hard and I crash into the dresser.

I squat, dazed, a bottle of Chanel and a half empty tin of Bufferin in my lap. I taste blood as I reach up to right a bottle of cough syrup that's about to roll off the dresser and into my lap along with everything else.

He looks at me and for an instant I think I see regret. But he says nothing, and then very deliberately he leaves the room. I hear him grabbing the banister as he takes the stairs, the palm of his hand smacking the mahogany.

And I am more afraid than I have ever been in my life.

I bend over to wrap my hair in a towel, then open the bathroom door. I hear Jaime's slippered feet whisper over the polished wood floor. He appears in the doorway. "Uncle Philip's here," he says.

Goddammit, I don't need this, I think. To Jaime I say, "Tell Uncle Philip I'll be right down." I throw my robe on and tie it tightly at the waist.

Philip is standing at the sink, looking out the window. He turns when he hears me. He looks like hell, his face creased as if he's been sleeping with a waffle iron—he's probably slept in his car, his head lolling between seat and window.

"How long has it been going on?" he asks.

"Right to the point," I say. I squat and peer under the table where Jaime is tending his brood of dinosaurs. "How about checking out *Sesame Street,*" I say. It takes me a moment to stand straight. My right hip is stiff, bruised from waist to thigh from colliding with the dresser.

I watch Philip watching Jaime as he dallies. "Let me help, Jaim'," I say. I gather his stuff while he balances a mug of dry Cheerios.

After I've settled him in front of the TV, I take a deep breath, bend to rewrap the towel around my wet hair, and wince when I straighten.

Philip is sitting at the table, his forehead resting on his tightly clasped fingers.

"You look like you could use a cup of coffee," I say, "and something to eat."

As I make a fresh pot of coffee and slide slices of oatmeal bread into black toaster slots, he talks. His voice is flat and thready. I listen to him and watch the coiled toaster elements take on an orange-red glow. He slams the table with his fist, startling me, and I look up to see his anger, finally: "I'm just gonna leave them to it. That's what she wants. That's what she'll get. But we're gonna have to sell the fucking business or they're gonna have to buy me out, because I'm not going to work with that bastard brother of mine."

I pour the coffee slowly, careful to keep loose grounds from escaping into the cups. Despite that, when I pick them up I notice that one has a clump of grounds floating on the surface like magnetized iron filings. I claim that cup for myself and set the other in front of Philip.

He looks up at me, his chin resting on his knuckles, the hair on his hands glinting like fine copper wire. "He wasn't happy with you, you know. Never came right out and said it. But it was apparent. You kind of lost it, didn't you? In Vietnam."

This is plainly an accusation. He is making me culpable. Wants it to be my fault. Not Ben's or Rachel's. I get up from the table. Dump my coffee into the sink. "I see no point in continuing this conversation. I didn't put a gun to his head. Make him fuck Rachel."

"Forget it," he says. "It really doesn't matter a good goddamn now, does it?" He stands then, snatches his coat from the back of the chair, and stalks out.

I watch him back down the driveway. In a sort of suicidal maneuver he fishtails out into the road.

That was a lousy thing for me to say. And if I thought I had an ally I was sure as hell wrong.

It's nearly dark when I back down the driveway. As I wait for a car to pass, I glance in the rearview mirror and see Jaime yawn and rub his eyes with balled fists. He should be in bed. And I should be trying to figure this out in a reasonable fashion. Should be.

I am more and more aware of how small my world is. Most of my connections have to do with Jaime, directly or indirectly: the mothers of the children in his play group; the ENT man and his receptionist, a woman with mustache and chin whiskers, who never fails to call me "dear"; the librarian who sits behind a metal desk in the children's reading room, her hair arranged like soft ears, falling rabbitlike over her bony shoulders; the pharmacist who's become more than an acquaintance, calling me "Doc" and seeing to it that we get the meds for Jaime when we need them, no questions asked.

Small world. Growing even smaller. I can't even make myself call my mother. Or my brother. I'm afraid they wouldn't be surprised: Ben's left, I'd say, and I think he's going to try to take Jaime away from me. They would defend me and do what they could to help. But they would not be surprised: I'd hear it in their voices, the resignation, especially my mother's, though God knows she'd always been there for me.

I'd stayed with her the night before my wedding because the ceremony was going to be in the back orchard. I got up to find her up to her elbows in flowers. Explosions of yellow-eyed daisies and lupin, all purply-blue blossoms, filling the deep sink.

She looked over her shoulder and said, "There you are. I thought I was going to wake you up." She put her scissors down and eyed me for a moment, in the way only a mother can. "I'd forgotten how beautiful you are," she said. "You're going to be a lovely bride."

"Even with these bags?" I said, gingerly touching the sleep-swollen skin under my eyes.

"At your age," she said, "nothing's permanent. By the time you get out of the shower, they'll have vanished."

"I'm not all *that* young, Mum."

"It's relative," she said, "believe me."

I poured myself a cup of coffee and sat in the battered red rocking chair that always reminded me of my childhood.

To razz her, I said of the flowers, "Those are gorgeous. You haven't been trespassing on your neighbor's land again, have you?"

"You're so suspicious, Lily," she said, "and for your information, I asked John this time. Caught him as he was leaving for work. He said to tell you he's looking forward to the wedding."

"Have you ever thought about asking him to dinner, Mum?" I said to her.

"Oh, I don't know about that, Lily," she said. She tucked a strand of hair behind her ear. Wiped her hands on her khakis, then wrestled with an arrangement, a work in progress, taking stems of lupin out and adding daisies.

"Mum," I said, "it's only dinner. We're not talking about sleeping with him, for goodness' sake."

She made a face, a kind of exaggerated wince. "Lily, please," she said, "you're embarrassing me. The last thing I want to talk to you about is dating."

"You mean sex?" I said.

"That too, my dear daughter," she said, with some irony.

"You should take lessons from Aunt Fay," I said.

"Three husbands in ten years?" she said. "I love my sister, but her appetite amazes me."

And for some reason that remark made us both howl with laughter.

"Appetite," I said, after I'd caught my breath, my stomach hurting from laughing so hard. "God, Mum, *you'd* do better talking about peanut butter cookies. And who's embarrassing who now, anyway?"

"You started it, Lily," she said, "and you're slowing me down here. You want flowers for the banquet tables, don't you?" She dried her eyes with the dish towel and patted her chest, a gesture of relief. "Go take your shower," she said. "You're awfully relaxed for someone who's getting married in a few hours."

I don't know why that conversation affected us so, made us laugh with the abandon of adolescent girls. Maybe it was the sense of uneasiness we both felt. Though we'd avoided talking about it, we both knew why I was marrying Ben. I know my mother was hoping that it would work out, that she could take solace in the fact that a good man would love and look after me. Share the burden, the worry and responsibility, for her sometimes fucked-up daughter.

And it was because of this that I loathed the idea of telling her that she was, again, alone with that burden.

I'd promised myself I wouldn't smoke in front of Jaime. But panic hums in my ears. Vibrating like a high-tension wire. Just one, I tell myself. I depress the cigarette lighter and rummage in my bag, feeling for the cellophane-covered pack. Bits of tobacco crackle and flame as I light the tip. I roll down the window and blow smoke into the night. I hear peepers trilling and remember the lavish fretwork of frog eggs Jaime and I saw floating in the shallows, glistening in the sun. Now the smells of pond water and muddy banks only seem to heighten my sense of panic.

Jaime says, "Mum, you have a fire on the end of your cigarette." His nonchalance is somehow reassuring.

The tobacco, for some reason, flames up and burns furiously. I take one last drag, igniting a shower of sparks that fall like fiery glitter on my skirt. I slap them out with the flat of my hand. Stub out the Tareyton in the ashtray. And pull over to make sure nothing's smoldering. When I've got things under control, I twist around in my seat. "Sorry about that," I say to Jaime. "Mum shouldn't smoke. I'd be better off sucking my thumb."

Jaime pops his thumb out of his mouth and cocks it like a determined hitchhiker. "You can try my thumb," he says.

In the time it takes to get to the bridge, Jaime's asleep. When we arrive at the intersection of Silver and Greenleaf streets, he is snoring. Flowering chestnuts obscure the library parking lot. I realize I've passed it, in fact, so I turn around and double back. The driveway is more visible from this direction.

When I pull in I realize it's Wednesday. The library is open on Tuesday and Thursday evenings. Not Wednesday evenings. I cross my wrists over the wheel and rest my forehead against them. Now what? I put the Peugeot in gear and back up, checking the rearview.

I head in the opposite direction of home, passing a stretch of houses built at the turn of the century, a multitude of turrets, mullioned windows, stained-glass sidelights lit from behind, a shimmer of color: vermilion, tangerine, turquoise. Their lawns, once broad and tree-lined, have been sliced away like a sheet cake at a fiftieth-wedding-anniversary party, giving way to a four-lane boulevard in the name of urban renewal. The half-light of dusk restores the houses to their former splendor; wood rot blooming through paint and the odd missing slate shingle, like a missing tooth, are not visible.

Caught up by Victorian architecture, fabulously backlit by a ruddy afterglow, I don't see the cat till it's illuminated by my headlights. A sleek marmalade body, legs scissoring, bearing it forward into the path of the Peugeot. I jam my foot down on the brake pedal. The terrible screech of rubber grabbing pavement is deafening. The force of braking drives my head forward, then back, as if it were mounted on a spring. But it's too late: I have felt the left front wheel strike the soft body.

I sit dazed for a few seconds, then shift in my seat, turning to check on Jaime, ignoring the tingling sensation that runs up the back of my neck, bisecting to converge at either joint of my jaw. "Jaime, are you okay?" His face, softly illuminated by the streetlights that have only now come on, looks ethereal, as if he might fade away right in front of my eyes.

"I'm okay," he says finally, his voice giving him substance. "What was that?"

"Oh God, Jaim', I think I hit a cat." My leg begins to tremble and I realize that I'm practically standing on the brake pedal still. I ease off, feeling the needling of flesh, lack of sensation in my foot.

"I'm going to pull over," I tell him. "Stay in your seat while I check."

"I'll stay here," he says.

I hear the fear in his voice. "Maybe it got across the street. Maybe it's okay," I say. I pull over, cut the engine, and get out of the car.

I am sickened at the sight of the cat, the smell of burned rubber amplifying the visceral static I feel as I squat next to the animal. It is stretched out on its side, head back, revealing a bright triangle of white fur under its chin. Its pose is oddly relaxed, that of a house cat stretched out in the shadows. There is no sign of blood. I slide my hands under the still-warm body and pick it up. Its fur is agonizingly soft. Its weight terrible to bear. Someone loved this cat. I cannot just leave it on the roadside.

I stop to wait for a car to pass and then head for the Peugeot. The driver's-side window is still down. I call to Jaime: "Jaim', can you get out of your seat? We have to find the owner of this cat."

With swift efficiency, Jaime gets out of his car seat, crawls into the front, and manages to open the door. I help him by using my shoulder to lever the door open wider, securing it to keep it from swinging to as he slides out.

He reaches up to touch the cat. "Is it dead?" he asks, his voice a whisper.

"Yes, Jaim'," I say. "I'm afraid so."

We walk along the curb a bit, then step up onto the brick sidewalk. The house closest glows with yellow light, its windows like rectangles of butterscotch-colored cellophane. We find our way up the dark walk and manage the wide run of granite stairs.

The front door, oak, set with an oblong of beveled glass, is illuminated by light spilling from a bay of windows to its right. I support the cat's head in the crook of my left arm and cradle the rest of its body, holding it to my chest. I rap on the door with my free hand.

A woman calls out. And a light goes on, revealing the glossy pale gray floorboards of the porch, the white columns supporting the roof, their Ionic capitals made more distinct by a play of shadow and light, the beadboard ceiling painted a robin's egg blue. The woman, tall with wispy hair the color of ash, makes her way to the door. She fumbles with the lock and, when she opens the door, I see confusion on her face. "I'm sorry to bother you," I say. "But I'm afraid I've had an accident."

The woman looks at the cat and reaches out tentatively as if to touch it, then withdraws her hand. "Oh my, not that bad boy," she says, shaking her head. "He got out on me, and I didn't even know it."

She swings the door open for us. "Come in," she says, "I've got to make a call."

We stand on a faded runner, a Persian. The woman picks up the receiver of the black rotary phone that sits on a diminutive gateleg table. She turns her back to us as she talks. I can't make out what she's saying. When she's through, she pivots around in a surprisingly agile manner and says, "He'll be right over."

"Who?" I say.

"My neighbor up from the carriage house."

We go back out onto the porch to wait, not wishing to upset the woman further.

Hardly a minute or two later, a man comes up the stairs. I can hardly believe my eyes. Callahan.

He doesn't act at all surprised to see me standing there.

"It was only a matter of time," he says. "He was a wild one. A neighbor's cat. They're away for a few days. Mira was taking care of him. He must have slipped out on her."

"I'm so sorry," I say.

When he lifts the cat from my arms, the old woman comes to the door. "I'll take care of it, Mira. I'm sorry it happened on your watch. But it was inevitable. You know that."

"Never even saw him," she says.

"Don't feel badly," he says. "I'll talk to the Simpsons."

After the woman has closed the door, Callahan says to me, "You look a little shook. Why don't you wait here a minute while I take care of this."

We wait in the dark, the old woman having shut the door and switched off the porch light. Without the weight of the cat in my arms I feel strangely untethered. I sit on the top stair and pull Jaime into my lap. "I'm so sorry about the cat," I say. "So sorry."

He reaches up to touch my face. "It's all right, Mum. It wasn't your fault."

The sympathetic tone of his voice makes me think of Ben: "Jamie's more a parent to you than you are to him."

"Let's not say anything to your dad about this," I say.

Callahan appears again, having taken care of the cat. "Why don't you come in for a minute? Till you get your bearings."

Light diffused by panicles of lilac shines over the path to the carriage house. "You live here?" I ask. Stupid question. Because obviously he does.

"Have for about twelve years," he says. "A long time before gentrification. It wasn't fashionable when we bought it; it was affordable."

We follow him as he takes a brick path that winds under an arch of honeysuckle branches. It is treacherous going, the edges and corners of bricks sticking up, having been shifted by frost. The scent of lilac is heady, and becomes more intense the closer we get to the house.

We pass an enormous pair of stable doors, crowned with a sequence of leaded-glass rectangles. "What interesting doors," I say, reaching, really wanting to do nothing more than to thank him for his kindness and tell him I think it'd be better if Jaime and I went home. But I don't. It seems so impolite. After he showed such humaneness, with the old woman and the cat and us.

"My wife found them in a little town above Ellsworth. Bartered with an old farmer for them. Traded my services. I put a shower-tub enclosure in for him and his son."

Beyond the elaborate doors is a nondescript four-panel door. He opens it and stands aside. "After you," he says.

We make our way up the pine stairs that open onto a loft. A gold-eyed Weimaraner sits at the top. He cocks his head and lifts his ears. The stump of his tail beats double-time against the floor.

"This is Max," Callahan says.

Like a polite host, Max comes forward to meet us, softly nosing Jaime's hand, patient when Jaime stops to stroke the velvet of his muzzle.

"He's lovely," I say to Callahan.

The furniture is faded. Under enormous exposed beams it seems to huddle together like timid farm animals.

"If you sit on the sofa, Jaime," Callahan says, "Max'll park himself right in front of you so you can scratch his head."

Jaime does as Callahan suggests, sinking into the cushions. Where there were once covered buttons, there are now only deep indentations, as if the buttons had retreated, like rabbits down a hole. Max does insinuate himself, daintily sniffing Jaime's knees before turning and backing up against the sofa.

"What'd I tell you?" Callahan says.

I am both grateful to and wary of him in this domestic regard. With Jaime occupied, Callahan turns his attention to me: "You look like you could use a drink," he says. "Scotch?"

"Yes, please," I say, amazed at myself. What *am* I thinking? I've run over a cat while trying to figure out my fucking life and now I'm at my plumber's house accepting a scotch?

"Sure thing," he says. "Follow me." He stops at the doorway to ask Jaime if he'd like a glass of juice or milk. Jaime, enthralled with the softness of Max's ears, says, "No," and after a second, "Thank you."

I follow Callahan through a narrow hall, at the end of which I can see glass door fronts, kitchen cabinets illuminated by overhead light. And so busy am I gawking that I nearly run into him when he turns to go into a room immediately to the right of the kitchen.

It is a library of sorts, a long narrow room lined with bookshelves that are crammed with hardcovers running horizontally, topped sporadically with chimneys of paperbacks. Next to a particularly well-used wingback chair is a cardboard carton of old books.

"You're quite a reader," I say.

"Keeps me occupied," he says. "Half belonged to my wife's father. I'm not much good at weeding things out."

That he would be left with the house and everything in it makes me suspect that his wife is dead.

I watch him open a pair of doors under a dry sink painted an oxblood red. He takes out a fifth of scotch, unopened. Turns over a glass, one of the three placed on a lacquered Chinese tray sitting in the sink itself. Before he opens the bottle, I ask if I can use the bathroom and he directs me to a room across the hall.

The closet-size cubicle, lit by diminutive flame sconces mounted on either side of a mirror the size and shape of a porthole, is a study in the use of small spaces. I wash my hands, taking the last drib offered up by a squat liquid-soap dispenser. The slim brass rod above the pedestal sink is draped with a carefully folded gray silk necktie in lieu of a towel. I gently shake my hands over the sink and then wipe them on my skirt. Denim comes in handy at such times. When I look up, I see my reflection in the mirror and for a moment I am startled: I remember my mother saying that I might as well tell the truth because I wear my guilt on my face.

As I leave the bathroom I notice dust along the mopboard. This is a guest bathroom. Seldom used.

Jaime and Max have joined Callahan. They are on the floor, Max with a fluorescent-green tennis ball in his mouth, Jaime with another in his hand.

"This game's called switching." Callahan nods as the swap is made: Jaime throws the ball he's holding, Max lets drop the one in his mouth. Jumps up and snatches the other out of midair as it flies circuitously past him. Callahan passes me my drink. "I took the liberty of adding a little water," he says.

"Thanks." I take the glass and swirl the amber-colored liquid, then sip gingerly and say, "That dog's incredible."

I sit in the wingback chair, on the edge of the seat, since sitting back would give the impression that I am relaxed. Which I am not. But I am grateful for the temporary distraction, the play between Jaime and Max. While Jaime's busy with the dog, I thank Callahan again and ask him what he'll do with the cat.

"The owners will be home tomorrow," he says. "Until then he's resting peacefully in the toolshed."

I am sickened at the thought of the beautiful cat growing cold and stiff in the dark, the smells of the spring night incongruous.

Callahan sees my uneasiness. "It wasn't your fault," he says. "It really was only a matter of time. I'm sorry it had to be you."

When we go to take our leave shortly thereafter, I notice, as Jaime says his good-bye to Max, photographs atop the piano in the living room. A boy. Wavy-haired. Handsome. A child looking strikingly like his father.

I turn to Callahan. "Is that your son?"

"Yes," he says. And in the few seconds it takes him to respond, I decide that the boy's mother must have left, taking him with her, and is not dead.

"We lost him when he was six."

"Oh, I'm so sorry," I say, wondering about his wife, what happened to her. There's still so much of her in this house, her father's books not the least of it.

Callahan stoops to pick up the tennis ball Max has lost interest in. Obviously not wanting to elaborate. I feel my face heat up. I really put my foot in it. "Well," I say, feeling awkward, "we'd better get going."

Max does an almost-itch, his left hind leg cranking frantically in midair, his metal collar tags jangling madly. We all watch. Finally, the leg stops and hangs suspended for a moment before joining its three comrades in the work of supporting the usually elegant animal. Then, with a vigorous shake, Max regains his poise and noses Jaime's hand from his jacket pocket. Jaime, well aware now of what the gesture means, strokes the narrow furrows atop the dog's head.

"Quite a show," I say.

Callahan pats the dog's rump. "You bet."

"Again," I say, "thank you for coming to our rescue."

"I was glad to help," he says.

He follows us down the stairs. "I'll get you to your car," he says. "Walking around here after dark can be perilous."

As we walk toward the boulevard, I remember the weight of the cat in my arms. I am both relieved and pained to see the Peugeot. Max, who has followed us, stands next to the car, waiting patiently for us to take our leave. He yawns with complete abandon, his teeth clicking when his jaws close, making a sort of toothy crocodile sound. "Looks like you've got a tired pooch," I say to Callahan. "Best get him to bed."

CHAPTER 10

Ben has Jaime for the weekend. They're staying at a hotel in Brunswick where Ben has been renting an efficiency suite. Jaime was beside himself with excitement: "Dad's taking me to the pool!" he kept singing. I dug his bathing trunks out. He packed them in a canvas tote along with his dinos, a pair of pajamas, and a toothbrush.

It is our first warm June evening. I sit on the front stairs in the dark, an iris blossom grazing my leg. I touch a ruffled petal. The fist-sized bloom seems to radiate white light. It reminds me of Vietnam.

I don't miss Ben. Don't miss the feeling of being scrutinized, the tightening of gut, muscles contracting in calf and arch. I'll be better off without him. I won't let myself fall into another funk. I'll think only positive thoughts before I go to bed, garrote the source of the dreams. Imagine the Montagnard child back in the Highlands, where, after everyone has gone to bed, starlight is the only illumination. I cup the iris blossom with spread fingers and breathe in its scent. I stand then. Raise my arms high above my head and stretch.

I wake with a start. I feel her. I will have to turn over onto my right side to see her. I slowly disentangle my body from the sheets; they are wrapped tightly around my legs, like a cerecloth.

I see her quite clearly, her gauze wrappings white in the darkness. I remember what he said, the corpsman who found her huddled next to her mother's body. "The corpse looked like a larval sack," he said, "limbs fused to the trunk. Hair and clothes burned away."

I turn. Face the wall. Determined.

I wake feeling stiff. I stretch and encounter resistance, my muscles like thick bands of rubber, dense and tight. I will stick with my strategy, even as I feel the residue of the nightmare settle like grit between my teeth. I wish I hadn't agreed to let Ben take Jaime for the whole weekend.

The bathwater's so hot, I have to sit on my haunches for a bit before lowering my body. I close my eyes and feel my muscles elongate in the warmth.

I rifle through my bag. Can't imagine where I left the checkbook. I try to think. When was the last time I used it? Gloria waits patiently. Double-bags the ice cream as I disgorge the contents of the satchel finally. "Not there," I say. The pile of pens, old grocery lists on envelopes, wallet and loose department-store charge slips, crayons, and paper clips depresses me. I drop everything back into the abyss of the bag and look up at Gloria, her beautifully rouged mouth dramatic against Crisco-white skin.

"I can cover you," she says.

Eighty-two dollars and fifty-two cents. Probably more than she makes in a week. "I can't let you do that," I say. "I'll run to the bank and be right back. All right if I leave the cart over here?" I nod at a space beyond the counter.

"That's fine, Mrs. Townsend," Gloria says. "But I wouldn't mind helping you out."

I thank her again for her kindness and head for Maine Savings, just up the street from the IGA.

———

I got cash and went back to pay for the groceries. I figured the checkbook was at home on the counter or in the pocket of my coat. And then I realized the coat was missing too. The last time I wore it was the night I hit the cat. So.

I walk away from the wall phone, stretch the coiled cord as far as it will go, then walk back and watch it recoil like a snake. I do this a few times before Callahan answers. "I'm sorry to bother you," I say, and then, "Oh, sorry, this is Lily Townsend. I wonder if I left my coat the other night? I can't seem to find it."

"Hold on a minute and I'll have a look," he says.

I can hear the radio in the background. A female news host. I can't make out exactly what she's saying, though I can tell by the rhythm that she's reading from a court transcript, the he-said, she-said deal.

Max barks and Callahan shushes him before picking up the receiver. "It's here," he says. "It was behind the sofa. Must have slid off. I hope Max hasn't been sleeping on it."

"As long as he's not written any checks," I say. "Would you see if my checkbook's in the pocket?"

I hear the slide of acetate and twill. "One checkbook," he says, "with a twenty-dollar bill acting as a marker."

"Finder's fee," I say.

I talk to myself all the way to Callahan's house: You're being paranoid. Do you think Ben's going to take off with Jaime? No. Can he prove you're an unfit mother? No. Not if you get your act together. But it is of little help, this self-talk. It doesn't make the visceral feeling go away, the feeling that seems rooted like a tree in the nether regions of my body. There have been times when I've disregarded my intuition and paid dearly for it and other times when it's turned out to be wrong.

When Callahan answers the door, Max scuttles out to greet

me, wagging his whole body as if it were articulated. He allows me to stroke his fur, which is damp from an apparent bath, before pushing past me to look out the door.

"No Jaime this time, Max," Callahan says. "Sorry."

Max responds by bounding back in and up the stairs as if he has understood Callahan perfectly. He waits on the landing, sitting aristocratically, using the stump of his tail as a kind of rudder, a kind of furred wedge, to keep him aligned on the waxed wood floor. When we reach the top, all aristocratic bearing goes to hell as he winds himself around Callahan in a show of adoration, nails ticking frantically on wood floor. After patting the dog's rump a few times, Callahan tells him to sit. And so he does. I notice a dab of shaving cream pillowed between Callahan's earlobe and jaw as he halfheartedly scolds the dog.

The living room smells of lemon oil and clean, damp dog. "Smells like you've been housecleaning," I say.

"I put things off," he says. "I decided to catch up. Let me get your coat."

He makes me feel slovenly. I realize I've done only the bare minimum for days now: shower, dress: khakis, T-shirts, anything that doesn't need to be pressed. And then the house. I've barely kept up with the dishes and the laundry.

With great delicacy, Max steps onto his mushroom-colored bed, circles tightly a few times, stops, looks at me, and then circles again. Finally, he settles fawnlike into the cushion, which rises up around him, a giant marshmallow. He groans luxuriantly. There is a sort of warm corn-chip smell coming from the bed; actually, there is an effluvium of smells in this corner of the room: warm corn chips, furniture wax, damp dog fur, and vacuum exhaust tinged with some sort of carpet freshener. Scented baking soda, I would guess. So he didn't wash the dog-bed cover, which makes me feel better.

Max adjusts himself again, and as he does he jars the mahogany upright, which glows, so thoroughly has it been polished. I reach out to touch the keys. Keys the color of buttercream. The muscles in the arch of my left foot draw up: I have an image of Jaime learning "Chopsticks" on my mother's harmonium. Christ, stop it. He's only gone for the weekend. But I can't seem to shake the sense of desolation I feel, can't talk myself out of it.

When I look around the room, the order I see only magnifies my own sense of chaos. And I'm afraid. Terrified of losing Jaime. Can't even keep the house clean or focus on tasks at hand, paying bills, watering the plants, registering the car, renewing the subscription for the goddamn *Sunday Globe*.

When Callahan comes back into the room, my coat neatly folded over his arm, I feel a lump in my throat, because he is kind, simply goddamn kind. And when he hands me my coat, I have to fight to keep from crying. I know he can see me struggling. I avoid his eyes and put on my coat, looking down at the buttons as I slip them through the buttonholes. It's your clean house, I want to tell him, the sense of order, and the way you smell like supermarket carnations and the way your goddamn dog is curled up all snug on his bed.

"Lily," he says, his voice even and sympathetic, "what is it?"

I feel tears welling up and running down my face. No sobbing. No sound at all. Only tears running.

"Come, sit over here," he says. And he takes my arm and steers me, like you would an old woman, to the sofa. I sit down, feeling a fool, and he sits in a chair across from me. "What can I do to help you?" he says. His kind tone only makes me feel worse. When I don't answer he says, "Your husband called to tell me to call him at work or at the Executive Inn if I needed to talk to him. Which tells me you two are separated. Is this why you're upset?"

I find myself laughing as tears roll. I reach to pat Max's bony head, since he's gotten off his bed and backed up against my legs. "That's not the problem," I say. "I only wish it were." But there's no way I can tell him what the problem is. No way that I can say aloud that I'm afraid of losing Jaime. I feel sick with shame just thinking about admitting it.

So I don't say anything. Afraid that if I open my mouth I'll completely fall apart. So I stand. As does Callahan. And he touches my shoulder. And I think maybe I could tell him, because I have to tell someone. I fish in my pockets, finding the McDonald's napkin I used for Jaime's hands. I dab my eyes and wipe my nose. And I smell catsup.

And out of the blue, Max barks and makes me jump, and at first I think I've agitated him in some way. But he lopes across the living room to the landing and bounds down the stairs.

"I was expecting someone," Callahan says. "Bad timing, I'm afraid."

"I'm sorry," I say, wishing I could disappear into thin air. "I've got to go."

"Are you sure you're all right?" Callahan asks. "You don't have to leave."

"I'll be okay," I say. Max sits patiently at the door but stands when I start down the stairs, his ears lifting in anticipation. Callahan stops on the stairs behind me as I open the door to find a woman standing there; she is holding a foil-covered bowl, atop which are balanced a half dozen fat biscuits wrapped in plastic. I excuse myself and rush past her. When I get into my car I see her and Callahan watching me from the stoop. I try to demonstrate my sanity by backing into the turn-around with absolute precision.

Once on Silver Street, I look at myself in the rearview mirror. My face is red and swollen. Distorted. I snap the mirror down and tell myself to get a grip. Say aloud, "You're not going to win the battle if you keep this up." I stop at the light, hear music, the thump of bass drums coming from the car in front of me, a baby-blue Bonneville. And then I think of the woman, a fleeting impression: skin, apricot with fine freckling. Hair, voluminous Irish-setter–red hair.

Well, good for him, I think. Good for him.

———

I scrape the remaining peanut-butter batter out of the bowl, thumb it off the spoon, roll it lightly between my palms, and set it on the cookie sheet. Then slide the tines of a fork through flour and carefully press and crisscross it, the last of a dozen. It is suddenly dark, as if the sky has been tilted and emptied of its milky light. I feel bereft without Jaime. So I've made his favorite cookies. They will keep in Tupperware. Though I have never learned to burp the covers properly.

I hear the sound of a diesel engine: Ben's Mercedes. I watch from the kitchen windows as the car pulls up behind the Peugeot, which I've not bothered to park in the barn.

When I open the door, Jaime's there grinning at me. I scoop him up, twirl him around, kiss his face, which smells of butterscotch. "Boy, did I miss you," I say.

Ben comes in, carrying Jaime's bag. "We stopped at the Dairy Queen," he says. "Jaime had grilled cheese and a sundae."

"So that's what I taste on you," I say to Jaime.

He smiles and then rubs the back of his hand over his mouth.

"You better go wash your face."

"Here's your bag," his father says, handing him the green and white canvas bag.

He takes the bag and makes for the bathroom, calling behind him, "I saw the cookies!"

"Peanut butter," I say.

When I turn back to Ben I see by his face that it is hard to leave Jaime. Since the incident, which has branded itself on my brain—the Chanel bottle in my lap, the metallic taste of blood in my mouth—we are wary of each other. I feel like an animal that's been maimed by one much bigger and stronger. So I know enough to stay in my own territory. To be cunning. To try to find a way around the source of struggle without being bloodied.

"Maybe you'd like to take him Wednesday evening," I say. "I realized this weekend how hard it is to be without him."

I feel like I'm making the ultimate sacrifice. If he has Jaime on Wednesday evening, it will mean that I'll be alone. But I know it behooves me to be rational, to make it difficult for him to build a case against me.

"Let me think about it," he says.

I am surprised at his response. But I just shrug my shoulders.

He says good-bye, opens the door, hesitates a moment. "By the way, I've talked to an attorney. I'd like to get this over with."

"So would I," I say. I stare at the door after he's left and suspect that he and Rachel have been involved a lot longer than I figured.

I turn off the fluorescent tube over the sink, putting an end to the annoying flicker, and before heading upstairs I lock the door. Fuck you, I say, at the exact moment that Ben's car lights wash over the kitchen cabinets. Fuck you.

At noon, I decide to pack up Jaime for a trip to the library. We stop off at the drugstore for Benadryl. To be taken more as a sleep aid this time.

Just before the turn onto Silver Street, I stop at a red light. As I wait, traffic coming from the west serpentines like a mechanical snake, winding across the black expanse of newly resurfaced pavement. The mustard-yellow curbing pulls my eyes, the color so intense it almost hurts. I glance in the rearview mirror to see Jaime creating a quiet drama between T. Rex and Stegosaurus, as if the dinos are stand-ins for people. When I look back out at the intersection, I see Callahan's van crossing in front of me. He does not see me. Or does not *want* to see me. He looks straight ahead. The driver behind me lays on his horn. The light has turned green. I accelerate too quickly. My tires squeal. I forget to use my blinker signal when I pull into the library lot. I hear the car behind me brake. I do not look back. I pull into a parking space. Look in the rearview. "Mum's not with it today," I say. Jaime grins and throws up his hands as if to say, Oh well.

By the time we reach the children's reading room, I have tripped on the stairs, hit a revolving display rack, and walked over on the side of my foot. Jaime takes my hand, whispers loudly, "Mum, it's okay." I squeeze his hand.

As he peruses the shelves, I sit, knees knocking the edge of the child's table, back ramrod-straight in the child's chair. Wondering how I'll figure this out. Work it.

I stir the pudding, thinking I've added a little too much cornstarch.

"We have whipped cream?" Jaime asks.

I can't seem to get the heat right. It feels like it's catching. I turn the burner down. "Sorry. No whipped cream. How about a dollop of marshmallow?"

He nods enthusiastically. Throws his arms around my hips, hugs me, asks, "Can I help stir?"

"Get a wooden spoon from the drawer," I say, "and pull up a chair."

He drags a chair from the table to the stove. I help him up. "Careful, now," I say.

"I can do it," he says, indicating that he wants my spoon out so he can do the stirring by himself.

I hold the handle of the pan and let him stir. "Maybe you'll be a famous chef someday," I say, nuzzling his hair with my nose. And the phone rings, of course.

"Would you please get that?" I say.

He relinquishes the spoon and I take it and continue to stir as he scrambles down from the chair and heads for the phone.

He answers it on the fourth ring. It's his father. I can tell by the conversation. They talk about swimming. "I'll pack my bathing suit," Jaime says, "and bring my goggles." Finally, after the logistics have been figured out, Jaime says, "It's Dad, Mum."

I slide the pan to the adjacent burner, so the pudding won't scorch, wipe my hands on the dish towel, and go to the phone.

"Just calling to tell you I can't take Jaime on Wednesday," Ben says. "I'll pick him up on Friday afternoon, if that's okay with you."

"Fine," I say, and, seeing no need for niceties, I tell him I'm cooking so I need to get off, and ask if there's anything else.

"Yes," he says, "I called Kevin Callahan last night. Things are a little tight with paying the mortgage and renting a suite here, so I asked him if he minded if we paid him the balance in installments. He seemed amenable. So would you mind writing him a check for six hundred dollars the next time he comes?"

"Fine," I say. "Fine."

After I rinse the pudding dishes, I dry my hands and head upstairs, but before I can make my way through the dining room, I see car lights sweeping over the barn doors, creating an optical illusion, shadow and light shifting alternately, making the doors appear as if they are sliding open. I recognize the sound of the engine. I go back to the kitchen and watch through the window as Callahan strides through light thrown by the cockeyed fixture mounted above the outside door. I let him knock before I answer. His hair is damp. I smell bath soap and a subdued version of the scent he wore the day I fell apart in his living room.

"Sorry for not calling," he says. "I know you expected us today. But we had a little emergency." I think he must be here for the $600 installment, the check I'm supposed to give him.

"That's okay," I say. "Come on in and I'll write you a check."

"Thanks," he says. "I intended to talk to you today, but my apprentice hurt himself on the job this afternoon. Nearly took off a finger trying to cut pipe. It was a little hairy for a while. I stayed with him at the hospital till I knew he was going to be okay, but it's been a long day."

I move back to let him in. "His folks aren't around?" I say.

"It's only his dad and he's on the road," he says. "Drives a car carrier."

"He's going to be all right, though?" I ask.

"They say he'll be fine," Callahan says.

"Want a drink?" I ask. "A beer?" This seems a halfhearted gesture to make up for being curt.

"A beer would be good." He pulls out a chair, sits at the table.

I open the refrigerator door, push various jars and cartons out of the way till I see a green bottle lying on its side.

"You didn't see me at the Silver Street intersection this afternoon, did you?" I open the bottle and pour the beer into a glass.

"No," he says, "I didn't. I must have been on my way to the hospital. I was pretty focused on getting there."

I set the glass on the table in front of him, pull a chair out, and sit.

He leans forward, reaches for the salt shaker, strokes the wooden base with his thumb. "I wanted to tell you that I felt badly," he says, "about the other day. The poor timing. I don't want to get too personal here, but it seems that you need someone to talk to. And I wondered if you'd considered seeing a doctor?"

"I am a doctor," I say, "for what good it does me."

"Really?" he says. "I guess that explains a lot."

I know he's mulling it over, the thing about doctors being their own worst patients.

"I haven't practiced for a while." I don't tell him *for a long while*. Not since Vietnam.

"Well," he says, "you want to talk about it? It seems to me you were on the verge the other day before Philamena arrived."

Yes, I think, Philamena, of course, goes with the Pre-Raphaelite hair.

"It's a long story," I say. "One I'm not sure I can tell."

"Well, Lily, you've got a problem." He sits back in his chair, takes a sip of beer, sets the bottle on his knee, and looks at me.

I lean forward, put my elbows on the table, and rest my chin in the cradle of my palms. "I think I need an attorney more than I need a doctor."

I am surprised at how easily I proceed to tell him about my fear of losing Jaime, but I am not surprised at the shame I feel after.

He sets his beer down, clasps his hands loosely on the table. "Forgive me, but frankly, I'm a little confused," he says. "Your husband would have to prove you unfit in order to seek full custody. Wouldn't he?"

"That's exactly why I'm afraid," I say. "I think he'll try to distort things. One particular incident, anyway."

Callahan leans forward, crossing his arms on the table. "It can't be all that bad," he says.

He reminds me of a Sunday-school teacher I once had who convinced me that "talking about it" always made things better. And so, in the relative safety his presence seems to have created, I begin at the beginning. Telling him what I have never told anyone about Vietnam, feeling vaguely disembodied as the words follow one upon the other, creating a strip of freeze frames: Ian and the surrealism of Saigon. Tet. And then an image of Pleiku: a pregnant Montagnard woman, her belly full of shrapnel, the fetus like a dead bird in a cracked shell. The delicacy with which the nurse received the tiny body, swaddling it and holding it to her as if it were still alive. And after, in the late evening, the OR crew sat in a makeshift bunker listening to Jimi Hendrix, and smoking dope and laughing. And my own laughter, which had begun as an expression of high hilarity, transmuted, and I heard in it, as I floated far above myself, the unmistakable sound of hysteria. And so I drank. Whiskey. Straight. To drown it out.

I cover my mouth with the tips of my fingers for a moment before continuing. Feeling strangely removed, I say, "I dissociate sometimes. Become lost. Like the time in the cellar. Remember?"

"Yes," he says, "I do." He reaches across the table and takes my hand. Squeezes it. "What can I do to help you, Lily?" he says. "Tell me, what can I do?"

CHAPTER 11

Before Callahan left that night, he told me he'd seen a car parked on the other side of the road opposite our driveway. Someone coming through our fields had crossed and gotten into the car just as Callahan had pulled in. I hadn't a clue, I told him, who it could have been. He took a walk around the outside of the house and down the driveway. Came back to tell me he'd found nothing, but to make sure the doors and windows were locked anyway.

I slept like the dead that night. No nightmares. The next morning, at seven-thirty, I was served with divorce papers. The sheriff hadn't wanted to miss me, apparently. I'd just made coffee. Jaime was still sleeping, and I looked out to see a big Chrysler lumbering up the driveway. Couldn't mistake the fact it was an official vehicle, sheriff's seal on the driver's-side door.

"Sorry to bother you, ma'am," he'd said.

"It's all right, Sheriff," I said, "one of us had to do it. Get the ball rolling, I mean. It may as well be him." He'd looked relieved. He was tall and bony and kind-eyed.

He'd tipped his hat before he left, said, "You'll do all right, ma'am."

As I watched the Chrysler being maneuvered like a boat out of dry dock, backing down the driveway, I felt sick to my stomach.

The moon floats above the branches of the center oak like a pale balloon caught up by its string. I sit on the porch stairs and watch it. Jaime is lying on his belly, playing with a Matchbox car, guiding its hard rubber wheels over the hill of a battered threshold.

"How about a walk?" I say.

"Just one minute, Mum," he says, "till I get this Cobra parked."

He maneuvers the car carefully into a space between a porch column and the balustrade, and says, "Ready to go."

"Let me button your sweater," I say.

"I can do it," he says. "Thanks anyway."

We stroll down through the fields, the grass already tall and fragrant; spreading my fingers, I hold my hand flat just above it. I feel it touch the skin of my palms like cats' whiskers as I walk. Jaime wants to check the cemetery out first. For ghosts.

When we get there he steps in front of me and unlatches the gate, easing the metal tongue out of its rusty groove. Before we go in, he holds a finger up to his mouth, then takes my hand and leads me to the obelisk with great care, as if he were leading an ancient animal. In the moonlight, he pats the base of the monument, indicating I should sit. I settle on the smooth granite, my palms flat, my fingers spread wide, a spatter of mica twinkling between them. I look out over Browns Head and am momentarily dazzled by the foil of the sea, its crinkled surface refracting moonlight. Jaime crawls up next to me, whispers loudly, "Don't look now, but there's a ghost by the gate." He puts his hands to his mouth and snorts, a kind of nasal laughter, and then says, "Now. Now you can look."

I look over my right shoulder and for a split second I am

wary, as if I'll see her standing there, the Montagnard child. But of course there's nothing. "I think it's disappeared," I say, going along with the charade, humoring Jaime.

He slides down from his perch and crows, "You believed me, Mum! You believed me!"

"You really fooled me," I say. I stand then, scoop him up, twirl him around, say, "I guess it's time to go for a little hike. Don't you think?"

We take the long way back, strolling along the edge of the field closest to the sea, the grass closing behind us like a tasseled gate, the momentarily silenced crickets recommencing their incessant chirp. Within sight of the house, I stoop to pick up Jaime. He lays his head on my shoulder and slips his thumb in his mouth. I list slightly as I make my way through hip-high heliotrope.

At first, when I see movement at the back of the house, I stare stupidly. It takes me a moment to figure out what I'm seeing: a man near the bulkhead, his back to me. I squat awkwardly, nearly falling over, Jaime's weight throwing me off balance. I watch as the man disappears around the side of the house. The hair stands up on the back of my neck. Who could it be? Someone trying to break in? That couldn't be the case, since I left the doors open, the windows up. A peeping Tom? Some pervert looking to get a thrill? I ease Jaime into my lap. He continues to sleep as if he were tucked in his own bed and not crumpled like a disjointed marionette. I try to situate him more comfortably, hold his head against my chest.

What are my options here? I could walk back through the field to the main road, go to a neighbor's house. Call the police. Or I could wait awhile. Give him a chance to figure out there's no one home, then head for my car. It's parked at the top of the driveway, in front of the barn doors. Coming from the back of the house and around the side, I'd not be obvious. The Peugeot's dome light is out. The key's in the ignition. I could ease open the door, slide Jaime into the backseat, get in after him, crawl over the seat, hit the central lock button, start the car, and head for the neighbors'. And that's what I decide to do.

The Peugeot's headlights illuminate trees, lawn, sweep over the ell of the house. No sign of the man. I've turned around on the lawn so I won't have to back down the driveway.

There is nothing on the main road. No car parked on the side. Nothing.

My closest neighbors, the Arnolds, Otis and his daughter, Fran, are watching television. As I go up onto the porch I can see them through the window, sitting in chairs opposite each other, Fran knitting and Otis ramrod-straight, deeply absorbed in his program.

I knock on the screen door and call out, "It's your neighbor Lily."

Fran comes to the door first, her father, hard of hearing, following but hanging back, leaving it to his daughter.

"Lily," Fran says, "what's the matter? Is Jaime okay?" She opens the door to let me in.

"As a matter of fact, Jaime's fine," I say, "sound asleep in the car. But it seems we have a prowler. And I think I ought to call the police. May I use your phone?"

"Of course, of course," she says, "absolutely."

I slide down till I feel the water at the hollow of my throat. I try to empty my mind, but it's no use. There's too much static. After I pick up Jaime at play group, I'll swing by the police station. Ask if anyone else in the area may have seen something. Two cops followed me back from the neighbors' house last night, checked everything out. No trace of the guy. They patrolled the area till dawn. I slept hard. No dreams. That I remember.

I use my toes to manipulate the faucet, adding more hot water. I think about those cops. The one who did the talking had the distinct manner of the military about him; the way he spoke to me, yes, ma'am, no, ma'am, the way he stood, looking straight on, his muscular body reflecting a determined self-discipline. He had an air of authority that was undeniable, his subordinate deferring absolutely. He could have been that MP outside the Continental in Saigon. Except he was too young; he'd have been in high school.

How many times have I thought back to it, that last week in Saigon, like touching a tender spot and being instantly reminded of the wounding? Ian returned to the Continental three days after the Tet Offensive began. I had to leave for Pleiku the next morning. Other journalists had made their way back to the hotel and I'd interrogated them. Had they seen Ian Morris, and if they didn't know him by name, I'd explained that he was an Aussie, a tall guy affiliated with Reuters. No one knew anything, most saying that it was a mess out there, the Vietcong still fucking things up. Ian could be stuck somewhere, in hostile territory where the VC had dug in. One guy, an American, a sloppy loudmouth drunk I'd seen at the Caravelle, was insensitive enough to say, "The VC don't give a fuck if you're a journalist, they'd as soon shoot you as not."

I'd even gone back to Reuters late the night before. But there was no one there. The door locked. A bullet hole through the Reuters sign. A recent happening that made my mouth go stone-dry. I proceeded to walk back to the hotel, not giving a damn if the MPs or the VC saw me. I was so disheartened that I didn't care if I got picked up or shot. I couldn't imagine how I was going to go back to the chaos of Rocket City, good old Pleiku, and be able to concentrate.

When Ian did appear, looking like hell, unshaven, red mud under his fingernails and in the creases of his knuckles, red dust in his hair, I experienced a wave of relief that made me sit down hard on the bed. And then I got up and put my arms around him. He held my head against his chest and said, "I'm a mess, Lily, I need a bath."

I ran the water for him while he peeled off his clothes; the red dirt had permeated his underclothes, sifted through his pubic hair, and into every other crevice he possessed. He looked as if he'd rolled in the dirt. He was exhausted, too tired even to talk. He stepped into the tub and eased himself down. He closed his eyes and I used the water glass to wet his hair. The shampoo created a pathetic lather, the dirt and hard water resistant to soap. I ran the tap and filled the glass with clean water over and over and shampooed his hair two more times before he said, "It's all right, we'll get it next time." He let me wash his back and shoulders and neck. I ministered to him in silence, using my hands to comfort him in the way that you'd use your voice, softly, but pressing now and then, changing the rhythm and inflection to soothe and console. When the tub was nearly full again with mostly clean water, he said, "I just want to soak, Lily; how about pouring me a drink while I finish?"

I left him, closing the door behind me, feeling a flicker of fear. Knowing there was something different and that whatever it was could change things irrevocably. I poured an inch of scotch in a clean glass, noticing that my fingers were puckered from the water, the residue of red dirt finely laid in the creases of my palms. I sat on the bed that I'd turned down. Room service had resumed. The fresh sheets were smooth, tucked tightly. I waited for Ian. I heard him turn on the tap again. It ran for a long time. I lay back on the bed. There was nothing I could do but wait.

It is already sultry, the cicadas buzzing. Though it is barely nine o'clock, the traffic on Silver Street is heavy, people heading for the beach, their cars packed with coolers, chairs of plastic webbing and tubular aluminum, and canvas bags bulging with beach linens: towels of schizophrenic color and design, thin waffled blankets, sheets grown nappy and threadbare. I depress the COOL-ATMOS button. Feel jets of air first blowing hot, lifting the hem of my skirt, then growing needle-cold so that I have to adjust the baffles, directing them upward. I have a semiaversion to air-conditioning, so keep my window half open.

I glance in the rearview mirror. Jaime mashes his fists into his eye sockets, the string of a Maine Savings balloon around his right wrist sliding lazily up and down as the balloon itself bobs naked and pink in the back window.

"Are you sleepy?" I ask, knowing he will ignore the question. The *S* word is anathema to him. And indeed he doesn't answer, only rests his head on the padded tray of the car seat.

After slow going, we manage to get to the bridge, but it is bottlenecked. The driver of an old Plymouth, coming up on the right, insinuates the bulbous fender of the car into the space between the Peugeot and the pickup in front of me. I allow the driver, a bald man, to maneuver the dull green wreck into the space.

I can see that we're going nowhere fast, so I lay my head back against the headrest, close my eyes, and yawn. Think about the fact that I've managed to maintain a kind of normal daily routine since Ben left; the idea that I can will my life to be what I need it to be is working, somehow. I yawn again and begin to drift, the heat lulling me, drawing me down, and for a few seconds I doze, feeling a pleasant weightless sensation, as if I were floating free, gravity having lost its hold. I am aware that Jaime is snoring, given in to the stupefying white noise of the car's idle and the warm air.

I am nearly asleep when a horrendous crack and boom brings me to. There is no time to think. I lunge sideways, reacting to the explosive sound, grabbing for the door handle, releasing the latch, the door swinging wide, but I am brought up short, the seat belt throttling me, holding me back. I fumble for the release and when I finally find it I propel myself out, landing hard on the pavement, the nubble of blacktop searing the palms of my hands and the skin of my knees. Another crack and boom deafens me and I flatten my body against the scalding pavement and scuttle under the Peugeot. I pull my knees into my chest, eyes pinched together, fists over ears, the thundering bass of my heart deafening me further. *Incoming.*

And for a moment I don't want it to be over—don't want to open my eyes to see the grunts who got caught. Outside the wire. But I see them anyway. They lie broken. Like discarded dolls, arms and legs akimbo, the stuffing spilling out of their bellies. They smell of blood. And of shit. And of the briny liquor of brain and spine.

When I open my eyes, I see Ben standing in front of a wide window flanked by floral drapes, the flowers fleshy and overblown, mustard-colored blossoms fastened on vines like scaffolding. Leaves sprout narrow and serrated-edged. Something out of a nightmare. And then I remember. "Oh, Jesus. Is Jaime all right?"

Ben turns. "Awake, finally?" he says.

I kick off the sheet, but when I attempt to sit up my head reels and I have to lie back against the pillow and close my eyes. I tell myself to be calm. Be calm. I wait for equilibrium to return. "Where is he, Ben? I don't need you to be castigating, please. Just tell me where he is."

"Jaime's okay, Lily," he says. "You're the one with a problem."

He stands with his arms folded. "Do you remember what happened?" he says. He waits a moment for me to respond, and when I don't answer, he continues. "You crawled under the car in the middle of a traffic jam and went into one of your funks."

I open my eyes and watch his expression go flat, as if a shade had been drawn. "I remember," I say. "I remember."

"It was simply the car in front of you backfiring," he says. "I wish you could have figured that out."

I try to ignore his rising antagonism. "But Jaime is okay? Yes?"

"He's with Rachel," Ben says. "Where he'll be safe."

"So you're saying Jaime's not safe with me? Is that right?"

"I don't think I need to answer that question," he says. "It's obvious, isn't it?"

He's quiet for a moment, not thoughtfully quiet, more a careful self-monitoring; he knows what he's going to say, so it's more about how he says it.

"I don't want to hurt you, Lily," he says finally. "You must know that. But you need to understand the problem we have here. You can't be trusted with Jaime anymore." He rubs his jaw and scowls, and I know what he's going to say next.

"I've taken legal action," he says. "I have temporary custody of Jaime, and I intend to make it permanent. I think it only fair that you know this while you're here. Where there is support. You must agree that Jaime's safety is paramount here."

I try again to lift my head. There is a delay between the will to move and the movement itself. Every motion feels robotic, the effects of an antipsychotic: Thorazine, no doubt. Ben watches me, and I see pity in his eyes. I pull myself up to a sitting position, using the bed rails for leverage. Once I have gathered myself, I slide my legs over the side of the bed and for a moment stare down at my feet, which look pale and childish, toenails cut too short, remnants of red nail polish above the ghosts of cuticles.

When I stand, waves of vertigo wash over me. Ben watches as if he were witnessing something grotesque, something that compels you to stare, something you'd see on a carnival midway.

Unsteadily, I work my way around the bed, like a drunk, finally reaching the narrow metal locker on the other side. I've got to get dressed, see if I can figure a way out of here. My head reels again and I close my eyes for a few seconds, then will myself on. I am vaguely aware that Ben is leaving. He says nothing, and when he has gone, I say aloud, "You won't keep him from me."

I try to concentrate, try to remember how to release the simple iron latch of the locker, but my mind seems unable to fathom even the most elementary task. Finally, after fumbling, I abruptly flip the catch, causing the locker door to fly open and slam against the wall with a metallic crash. My clothes hang from hooks, the skirt ripped up the left seam, the blouse smeared with grease. I fumble with the strings of the hospital gown I wear, trying to untie them, the effort useless. So I pull the gown over my head, catching strands of hair that tangle in the knot.

I manage the blouse, but before I can button it, a nurse comes in. Ben must have told the staff that his crazy wife was trying to get up. She looks at me, at the nakedness below my waist, and before I can speak, she says, "Mrs. Townsend, you need to rest. Let's get you back to bed." She hovers close, a stark white-winged bird, eyeing the buttons of my blouse as I try with useless fingers to slip them through the buttonholes.

"I know my rights," I say. "You can't keep me against my will." The buttons undo me. I give up on them and lift my skirt from the metal hook.

She moves closer and I smell perfumed skin cream, citrusy and clean-smelling, and white shoe polish, still tacky. I concentrate, trying to get the skirt on, stepping into it, sliding it up over my legs, nearly losing my balance before I can pull it up over my hips, steadying myself. I zip it up.

"You can't leave of your own volition," she says. "A relative has to sign you out." She slides her hands into her uniform pockets then, a gesture that humanizes her. "And maybe that's an option, but first you've got to let the medication wear off."

I know that's the case. But who's going to sign me out? Not Ben, certainly. And my mother only as a last resort. The idea of her seeing me on P6 again makes me ill. I don't want to see the sadness in her eyes.

"Look," I say, "I'm a doctor, and I refuse to be treated like this. I need to leave and my shoes aren't here. Where are my shoes?"

"Dr. Townsend," she says, addressing me respectfully if somewhat ironically (maybe wondering if I'm delusional, a doctor?) but maintaining her position still, "I understand your wanting to leave, but you've had a bad time of it and you have to get it together a bit before we can let you go."

It is hard not to respond to this woman, who is not at all a paradigm of cold efficiency; in fact, her compassion is intensified by her flaws, lipstick on her teeth, frilled pillbox of a cap sitting back jauntily on her head, some of the pins securing it having been sprung like tiny traps.

I blink back tears of frustration. "Look," I say, "you seem like a reasonable woman. But you must understand that it's imperative that I leave. I have a child I need to get to."

"I can understand how you feel," she says. "I have kids myself, but you're in no condition, Dr. Townsend, to leave. Why don't you sit down and I'll ring for a cup of tea and we'll talk. Figure things out."

She turns from me, the swish of her white hose like fine-weight sandpaper buffing the stillness; purposefully, she makes her way to the steel panel over the bed, presses the intercom button, and, when someone answers, says, "Send a pot of tea down, will you?"

To hell with my shoes. I leave the nurse standing at the intercom. I walk out the door. Down the hall. The sound of my bare feet on the cool waxed floor echoey, like something out of a dream. The pale linoleum diffuses the lozenges of light that fall from a series of slotted windows. As I walk it seems to brighten, like stage lights coming up. I don't even make it to the elevator; they come, the nurses and aides, like a gaggle of geese sweeping me up, fluttering around me, bustling me in a white flurry back to my room.

They hold me down. Wrap my wrists in gauze, then slip on

leather cuff restraints, buckling them tightly. One of them explains that this is for my own protection. I simply can't just up and walk out. There are certain procedures that have to be followed. They are, after all, responsible for me. After they have left, I struggle against the restraints. But it is useless. I am a *psych casualty,* after all. Everything's reversed. Now I am the patient. And this time I cannot sign myself out. My worst nightmare come true. And within minutes two of them reappear. One with a blue plastic syringe in her hand. I can see that there is no point fighting it; I will only get out of here if I cooperate. I feel the prick of the needle and a burning sensation as the solution is injected into muscle. Not long after they leave, I feel my consciousness dimming as if it were being funneled down a black hole. I try to resist it, but finally I am powerless.

"I told them I was a cousin," Callahan says.

We sit in the visitor's lounge, he in a rocking chair across from me. My calves stick to the mustard-colored vinyl sofa, and I can feel the loose buttons in the upholstery making weals in the flesh of my thighs. I wear two hospital gowns, one as a robe. I pull them down under me and sit closer to the edge of the sofa. "How'd you know I was here?"

"Pointe Blue's a small town," he says. "Things get around."

The sound of his voice makes tears well up. I feel them slide down my cheeks and follow the angle of my jaw.

He gets up, sits next to me, puts his arm around my shoulders.

I feel shame. I can smell my own body. I didn't come prepared for this little visit, no overnight bag, no deodorant, no mild-smelling Portuguese soap. No money to buy toiletries at the coffee-shop store. I have been issued a hotel-size bar of Ivory and a minuscule bottle of shampoo that smells like cleaning fluid.

"You must have family, other than your husband. Have you called anyone?"

I look down at my hands resting on my knees, see snot on my knuckles. I tuck my fists under my arms. "I don't want my mother to see me like this," I say. "Though I'm surprised Ben hasn't dumped it in her lap."

"We're going to have you out of here in no time," he says. "Let me see what I can do."

After he leaves me, I get up and walk around the room, wishing I had a cigarette. The med cart rumbles past the door. I hear the nurse talking to a patient, saying, "Open your mouth, now. You're not hiding it under your tongue, are you?"

The woman balks, tells the nurse, "You can go to hell," and then there's a commotion and I hear the cart being wheeled speedily down the hall, the patient yelling after it, "That's right, go tattle!"

Just when I have given Callahan up for lost, he is back. "Had to talk with the doctor," he says. "They finally located him. Just in from eighteen holes. Tough life. Anyway, we sprung you." Callahan exudes a kind of easy self-confidence, I realize, and, of course, would have no trouble convincing anyone that he is a concerned relative willing to take responsibility for a half-baked cousin.

"I've got to sign a waiver, and while I do that, why don't you go get dressed?"

"I've got to get an attorney," I say.

"One thing at a time," he says. "One thing at a time."

CHAPTER 12

I stand in line at Gloria's register, the ingredients for pudding—sugar, eggs, Baker's chocolate, cornstarch, whipping cream—being moved along on the smooth rubberized conveyor belt. Everywhere I look I see reminders of Jaime: racks of candy and chewing gum: Tootsie Pops, cinnamon-flavored Dentyne. My attorney has petitioned the court to restore custody until the divorce proceedings. In the meantime, I have to be content with the four hours a week that I have him, though even that is conditional: He must stay on the premises. I am not allowed, of course, to take him in the car.

The woman in line ahead of me insists she should be given the sale price on the three packs of pantyhose she keeps playing out on the counter in front of her as if she were dealing cards. Gloria calls to the assistant manager, a man in his twenties, so painfully thin that his neck projects from his collar like a straw from a bottle.

"It's okay," he tells Gloria, "this once." It is obvious that he is intimidated by the frowsy-haired woman. I want to confront her, say, You've been aggressive and rude only to save a few pennies. But who am I to question anyone else's behavior? A grown woman who dives under cars and hides under beds.

"It takes all kinds," Gloria says, after the woman has left. "And how are you, Mrs. Townsend?"

"I'm fine, Gloria," I say, thinking how easy it is to say one thing and feel another. "How are you?"

"I'd be great, Mrs. Townsend, if it weren't for this damn sciatica. You know how it is. Always something."

"You're right," I say. "Always something."

I watch her hands, how her fingers deftly open the egg carton and turn each brown-shelled egg. Finding no cracks, she closes the carton, the great white wattle of her arms swaying slightly. Her hands are beautiful, I think. Extensions of her being.

After she has bagged my groceries, she looks me in the eye. "Things have a way of turning around, though," she says, "just when you're ready to hang it up."

If I believed in God, I'd thank Him for putting Gloria on the register this day.

The parking lot is crowded, people driving around looking for spaces. Saturday-morning shopping. Just as I get into the Peugeot, a woman leads a little boy about Jaime's age to the pickup parked next to me. I watch as she unlocks the door, puts a bag of groceries in the back of the cab, then lifts the boy up into his car seat. I hear her talking to him as she buckles him in, teasing him for a taste of his red Tootsie Pop. He holds it out to her and in a tone of conditional generosity says, "We have more in the bag. Right, Mom?" She laughs and delicately licks the red candy shell.

My heart sinks.

I start the car, use a napkin I find balled up in the console to blow my nose. Maybe if I appeal to Ben, he'll see how bad it is to keep Jaime from me, from his own bed and the nooks and crannies where he tucks T. Rex and Stegosaurus.

We're just finishing dinner when Ben arrives. "Would you like something?" I ask, trying to play it cool, knowing that it will do me no good to be hostile.

He looks at me warily, as if there might be cyanide in the whipped potatoes.

"No thanks," he says, and to Jaime, "Finish up and we'll go for a swim at the hotel."

Jaime grows quiet, slowly stirs his pudding, eyes riveted on the satiny chocolate stuff. He speaks to his father without looking up. "Why can't you stay here with Mummy and me?"

Ben squats next to Jaime's chair, says matter-of-factly, "Your mum and I aren't going to live together anymore. You know that, Jaime."

Jaime stops stirring, considers what his father's said, says, "I don't want to go swimming, Daddy. I want to stay here with Mummy and maybe, just this one time, you can sleep over."

"I can't do that, Jaime," Ben says. "Now, finish up so we can go. Maybe Nina would like to go swimming too."

Jaime lets his spoon slide down into his pudding. His face crumples and he cries softly.

I take him in my arms, hold his head against my chest, tell him it's going to be okay, I promise, it'll be okay. He holds me tightly, his face hidden in my neck, my hair. I sit, cradle him in my lap, kiss his head, rock him. The peppery smell of his hair and the soft skin of his neck make me feel fiercely connected to him, as if my body were molded for him, my hands made to hold the heart of his face, my hip to carry him.

Ben stands stiffly, ill-equipped to deal with the emotionality of the moment. I cup the back of Jaime's head with my palm, say, "Can't you let him stay with me tonight, please? He'll feel better tomorrow. He's just overtired right now. It would be good for him to sleep in his own bed, don't you think?"

Ben slides his hands into his pockets, draws a breath, says, "We can't set a precedent here, Lily. You've had him for the time allotted. Now, please get his coat."

I struggle to keep my composure, though I can feel my face flush, my heart beat hard and fast.

"Come on, sweetie," I say, gently taking Jaime's arms from around my neck.

"I don't want to go," he says, his voice tremulous. He tucks himself, doglike, into a ball in my lap, his face buried in my belly.

I look at Ben.

Jaime begins to cry again, and asks his father yet one more time, "Please, Daddy, I want to stay."

"No, Jaime," Ben says. "It's time we left. You can visit your mother another day." And with this he attempts to lift Jaime from my lap. "Now, come on," he says. "Let's get going."

Jaime wails, "No, Daddy, no!" He holds on tightly and so do I.

My face is close to Ben's and when he finally looks at me, at what is apparent in my eyes, he backs off abruptly. In a voice so controlled that it surprises even me, I say, "You've upset him enough. Now why don't you just go."

His face flames. "You're not going to get away with this, Lily," he says. He turns tightly and nearly crashes into the empty chair I'd pushed back from the table.

I keep rocking Jaime even as I hear the Mercedes spin out, and I keep rocking long after Ben has left.

Shortly after ten, I see a car drive in. Pointe Blue's finest. When I answer the door, I recognize the cops who came the night I saw the peeping Tom.

"Mrs. Townsend, ma'am?"

"What can I do for you, Officer?" I say, knowing full well why he's come.

"Your husband, ma'am, is here for his son."

In the half-light, I see that the subordinate is extremely uncomfortable. His fresh haircut, an attempt to subdue a whorl of cowlicks, makes him look more boyish than he really is.

"I'd like to speak to my husband first, please, if you don't mind," I say to his superior.

He steps back to let me by.

Ben stands next to his car.

"You can go drag Jaime out of bed," I say. "I'll have nothing to do with it."

He doesn't answer, only walks past me into the house.

I cover my face with my hands for a moment, then wrap my arms around myself, trying to quell the trembling that has invaded my body.

"Are you all right, ma'am?" the older officer asks. He approaches me cautiously, like a dog wary of being kicked.

I wave him away. "I'm okay," I say. "I'm okay."

Ben shoulders the screen door open, Jaime asleep in his arms. It takes all my strength to keep from going after him. I watch him maneuver the rear door of the Mercedes, using his hip to hold it ajar while he slides Jaime into the backseat. After he has slid behind the wheel, started the engine, and backed down the driveway, the cops follow, the younger one nodding guiltily to me.

I stand barefoot, arms at my sides, robe fallen open, watching till the car lights disappear. When everything is dark and quiet again, I sit on the stoop and cry and hit the cold granite with my fists until they go numb.

I nearly run into the old woman crossing in front of the Peugeot. She clutches her bag under her arm and glares at me. I cut the engine and get out. "I'm so sorry," I call. She does not acknowledge me, only continues across the street and onto the sidewalk.

I get back into the car. Tell myself to concentrate. Keep it together till you get home. Then what? Fall apart? I keep hearing my attorney's words: "It's going to be tough. The fact that you've been on a psych ward makes it that much more so."

It takes all my concentration just to keep the car in the right lane, to brake at the lights, to think far enough ahead for the next turn.

After I make the driveway, I hit the brake halfway up, shift into first, cut the engine, set the emergency brake. For a few seconds, I close my eyes, then open the door, slide my legs out, sit with my hands on my thighs, my feet flat on the gravel. I think about the Montagnard child, how I couldn't save her. And how I can't even save my own child. My muscles feel as if they are spring-loaded, adrenaline torquing them. I get out of the car and cross the driveway to the grass, to the stand of poplar where every year I first see spring, tender new leaves, heartbreakingly green.

I walk among the trees, touching the smooth gray trunks, stopping finally to look up. Leaves overhead shift in the breeze. I cover my eyes with my hands. It is Vietnam all over again.

It is Sunday. Callahan called out of the blue this morning. He wondered if I'd like to get out for a bit, go for a ride. Sure, I told him. I welcomed the distraction.

He'd been thinking about my situation. "Would you be okay with a little input?"

I'd be open to suggestions, I told him, of course I would.

"I'll tell you about it when I get there, okay?"

"Fine," I said. "See you soon."

I'm glad to be getting out. Everything around me seems to have a significance I don't want to remember: The waffle maker sits unused. Its mere presence is somehow chastising. I take it from its place next to the mixer, wrap the cord tightly around it as though to keep it still, and shove it deep into the narrow cupboard next to the stove. That being that, I can no longer endure the house or anything in it. I grab my bag and head out.

Callahan pulls in just as I reach the end of the driveway. He leans across the seat and opens the passenger door. I get in. Instantly apologetic, I say, "I know you must have other things to worry about. Thanks for thinking of me, on a Sunday, no less."

He pats my knee. "I have a stake in this," he says. "I lost a

son. And, consequently, a wife. Not that seeing you reclaim
Jaime will change that. But I can help you in a way that I
couldn't help us."

He has never named his wife. Or spoken of her, really. It is
clear now that she left not long after the boy died. Not, I suspect, because she didn't love Callahan, but because he would
forever remind her of the boy in the photograph that sits atop
the piano in the carriage house.

"You're divorced?" I say.

"Yes," he says, "not that it was my idea."

He goes quiet then and I'm sorry I asked the question. I
want to tell him I understand his reluctance to talk about it,
but instead I look through my bag for my sunglasses, making
an elaborate pretense, taking out my wallet, my keys, a ball-
point pen, a lipstick, and a nearly empty package of M&M's.
"Must have left my sunglasses at home," I say. "Oh, well."

"Maybe this'll help," he says, reaching over to flip down the
visor.

"Thanks," I say, feeling ridiculously transparent.

I change tack and ask him where we're going.

"To see a lawyer friend of mine, a guy I went to school
with," he says. "He practices maritime law but lives with a
woman who works for Pine Tree Legal, specializing in
women's issues. I talked with them last night. They said they'd
be home today if we'd like to drive to Durham. What do you
think?"

The idea of two relative strangers knowing, when I've not
even told my mother or brother, makes me sick with guilt. But
I can't stand the thought of telling my family that I endangered
Jaime's life, that I don't even remember him crawling under
the car after me, terrified when I'd abandoned him.

Ben made sure I knew that he had sought out and spoken
to the driver of the old green Plymouth. He told me that the
man was still shaken. Could still hear Jaime wailing when

someone crawled under the car to rescue him. Jaime held on to me so fiercely that when they dragged him out he had strands of my hair twined around his fingers. He still had black tarry scabs on his knees, and an elongated smear of a burn from the exhaust pipe on his forehead.

Callahan seems to feel my reluctance. "I'm sorry," he says. "I should have talked to you first before I called Tom." He takes my hand then, smooths my knuckles with his thumb. His touch causes an immediate and profound confusion in me, the deepest part of my body remembering what I haven't felt since Saigon fused with the all-consuming shame of losing Jamie. I cannot seem to speak while he's touching me, so I take my hand away, in a manner that could only be described as awkward, and carry on as if nothing had happened.

"It's okay," I say. "It's me. I feel like a pariah, like one of those pathetic women you read about in the papers. A woman who can't even take care of her own child."

"Jesus, Lily," Callahan says, "believe me, it could be worse. You've got to fight. Use whatever resources are available to you. Your husband's probably counting on your guilt to paralyze you. You can't let that happen."

I hear a real sense of frustration behind Callahan's words. Because of course he knows it could be worse. Much worse.

"I know, you're right," I say.

Not long after we leave Pointe Blue, the anxiety I've endured since leaving the hospital seems to abate, though I am not naive enough to think it won't return, like a flotilla of sparks in my blood, igniting muscles, making them coil, keeping them ready for the fray.

I glance at Callahan as he concentrates on the road; in his profile, I see stubborn resilience, partly acquired, no doubt, from the grief he has suffered and managed to survive, humanity intact. At that moment, almost as if he can read my mind and is uncomfortable with my observations, he matter-of-factly reaches to open the glove box and takes out a map. "Would you check the map? We're looking for Route Nine East."

"Glad to," I say.

I realize, after speaking with Callahan's friends, that I've avoided talking about Vietnam for almost eleven years. For good reason. If you haven't experienced it, you really can't understand it. That's not to say there aren't some compassionate people who try to empathize. It's just that if you're not an elephant, you can't know what it's like to be one. Simple, but there it is.

"Your attorney could get some real mileage out of the Vietnam vet factor," Margaret Tibbets said. "If it were approached in the right way." I was amazed at the fire of the tiny woman, someone who looked like she'd have to buy her clothes in the "Young Miss" department. I was heartened by her. Though I wasn't quite sure of her Vietnam vet strategy.

"Women who served in Vietnam aren't generally looked at in the same way as the men. We didn't experience combat, though it sure as hell felt like it sometimes. Pleiku, in fact, was called Rocket City."

"Maybe it was worse than combat," Tibbets suggested after I told her about the seventy-two-hour pushes, and how we had to take Dexedrine to keep awake while we slogged around in blood, wrist-deep in some kid's gut. "You had to remember to eat so you wouldn't get light-headed," I'd said. "Once, after eating half a sandwich, I noticed dried blood in the creases of my knuckles and between my fingers. I swallowed hard. Then I got on with it. Scrubbed, and went on to the next kid."

But I didn't tell Margaret Tibbets what most torments me. The Montagnard children. How napalm seemed to liquefy their skin, some like human candles, skin melting like wax, features sliding off faces. And how, even now, one dead child still haunts me, materializing in front of a church parish house, or near the trees on my lawn, or even in my bedroom. They'd think I was really screwed up, now, wouldn't they?

Ben is late dropping Jaime off. I scrape the cookie dough I made earlier from the metal mixing bowl, ball it up, swaddle it tightly in a sheet of plastic wrap, and put it to bed next to the leaf lettuce in the crisper drawer of the Amana. Anyway, I tell myself, it'll roll out easier.

I wash my hands, dry them carefully on a terry dish towel, line the cookie cutters up on the counter, the stegosaurus first, then the brontosaurus, and last, but not least, the Tyrannosaurus rex. I stand back and look at them and feel a rigor take hold of my muscles, making them rigid as barrel staves. It's six by the stove clock. They're an hour late. "We're gonna find out what's going on," I say aloud, for the benefit of who I don't know, maybe the dino cookie cutters. I pick up the phone, wishing I had a cigarette, and dial the cleaners. The phone rings six times before June picks up.

"June," I say, "let me speak to Ben, please, if he's still there." She hesitates before speaking.

"Lily, dear," she says, "Ben asked me to tell you that he won't be bringing Jaime over. He's worried about you. He doesn't think you need the responsibility of a child right now."

I feel my muscles coiling down, binding my diaphragm, making it difficult to breathe. I will myself to relax, take a breath, say, "June, they don't pay you enough to do this. Let me speak to Ben. Now, please."

"Ben's not here, Lily, and I'm afraid I have to hang up now."

And she does. I call back, but the line is busy. No doubt she's left the receiver off the hook.

My hands shake. Objects around me take on a reality that borders on surrealism: The frames around the windows glow, the panes absented, nothing between me and the greenness of the trees and grass, the obsidian blackness of the driveway. I move through the kitchen, past the jaws of the electric can opener and the toaster-become-looking-glass. Everything exquisitely alive, banks of glass-fronted cupboards through which a gleaming plate rim cleaves the eye like a golden sickle.

The Peugeot also seems oddly alive. I open the driver's-side door, slide behind the wheel, turn the key. The sound of the idle, particular to a diesel engine, seems new to me, as if this were the first time I'd really heard it.

My timing couldn't be better: As I head down Commercial Street, I see Rachel's car in front of the brick shoe-box–shaped building that houses Townsend Dry Cleaning. I pull up behind the gleaming Volvo, put the Peugeot in gear, set the brake, and get out. Rachel's belting Nina into her car seat and doesn't see me come up behind her. I call to her, and in the moment it takes for her to respond, I see Jaime in the backseat, though he doesn't see me.

I am momentarily taken aback by Rachel's expression. Hostility distorts her features, her eyes hard as the heads of tacks. Before she can say anything, I say, "You'd better tell Ben to think twice before he makes decisions based on my supposed state of mind." I walk around to the other side of the car to get Jaime.

Before I can open the back door, Rachel hits the lock button. "You're not capable of taking care of that little boy," she says. "Ben's only trying to protect him."

I vow to stay calm. I speak distinctly: "You realize this is kidnapping," I say. "Ben was supposed to drop Jaime off over two hours ago."

Rachel puts her fists on her hips. "Ben's at his attorney's office right now. You'll be lucky if you ever see Jaime again."

I feel almost paralyzed by the heightening of this strange clarity, the Volvo's gray glow pulsing, the dent in the hood where I'd smashed it with my fist an ugly perversion. Only when Jaime begins to cry and call to me am I mobilized. I walk deliberately around the car to where Rachel is standing by the front passenger door.

"God knows what you're capable of," she says, cocking her hip and pressing it against the door so that it closes with a muffled finality. "I've never felt comfortable leaving Nina with you. And let me tell you, since Jaime's been with us, I've seen some strange things. Sometimes we find him asleep under his bed in the middle of the night. Where do you think he learned that?" She stares at me, her back against the door.

Jaime's voice rises to a hysterical pitch. I am vaguely aware of cars going by as I use all my strength to shove Rachel away from the door. I smell her perfume, something cloyingly pesticidal, as she trips over the curbing and sprawls headlong onto the brick sidewalk. I bend and pick up the car keys she dropped and unlock the doors.

Jaime is sobbing so hard that he can barely catch his breath. I unbelt him, hold him to me, say, "It's going to be okay, Jaime. It's going to be okay." Nina observes us with great interest, strangely unaffected.

"You're telling me that the charges will be dropped if you basically sign away your rights as a mother," Callahan says.

I nod. My head aches fiercely; the simple act of speaking makes it worse.

Callahan puts a hand on my shoulder. "We'll figure it out," he says. "We'll figure it out."

I can't answer him. Can't even cry anymore. Can barely believe what has happened, being charged with assault and battery.

I'd resisted them when they came to arrest me. They jerked my arms behind my back. Jerked back and up. Dislocated my right shoulder. "Amazing strength," one of them said, "for a woman." What did they expect? They were taking me away from my child, leaving him in the hands of a young woman who wore the same uniform as her male counterparts, a stiffly starched gray short-sleeve shirt, straight-legged navy trousers, highly polished black oxfords. She appeared bored with the prospect of staying with a sleeping child till his father came. She put her hand on her hip and smirked when they told her she was to stay, making some comment about being the "token woman." Her expression was insolence itself, and she looked absurd in a uniform made for a man, slouching so that the spaces between the buttons on her shirt gaped, the garment unable to accommodate her overly endowed chest.

I knew Jaime'd wake and expect to find me there. It made me heartsick. He'd insisted on sleeping in my bed, afraid I'd disappear if he lost sight of me for a moment. I promised him I wouldn't leave. Stroked his hair, knowing I had only complicated things, created yet more obstacles for myself. I knew Ben would come anytime and there would be hell to pay. Even in his sleep, Jaime's fingers remained twined around the cording of my robe. When I heard them pull into the driveway, I carefully loosened his fingers, extracting the terry material. I knew before I opened the door that my luck had run out.

When they informed me that I'd been charged with assault and battery, I couldn't imagine what they meant, at first, but then the image of Rachel sprawled on the sidewalk came to me.

"I can't go," I'd said. "My child is sleeping. I can't just leave him."

"We've made arrangements for the boy," the older cop said.

I resisted still, and when they insisted, I fought going, flailing blindly, hitting one of them in the face, so that he reflexively cupped his nose, then looked at his hand to see blood. That's when they got me down, yanked my arms back, handcuffed me.

I cannot bear the empty house, everywhere reminders of Jaime: dinosaur magnets on the refrigerator door, plastic bath toys piled in a pail next to the tub: a red sailboat; an empty dish-detergent bottle; a rubber duck the color of a real chick.

The void creates an atmosphere that draws the Montagnard child. She is there nearly every morning when I wake, and always, always I am galvanized by her eyes, dark and knowing: what we are all afraid of, while we are living, *to know*. It is not the face of dread, not the face seared forever in our minds, of the naked girl running, napalm burning and burning, swatches of skin scalded white, distinct even in the black-and-white of a newspaper photograph. It is not that face.

It is the face of lost life, of what is known only to the dead. It cannot be deciphered by the living, cannot be forced through the conduit of the mind into words. Sometimes we may vaguely intuit it, but we always circumvent it, occupying ourselves, remembering that we must pick up toothpaste or that the car needs to be registered. It's what we do to live.

Callahan has, this day, given me a ride to my attorney's office, since the Peugeot, in need of a new battery, is dead. He is content to sit in his van and wait, reading an out-of-print book, no doubt found at his favorite used-book store in Portsmouth.

In a dove-gray office hung with watercolors, my attorney is trying to figure out the best way to use Vietnam to our benefit. "This will be tough," she says, "a real balancing act. We've got to present things in just the right light, and if we don't, you could be tagged just another screwed-up vet. One who's not capable of taking care of a child."

I sit forward in my chair, trying to remind myself of the fact that I got through a hundred or more pushes in Vietnam, choppers coming in after firefights loaded with maimed kids that we'd try to save, working without sleep, frantic to fix them up, to fucking make them live. If I did it then, I can do it now. I have to do it—the stakes are too high not to. I watch Honora Hudson-Whitman as she writes something in the leather-bound book she has taken from a canvas sack slumped next to her desk. Book and bag are representative of her, a mix of elegance and toughness. Two things that give me faith in her. "I am well aware of the magnitude of the situation," I say, "but it was an isolated event, in the car with Jaime. It's never happened before when Jaime was with me."

Hudson-Whitman closes the book, lays her hands palms down on either side of it. "But it was not the first time for you, only the first time it's happened with Jaime. And how can we convince the judge that it won't happen again when Jaime's with you?"

"I will be vigilant, find a way to avoid triggers." I convince myself of this.

"We have to have assurance," she says, "or else we could lose. We have eight weeks to get things together. It might behoove you to get into therapy. To show the judge you're serious about trying to prevent problems in the future."

I'm not thrilled at the prospect of therapy, but I figure I'll do anything I can to even the playing field. I stand, smooth my skirt, put my hands on my hips. "Whatever I have to do," I say, "I'll do."

After leaving Sears with a new DieHard battery under the hood, I find myself driving by the church nursery school where Ben has enrolled Jaime. I drive beyond the parish house, and in my distraction, when I pull over to park, hit the curbing. I take a breath, tell myself to relax, straighten the wheels. Sugar maple fruits like paper wing nuts whirligig through the air around me as I walk up the brick sidewalk shadowed by a thick green canopy. I cross the street just before I come to the parish house proper.

I sit on a stone bench to the right of the entrance of a small park that is dominated by a stainless-steel sculpture, reminiscent of a Calder, giant flat fish that seem to swim through the air, tails and bodies undulating on invisible waves. The park is situated down from the lawn of the parish house where the children are brought out to play on an elaborate jungle gym: rope ladders, tunneled slides, and all.

I did not plan to do this, but I am, nevertheless, here, waiting for morning recess. In the interim, I rifle through my bag and pull out an IGA receipt that has been accordioned beneath wallet, address book, a plastic tube of tampons, and a makeup clutch stuffed mostly with crayons and a lone lipstick. I read down through the lengthy register tape: *Cheerios, Jif peanut butter, Welch's grape jelly, Lincoln apple juice, Eskimo Pies.*

The frenetic laughter of children set loose makes me look up from the purple-inked tape. I stuff it back into my bag and watch a woman of imposing height lead a gaggle of children across the lime-green lawn to the jungle gym. At first, I can't see Jaime, but when I do, I feel as if the breath's been knocked out of me. He is perfectly dressed, everything matching right down to bright red canvas sneakers.

I watch him move away from the other children to a sandy patch adjacent to a tunneled slide. He squats and peers at something I can't see—an anthill perhaps, insects of some kind. The teacher is involved in the contortions going on on the jungle gym, her back to Jaime. I could walk over leisurely, take him by the hand, walk away with him. As I stand, the teacher turns, and in that instant Jaime spies me. The teacher has apparently decided to investigate whatever Jaime is observing, so she strides toward him in an awkward fashion, her long feet and legs making her look ungainly, a waterbird out of water. She settles herself into a squat, the better to watch insect activity. I realize that what I'm doing is dangerous; surely, I will destroy any chance of regaining custody if I continue on this path. Jaime does not give me away by openly acknowledging me; he glances in my direction, but mainly engages the teacher. He knows enough to be quiet to protect me. I stand, pick up my bag, walk down the street, and once beyond the parish house cross to the other side.

The Peugeot has stayed cool, the deep shadow under the

maples creating a cavelike atmosphere in the interior, peaceful and dark. I slide in behind the wheel, lay my head back, close my eyes. Feel as if I'm being emptied, like a bottle being tipped upside down. Finally, I start the engine, and when I check the rearview mirror before pulling out, I see the Montagnard child standing in the gutter next to the sidewalk, a rain of sugar-maple fruit floating down around her.

Dr. Moyer sits in a leather wingback chair, across from the outrageous orange and brown plaid love seat I sit on. It is my third visit and we've only now begun to talk about Vietnam. We've gone the gamut, discussed my relationships with my mother, my father, and my brother. It's been a waste of time to this point, in my opinion.

"Tell me," he says, "about the incident."

You mean how I went berserk and fled under the car, my kid following me? I want to say. But of course I don't. I just tell him what I remember before the backfire and what I don't remember after that. As I talk, I see his eyes glaze as if he's heard it all before. He stares into space somewhere above and beyond my right shoulder. I am taken aback at his obvious disconnection, and so abruptly stop talking.

He fastens his eyes on my face then, back in the world. He describes a "particular feature" of post-traumatic stress disorder: "You were, I believe, experiencing a state of dissociation, reliving a traumatic event, behaving as you had at that particular moment in time."

No kidding, I want to say. And I wait for him to go on, but he stops to write something in a green spring-bound notebook. You're not going to do me any good, I think, and in fact, I don't like you. I know it will be the last time I visit the good doctor.

During the day, the Montagnard child appears at a distance, on the bridge after I've crossed over; when I glance in the rearview mirror, she'll be standing at the granite abutment. Or I'll see her in the gray hours of morning on the periphery of the IGA parking lot, a wasteland of ashen-colored pavement spread out before her. It's as if she's holding sway over the emptiness, the wide swath of buckled pavement running with fissures. For an instant, I expect to hear the whistle of a rocket, to feel the concussion of the hit, and after the explosion to see she's there still, having somehow survived.

Because I am alone more and more, I think about Ian. Maybe to distract myself, maybe to exhume from the past what, at the time, had a similar weight, a similar power to wound. A power that finally got you to the point of no return. Of wanting your head to be cleanly decapitated. To decisively end the incessant wallowing in self-pity. The source of it cut off for good.

I go over the experience, examining each thread of it, what wove it into an imperfect pattern of being: the dense humidity of Saigon. The fecund smell of tropical nights. Exhaust hanging blue and sweetly deleterious on the air. The decay of elaborate friezes. Fleur-de-lis grillwork artfully rusting. Sidewalk cafés and bars secured by iron latticework. Shops along Tu Do, the former Rue Catinat, frequented by Western women in French-style fitted skirts. Diminutive Saigonese go-go dancers in thigh-high boots of glossy white vinyl. Scintillating neon signs pulsing electric-blue and psychedelic-cherry: Coca-Cola, Budweiser, Pepsi. A legless street kid haranguing guests at the Continental, gracefully maneuvering between the tables on the veranda, dauntlessly navigating his homemade skateboard, his ravaged body a paragon of agility. Bare-bottomed toddlers squatting to shit on the street. River rats the size of cats. Stalls of exotic fruits: mangosteen, *pamplemousse,* dorian fruit. Creamy orchids, femininely carnal. The whine of motorbikes. The cackle of far-off gunfire. The war from a rooftop. The drunk. The depressed. The adrenaline-driven. And, at the end of the day, the gore of the goddamn Vietnamese sunset.

I meticulously examine the memories of our first meeting at the Caravelle. How close I came to bolting seconds before Ian approached my table. The surreal light show of the war at a distance, the drunks watching it, their loud talk and frenzied hilarity grotesque, a testament to the degradation of humanity in war, the witnessing of which made me sick. And, at first, Ian was just a man providing a means of escape, a ride back to the hotel in an ancient Peugeot. But his Aussie vivacity, generosity, and candor were nothing if not seductive. Even his obstinacy come of growing up in Australia was appealing, its tenacity to be counted on.

I would wake in the night with his hand on my hip, palm against my skin, his fingers slightly relaxed, and just the warmth of him would make me emotional. The love I felt was a self-inflicted force that promised and delivered extremes, both good and bad. I later swore I would never allow myself to feel that kind of love again for anyone.

But I had not then considered the love for a child: There is no choice about whether or not to feel it; it is an inherent part of you, as much as the blood in your veins. Still, loving a man and loving a child seem different ends of the same continuum. Each can be equally euphoric and equally devastating.

As I lay on the bed at the Continental after the worst of the Tet Offensive, waiting for Ian to come out of the bath, I was trying to distract myself, fantasizing about going to Brizzie with him or him flying back to Maine with me. I wanted him to see the blue of a September sky, to feel the velvet branches of staghorn sumac, to marvel at its vermilion leaves and strange plush fruit. I wanted him to eat lobster tail red from the pot, the succulent meat drenched in sweet butter. I wanted him to lie in my childhood bed with me, a white pillow slip covering stained blue ticking I'd drooled on when I was small. I would catch his pajama bottoms at the waist and push them down around his ankles with my toes. And on white sheets I would lay my head on his belly, and touch the incredibly soft skin at the articulation of his hip joints, and then take him tenderly into my mouth.

But all the daydreams went to hell with a sound from the bathroom that rendered me immobile. I thought I heard Ian crying. I lay there listening, feeling my throat constrict. When I heard nothing else, I tried to convince myself that I had imagined it, the way you do when something feels ominous, something you don't have the heart to face.

I was relieved then to hear the sound of bathwater gurgling sluggishly down the drain, and after a minute or two, the metallic sounds of shaving: the intermittent tap of Ian's razor on the sink and water trickling from the faucet.

When he came out of the bathroom, he had a towel wrapped around his waist. His hair was dark and sleek, curling at the neck, his cleanly shaven face flushed, his eyes darker than I'd remembered, the expression blunted. I got up from the bed and put my arms around him.

He held me with reserve as if I were a stranger, someone who for some obscure reason needed comforting and he was too much a gentleman to offend by pulling away. I lifted my face. "Talk to me," I said. "Please."

He closed his eyes for a second and then spoke: "I can't right now, Lily. I can't." With a distracted gentleness he took my arms from around him, holding them briefly by the wrists at my sides as if he were putting off kindly an overly affectionate child. He left me standing and sat on the side of the bed, his back to me, the broad wedge of his shoulders an obstruction between us.

I persisted: "Please, Ian, talk to me. Tell me what happened."

He lay on his side. Was quiet for what seemed an eternity.

Then said, "I saw things in the street I don't even want to think about, Lily. All I know is that I'll feel better when I know where Bao-Long is."

I understood then that there was nothing I could do, and that my daydreaming had been just that, a pathetic attempt to imagine myself out of a hell that only promised to get worse.

CHAPTER 13

I choose not to see Callahan. I need to prepare for the fight alone. I have systematically unplugged lamps, stood on a wobbly stepladder, and loosened bulbs in overhead fixtures. Even the fifteen-watt appliance bulb that illuminates the white-shelved cave of the refrigerator has been loosened in its socket, like a tooth left hanging by a thread. I don't need light.

I smoke in the dark as I remember my mother doing on warm summer evenings, my brother and I spying on her, oblivious of her as someone separate from us. There is a tension that always exists between the need for seclusion and the need for connection, and I am walking proof of that: I hear her, the girl, her barely audible breathing, and then I see her in plumes of moonlit smoke. I speak softly to her, my resolve not to acknowledge her vanished.

"You're isolating yourself," Callahan said. "Not a good strategy." He had insisted on coming. And so I'm waiting in the kitchen, turned surreal in the golden light of dusk. My hand resting on the cool surface of the oak table has become part of the grain.

I see the headlights of his van. They play over the refrigerator door and the hood of the stove. He raps lightly at the kitchen door before opening it. "Lily," he calls out, "you there?"

"At the table," I say.

I can see him standing by the window, waiting for his eyes to adjust, his tall silhouette backlit by rose-colored light, before he moves to the table. He pulls a chair out and sits, reaches across the oak leaf, takes my hand and holds it as if he were holding something dangerously fragile. "How are you doing?" he says.

I withdraw my hand from his, take a breath, and close my eyes. "I don't know how to make you understand," I say.

"Look, Lily," he says, "I know you're trying to get through this the best way you can. But I don't think that seclusion's the answer. Have you even told your family yet?"

"Please, Callahan," I say, "I don't need a father. And I wish you wouldn't presume to come into my home and act like one."

"Well, then," he says, "I guess there's not a thing I can do for you, Lily. If you want to be on your own with this thing, it is your business. I wish you well." With that, he stands and leaves.

I watch from the window as he backs down the driveway.

I stand at the window in the third-floor bedroom and look up at the stars. They are so distinct, so bright, that I can almost feel their blue-white embers smoldering on my retinas, pin-pricks of fire. I just got off the phone with my attorney, who told me that a court-appointed child psychologist will be meeting with Jaime. "I'm not worried," I said. "Jaime's the best character witness I could have."

"Don't," she said, "underestimate the expert witness. These guys have a way of complicating things in ways you'd never believe. And because he's a so-called expert, he's got credibility."

Credibility. Being believed. I wonder if they'd believe me if I told them about the girl. How she lives at the periphery of my vision. How there's hardly ever a time now when she's not there: a flicker of movement, a hand lifted in recognition, downcast eyes that look up and catch me in their guileless depth, dark, and impossibly trusting.

The wind rises. Oak branches creak, replicating the sound of an old Buick with shot shocks. As I watch, the shadows sieve moonlight and a man appears. The same man, it would reason, that I saw the night I took Jaime for a walk.

I make my way down the stairs to the master bedroom, where I pick up the bedside phone and call the police.

About twenty-five minutes later the doorbell rings. I switch on the outside lights and see a cop, looking very much like a boy dressed for a costume party, not the guy who looked like an ex-MP or his partner. When I open the door, he takes his hat off and says, "We apprehended him, ma'am, the prowler. Turns out he's a PI who's been hired to watch your house."

"I bet I know just who hired him," I tell the boy. "No secret there."

I pull into the IGA lot and park across from a distinctly utilitarian street lamp, its steel shaft projecting from a square cement footing. A lone moth flutters in rapture around this source of artificial light, a work of metal and glass that is sorely uninspiring. It is spellbound, flying close to the white center of brilliance. It tumbles away as if stunned by the radiance, only to wheel about in a delirium of wingbeats. As I watch, I see a bat, graceful as a stealth bomber, glide into the frenzy.

I open the door and slide out. I dread schlepping the aisles of the IGA, tubes of fluorescent light pulsing overhead. There are few people out at this late hour: zombies, mostly, driven out for milk or bread or Hostess snack cakes, stuff for lunch boxes.

When I enter the front of the store, Gloria looks up from the magazine she's reading and waves to me. I wave back and wrestle a single cart from the neatly parked queue, and head for the cereal aisle. I pick up shredded wheat and oatmeal and a box of Cheerios. Then another box. I will get him back, I tell myself, I will. The lights flicker overhead.

I pass a lone soul perusing the bread aisle. Her tea-colored hair has been brushed straight back into a sort of whisk-broom ponytail; the wide rubber band securing it is twisted and I can only imagine the pain of removing it. When she turns to glance at me, I see that the fluorescent light has blanched further her already pallid face, and for an instant, I am reminded of the first boy I saw bleed out in Vietnam: There was a translucency about him; I swore you could almost see his heart through skin and bone.

There's something perverse in the way fluorescent light bleaches faces, annihilates shadow. As I turn down the next aisle I am struck by the labels on the canned goods, string beans gray-green as if they'd been boiled to mush; tomatoes depicted on jars of spaghetti sauce, too red, the overripe red of fruit gone bad. I walk faster, looking straight ahead at the sign-board hanging over the end of the aisle: CANNED VEGETABLES SPAGHETTI SAUCE PASTA.

When I turn the corner, too fast, I nearly hit a pyramid display of crackers. I pull the cart back a little, straighten the wheels, and when I look up, I see Callahan halfway down the aisle, a box of soap powder in his hand. I wheel the cart around then. Head to the back of the store, where I stop at the mostly empty meat counter. I pick up a lone package of lamb, then put it back. I walk away from the cart, heading for the produce aisle.

Gloria waves again, probably wondering why I'm leaving empty-handed.

My attorney eyes me. Takes in the skirt I wear, a subtle floral wrap. Too long now. Grazing the bone just above my ankles. "You haven't been eating, Lily," she says, "have you?"

I sit back in the chair, cross my legs. "It's dull, cooking for yourself," I say.

"You'll have to invest in some new clothes," she says. "Something that fits properly." She plants her elbows on her desk, rests her chin on her knuckles. "We want you well put together, healthy-looking."

Honora Hudson-Whitman looks at me, not without compassion. Her name suggests strength and integrity. It fits her.

"They're going to be ruthless," she says. "They'll make use of it all. Distort things. Try to make it appear that you're damaged, not fit to raise a child."

"I've prepared myself," I say, and in a fundamental way I mean it.

I can see that she is skeptical. "When you come on Wednesday, we'll begin preparation for the stand," she says. "In the meantime, I want you to buy something feminine. Classic and feminine. Something in a soft color that drapes nicely. That subtly accentuates your best features."

"You mean to use my feminine wiles?" I ask.

"We use whatever is available to us," she says. "Your beauty is a tool, simply a tool."

I stand, feeling my skirt slide against my calves. Honora Hudson-Whitman stands too and says, "It really is important that you look well. Try to eat a little better. I know it's the last thing you're worrying about, but it's important here."

I don't tell her that the thought of eating makes me nauseated. That I've stood at the counter in my kitchen, forcing myself to eat, taking small bites from a peanut butter sandwich, gagging them down, that I've looked at myself in the mirror more than once and, like her, come to the same conclusion.

The saleswoman carefully lines a navy suit box with sheets of cream-colored tissue paper. "Beautiful shade," she says, "especially with your coloring, your hair." I watch as she lovingly folds the things I've bought: a caramel-colored skirt and twin set; the sweater's cashmere, the skirt a blend of cashmere and lamb's wool. The woman reels off yards of cream-colored ribbon and proceeds to tie it around the box, finishing with a soft multilooped bow that resembles an exotic flower. "There," she says, "that should do it."

I adjust my sunglasses, sliding them up on the bridge of my nose. Out two days in a row. This time for shoes. Luckily, I found what I needed at the first store I went to: Village Shoes. A pair of buttery-soft ballerina-style flats, a few shades deeper than the sweater-skirt set.

The truck in front of me, waiting at a light, has its driver's-side mirror adjusted in such a way that it reflects sun back, momentarily blinding me. I use my hand as a visor and give the driver time to get through the intersection before I follow. Just after I pass through, I catch a glimpse of Callahan's truck parked in front of Glennda's. I take the next left, the graveled drive of a nursery. I pull into a parking space, easing up to a border of yellow chrysanthemums. In the rearview, I can see Glennda's across the way, Callahan's van parked in front, perfectly parallel to the curb.

I feel like I'm becoming transparent—only, unlike the boy I couldn't save, there is nothing to be seen through the transparency of my skin, no heart, no bone. I look into the rearview mirror again. My face is pale, my eyes oddly bright, the pupils dilated in the shadow of the car. I lever the seat back, unbuckle the safety belt, take the keys from the ignition, get out.

I peruse the line of mums till I see Callahan come out. I watch as he holds the door open for an elderly couple going into Glennda's. He smiles and nods, saying something in passing. The man nods enthusiastically, his bald head shining in the sun. When I see that he has seen me, I wave and with as much nonchalance as I can muster, I cross the street.

"I've wanted to talk to you," I say. "To apologize. I saw your van as I was heading home. So."

His expression is neutral.

"How are you doing?" he asks.

"As well as can be expected," I say.

"You haven't gone to court yet?"

"Next week," I say.

"I wish you well, Lily," he says.

I go for it. Humble myself, say, "Callahan, I'm sorry. About the other evening. How about tonight? I'll cook. To make up for my bad behavior."

Before he can answer, a young woman waltzes out of Glennda's holding a Styrofoam container aloft as if she were carrying something fragile and rare.

Callahan stands back so she can get by. "Let me figure it out, Lily. I'm working on a restoration in Brunswick," he says. "I'll call you later."

"Sure," I say, "no problem."

I cross the street, unlock the Peugeot, slide in behind the wheel, and start the engine. I wait till I see Callahan pull away from the curb before I back into the street. He won't come, I think. And suddenly I feel sick with disappointment.

I take a bath, shave with a blue plastic razor that has been hanging from the slotted soap dish for weeks. It drags as I try to slide it up over the bony protuberance just below my knee, and in my haste I disregard the dull blade and cut myself. I sit forward and watch the blood flow, a red rivulet. It reminds me of the 71st, of watching a kid bleed out faster than we could pump it in. I lay my head back against the rolled edge of the tub, pull my knees up, watch the blood still trickling, dripping into the water, eddying in rusty-colored waves.

Callahan calls at three-thirty. "Sorry I didn't call you sooner," he says. "Just only now managed to get away. No phone close by."

"That's okay," I say. "I know you can't walk off and make a call in the middle of things."

I hear him juggle the phone as if he has his hands full. "What time are you planning dinner?" he asks.

"Seven, seven-thirty," I say.

"I have to go home and clean up," he says. "I'll try to be there around seven-thirty."

"That's fine," I say. "See you then."

He hesitates for a few seconds and then says, "Do you need anything?"

"No," I say, "thanks."

"Okay, see you in a while."

It is ten to eight when I hear Callahan's engine. I put my paring knife down, take the dish towel from my shoulder, dry my hands, go to the door, open it, then go back to the table to finish slicing carrots. He knocks lightly on the door frame before coming in.

"A little wet out there?" I ask, looking up from carrots piled like orange Lincoln Logs, round on one side, flat on the other.

"We need it," he says, "just not all at once." He closes the door and, before taking his jacket off, says, "Maybe I should hang this in the shed; it's soaked."

I say, "No, you can hang it on one of those." I nod at the row of brass hooks mounted on a shellacked pine board, stenciled in green ivy, next to the door. "A little rainwater won't hurt *this* floor."

He hangs the jacket, walks to the table, pulls out a chair, and sits, his hands flat-palmed on his knees.

"Let me get you a beer." I lay the knife on the cutting board and push back in my chair.

"No," he says, "finish what you're doing and I'll get it."

I resume cutting, slice a carrot down the middle, place it carefully atop the pile, so as not to start a log slide. There is an edginess about Callahan. Like he's got something to say.

"Would you like a beer?" he asks before closing the refrigerator.

"No thanks," I say, "I've got one over there, next to the sink."

He gets himself a mug, comes back to the table, sits across from me, angles the glass, pours the beer. "It smells great," he says. "What you're cooking."

"Rosemary chicken," I say, "and roasted potatoes."

There's a curious tension that feels as solid as the leaves of the oak table we're sitting at. Callahan sips beer from his glass and looks at me in a way that makes me focus on the carrots in a fashion not warranted by root vegetables. And I hope that I'm not picking up what I think I'm picking up, that's he's got it wrong somehow, that he thinks I want something more than a friend, a lover maybe, and I can't even imagine that right now, though it has all to do with me, and nothing, really, to do with him.

I finish the carrots, spill them from the cutting board into a bowl, get up, cross to the stove, use the mitt to open the oven door, pull out the rack, lift the casserole cover, dump the carrots into the bubbling juices.

I pour the rest of my beer into the glass and sit down across from him. "Finished, for the moment, anyway," I say.

He thumbs the base of the beer bottle. "You seem to be putting on a good front, Lily," he says.

"Good practice, appearing normal, don't you think?"

"Just as long as you don't break under the strain," he says. "Though I've got to tell you, it's convincing."

"That's good to hear," I say. "Maybe I can inspire more of the same in the courtroom." I'm aware of Callahan's body, of the subtlety of movement, the way he sits slightly back, then leans forward, then back again. I feel a kind of unspecified anxiety in the muscles of my chest. On pretense of checking the carrots, I get up to try to alleviate the feeling.

He stands, beer in his hand, leans against the counter next

to the stove, watching me spoon caramelized juice over the carrots. "You know I'll do what I can to help, Lily," he says. "My only expectation of you is that you come out of this thing intact."

I close the oven door, feeling a sense of relief, which for some strange reason makes me start to cry. I dab my eyes with the dish towel, look at Callahan, and shake my head. "Sorry," I say, "sorry."

Callahan sets his beer on the counter, stands in front of me, and puts his hands on my shoulders. "Absolutely nothing for you to be sorry about, Lily," he says. "It's okay."

And this feels like déjà vu, like we've done it all before.

The warm weight of his hands is powerfully reassuring. But when he hugs me, it only makes me more emotional, to my chagrin.

Finally, I get a grip and say, "Will you excuse me for a minute, please?"

In the upstairs bathroom, I blow my nose and wash my face, and in the mirror I chide myself. "You're just a little schizoid, aren't you? It's Jaime you've got to think about. Everything else is irrelevant, including what's going on, if anything, between you and Callahan."

He's saved the potatoes from burning. And I have to laugh at him, with an oven mitt half on, too small for his big hand, clutching the casserole dish. "Why, don't you make a lovely Julia Child," I say, glad for the comic relief.

He gingerly sets the dish down on the top of the stove and says, "Why, thanks. I believe that's a compliment, is it?"

With the tension eased, we eat comfortably enough. Talking about *safe* things. No mention of Jaime or Ben or Vietnam.

Honora Hudson-Whitman calls a few minutes after Callahan has left. I answer her perfunctorily. My voice sounding distant to me.

———

The front hall is dark. And I am acutely aware that she is waiting. On the stairs. Close enough for me to smell the fruity sweetness of her breath, a manifestation of dehydration, the sanguineous fluid oozing freely from her burns. I leave her and go back to the kitchen. And for a time I stand in front of the wall phone before finally calling Callahan. I can tell that he has just walked in, Max happily vocalizing in the background, ecstatic at having him home. "I'm sorry to bother you," I say. "I know you must have just walked in. And I can't explain why, but I need someone here right now. Could you possibly bring Max and come back?"

I have no recollection of time passing. I am sitting on the landing. In the dark. And I hear someone calling my name. Then suddenly there is light at the bottom of the stairs and Callahan is standing on the carpeted tread of the first step, Max beside him. I hold my knees tightly to my chest and watch rainwater run down the front of his jacket and hear its muffled drip as it hits the thick wool pile at his feet.

I wake to see Max looking pensively out of the bay window, the stump of his tail doing a sort of semi-wag. I hitch up on my elbows, lean back against the sofa pillows. "Dog," I say, "what are you doing?" He gives me a cursory glance and refocuses his attention on whatever he's watching. I kick the throw off and get up to see what he's so interested in. Callahan pulls in, parks in his usual manner, and when he gets out, he is balancing paper cups of coffee set in a cardboard tray. Max's ears lift and tip forward as he watches Callahan maneuvering breakfast. I go back to the sofa and pull the throw up to my chin. Max gingerly slides his paws from the sill, giving me a sidelong glance, as if suddenly aware that this isn't his house and he might be in trouble for the impropriety. "It's okay," I say to him. "You are allowed."

And his sheepishness disappears instantly when he hears

Callahan coming through the dining room. He rushes to the door, cocks his head, lifts his ears, and listens. When the door opens he jumps back, playfully jutting his rear end up in the air, his doggy lips curling.

"Couldn't find your coffee this morning," Callahan says. He sets the cardboard tray on the end table, takes a Styrofoam cup out, and hands it to me.

"That's because I'm out. Thanks for going to Glennda's."

Max is still coiling around Callahan, no longer worried that he'd been left behind.

"Did he wake you up?" Callahan says.

"No," I say, "I woke on my own."

He rubs the dog's muzzle. Sweet-talks him. "Yes, Max, you're a good fella," he says, "a good fella."

I take a sip of coffee. It is black and steaming and slightly bitter. A little too hot yet, so I set it back in the cardboard tray. "Thank you for last night, Callahan," I say. "I was in a kind of panic after you left. It's hard for me to explain why, really." I look down at the floor, hesitating, momentarily fixing on the small dark eye of a knot in a length of pine. Then I try to get it right, try to make him understand: "I saw a lot of bad stuff in Vietnam. And it comes back sometimes. Ghosts, you might say. I know it sounds crazy, but it's the best I can do. The closest to the truth I can come."

He pulls the rocker close to the sofa and sits down. "You don't have to explain anything to me, Lily," he says. "I have an intimate understanding of ghosts myself. You don't have to explain a thing."

He's talking about his son, I think, and in a way, I realize, he does understand what I'm feeling; it's not such a long shot, after all.

"The last thing I remember," I say, "is you tucking me in."

"You were out for the count," he says. "The strain of putting up a front had finally gotten to you, apparently." He smiles at me and I think of his warning at dinner the night before.

I'd closed my eyes after he covered me, I remember. Turned on my side and drew my knees up. He sat in the same rocking chair, pulled close to the sofa. Max, for his part, had daintily climbed onto the cushions and curled like a fawn at my feet, a plush warm bolster. Callahan had rocked slowly, back and forth, back and forth, stroking my hair gently, like you would a child's. And I slept then, like I haven't slept in months.

He sips his coffee and lets his hand fall to the knob of bone atop Max's skull and absently thumbs the skin over it. "Oh yes, Max, that feels good, doesn't it?" he says.

And when he's through petting Max, he reaches under the throw to take my hand. "I could get used to sleeping in this rocking chair," he says. "It'd take a little doing, but I could."

"I hope I won't need you to," I say. "I'd like to think my ghosts would give up on me, get a little tired of hanging around."

He lets go of my hand and sits back in his chair. "That's just the way it is," he says. "The longer we live, the more people we know, the more ghosts we confront."

I hope he's wrong—otherwise, I will be walking with a legion of ghosts by my life's end.

I need to focus. To be ready, the hearing in less than two weeks. I am having a dress rehearsal of my own, standing before the mirror in my go-to-court clothes. The skirt drapes gracefully, falling mid-calf, the color warming my skin, neutralizing the sallow tone that I have chosen to dismiss to this point.

I feel sick with longing for Jaime, and it is there, absolutely evident in my face and my body. And beneath that longing is something darker: the sudden revelation that I am capable of violence, of doing something murderous to get him back. I sense him in my body, my breasts feeling strangely prickly and full, as if aching for the letting down, for the milk that no longer runs, the feeling intensifying, until I close my eyes tightly and wince, saliva rising under my tongue.

To distract myself, I fix on the task at hand: I undress, taking care to slip the sweater over a padded hanger and to zip the skirt and fasten the hooks before putting it in the closet. Then in bra and slip I reach back to fiddle with the clasp of the necklace, trying to catch the tiny lever under my nail. I labor unsuccessfully till my arms ache, and for a few seconds I let them hang loose at my sides before reaching up to snatch the strand at the hollow of my neck. I yank hard and watch pearls fire with surprising force, ricocheting off closet door and wall. I watch them roll across the floor and disappear under the bed.

I am determined, and though I still feel some anxiety, at least it is not paralyzing as it has been. I survived the interview with the court-appointed psychologist, though it felt more like interrogation than interview. He kept hammering me with the same question: "You acknowledge that you suffer from post-traumatic stress disorder. Has this not had adverse effects on your child?" It was hard to take the man seriously. Each time he asked a question, he sat forward in his chair, causing his rotund stomach to spread like yeast dough over his lap.

"No, I don't think so," I said. "I think Jamie feels safe with me. With the exception of what happened in the car; that was an aberration. We've talked about it a lot; he asks questions, and I tell him that I'm working on what frightened me that morning, that it was a kind of daytime nightmare. I promised him it won't happen again.

"He trusts me," I said, "and I'll do whatever it takes to keep us both safe."

I went on answering simply, trying to be honest. But I was repelled by his manner and treated him with barely cloaked contempt. After an hour of going over the same ground, he ended the interview. I thought it important to be decisive: "I am confident," I said lastly, "that I will prevail. No one loves that little boy like I do." I left him then, still in his chair.

I dreamed hard last night. Traveled through a nightlong hell pursued by Montagnard women. But there were no Highland mists smelling green and fecund in this dream, no mountain trails, no vines snaking up the buttresses of smooth-barked trees into triple canopy. Only the nineteenth-century buildings of downtown Pointe Blue. I crouched behind the columns of City Hall, my knees pressed into the fluted grooves of a shaft, my fingers spread over the sugary-fine surface of granite, balancing myself. Though I never saw the women, I knew they had followed me along the other side of Main Street where the shops backed the river, the rear of JCPenney, Sears Roebuck, and Goldstein's Jewelers all stark red-brick against which pallets and boxes were stacked.

I managed to lose them momentarily after slipping through what could be described as an alleyway, a dim antediluvian space between Sears Roebuck and the yard-goods store. The brick walls on either side, mottled with grime, were bedecked with the down of pigeon feathers, fine-quilled gray fluff that floated ethereally in the damp breeze.

Once hunkered down behind the columns, I saw them come through the narrow breach into the street. And there was not another soul about, no women shopping with bored children whining to go home, no salesmen in white shirts, cuffs rolled, out at noon for something to eat, hot dogs and fries from the lunch counter at Woolworth's or pickled eggs and corned-beef sandwiches from the beer parlor across from the Colonial Theater. There were no cars. No delivery trucks. No sign of life other than the women.

They carried machetes, all except the last woman, who cradled the body of a little girl whom I recognized. The girl's arms and legs were contracted in rigor mortis, drawn in to her chest and belly, her hair falling over the crook of the woman's arm like a dark silken fringe.

I knew they held me responsible for the death of the child. And so I decided to stand, to show myself. To try to explain that I couldn't have saved her, though God knows I tried.

I tried to talk to them, but they would have none of it and they mobbed me, their arms sinewy and strong, vines binding me as if I were a host, a living thing to bear their vengeance. The woman holding the child began to wail, a sound so fraught with grief that it made me tremble. I stopped struggling, sickened by the terrible keening.

I jerked awake then, my body anticipating the bite of blade.

And though I've been up for more than an hour, the dream still grips me, a bad omen come at a particularly inauspicious time, the night before the hearing. Even the steam floating above my bath feels menacing, like poisonous gas. My calf muscles contract and twitch, and my toes cramp, curling under painfully.

When I dress, I see that the skirt I had thought so becoming now fits loosely, unflattering. I button the cardigan so that it covers the slack waist. Never mind, I tell myself. Never mind. You'll carry yourself in such a manner that they won't notice. I stand taller, draw my chin up, look straight on.

The courthouse, a Greek Revival structure, complete with colonnaded portico, is one of the most elaborate nineteenth-century buildings in the state. I follow Honora Hudson-Whitman up wide granite stairs, feeling a sense of trepidation.

The lobby is lined with oak benches. Some people sit quietly, hands slack in their laps, eyes cast down. Others mill around like walleyed goats in a pen, oblivious of one another. It's impossible to tell who's who: Traffic violator? Shoplifter? Sex offender? About-to-be divorcée?

Honora Hudson-Whitman situates me on a bench close to

the courtroom, excuses herself, and goes off to see if the proceedings will start on time. Everyone I glance at looks guilty. A man across the foyer from me hangs back from an ashtray, waiting for a sullen-faced woman clutching a pack of Winstons to get out of the way. When she does, he moves in warily as if he expects the ashtray to suddenly disappear before he can grind his cigarette out against its metal lip. For a moment, I seriously consider looking for a cigarette machine, but I change my mind when I see Ben and Rachel come through the door into the lobby. They're so absorbed with each other that they don't see me.

I sit back against the wall in the shallow space created by faux-marble pilasters that stand a few feet beyond either end of the bench. I hardly have time to react before I look up to see the Montagnard child standing amid a loose knot of people who, like delinquent crows, seem obsessively drawn to the bright steel cylinder of an ashtray. It is uncanny, the way they carefully maneuver around her, as if they can see her.

I reach for my bag, slide the strap up over my shoulder, and at that moment she vanishes, and the woman who is bending to tap the ash from her cigarette straightens and steps into the space where, only seconds before, the child had stood.

I close my eyes, say under my breath, "Enough of this—no more goddamn ghosts. No more."

The courtroom is lit by electrified nineteenth-century wall sconces and chandeliers. Beautifully carved black-walnut panels rise chest-high, in contrast to the walls above them, which are painted a drab utilitarian green; life-size portraits of Washington and Lincoln hanging in gold-leaf frames against opposing walls relieve the eye of the dismal color. Before I sit, I see Callahan come in and stand to the side, just under Washington. He nods, and I find myself feeling grateful that he didn't take me for my word when I told him I'd rather go it alone.

I have not looked at Ben, who sits on the other side of the

room, next to his extraordinarily well-dressed attorney, a man who seems to have walked out of the pages of *GQ,* chalk-line suit, maroon silk tie, and all. Instead, I focus on the judge, a man who looks to be in his late sixties; his face, the color of ground sirloin, sports matching jowls that drape obscenely over his starched white collar. I wonder what became of the woman judge we were supposed to have. Honora Hudson-Whitman reaches under the table to pat my knee. I sit up straight, feeling the muscles between my ribs contract and go taut.

The first witness is called. My friendly child psychologist, whose belly looks less like risen dough today, his neatly buttoned double-breasted suit coat minimizing his rotundity, walks to the stand. Ben's attorney wastes no time. "Good morning, Doctor," he says. "Would you start, please, by giving us your name and address, and a rundown of your qualifications."

The doctor sits forward a bit, gives his name and address, then pauses for a moment before reeling off his qualifications: a degree in psychology from Colby College; a master's and PhD from Berkeley, graduating summa cum laude in 1960; received special training in psychology with regards to abuse of children; is a licensed psychologist who has been practicing for eighteen years and is a member of various societies in the psychiatric field. At which point, he identifies the three he considers the most distinguished.

Ben's attorney nods. "Thank you, Doctor," he says, "and in that capacity were you retained by the court to conduct a professional determination as to whether or not there was any history of any type of abuse or neglect of child Jaime?"

Again, the doctor sits forward; his hands, I notice now, are extraordinarily white. Spread loosely on one knee, they look strangely avian, his fingers fanned like tail feathers. "Yes," he says, "I was contacted by the court to make the typical determinations as to which parent would provide the best parental care."

I begin to feel sick to my stomach. I'd been wrong to dismiss the doctor. Here in the courtroom his authority is undeniable and I cannot take my eyes off him.

Ben's attorney continues. "And what did you do, Doctor?"

"The first thing I did was to contact the child's pediatrician in order to try to familiarize myself as to the child's medical history; then I conducted separate interviews, at length, with the father, the mother, and the child."

"And what did you learn, Doctor?"

"The major issue," the doctor says, "is the fact that the child was put in harm's way because Mrs. Townsend, suffering from post-traumatic stress disorder as a result of serving in a war zone, had a dissociative episode while the child was in her care."

"And how was child Jaime put in harm's way, Doctor? Would you describe what you know about the incident, please?"

"Well, I should explain that persons suffering from PTSD can actually relive a traumatic event as though experiencing that event at that moment. Often there is a trigger, as there was in this case. Mrs. Townsend responded to the sound of a back-firing car, and, behaving as if she were in a life-threatening situation, she sought a safe place."

As he described how I, in this so-called dissociative state, opened the car door and *flung* myself out, then *scrambled* under the car, I started to hear a frenzied buzz in my head, like bees caught in a jar. Jaime, the doctor continued, had somehow gotten out of his car seat, crawled over into the front seat and out the driver's-side door, where he followed me under the car.

"According to witnesses, the child was frantic, screaming for his mother, who, in the throes of dissociation, was not conscious of him or the possible danger he could be in."

Ben's attorney waits for what seems to me to be an eternity before asking the next question. "Could you tell us, Doctor, what happened to child Jaime?"

I close my eyes, the buzzing in my head growing more intense, sounding like panicked bees after the jar's been shaken.

"While trying to get to his mother, the child burned his head on the exhaust manifold and suffered abrasions to his hands and knees from the pavement."

I feel as if I've been initiated, that I am now part of an afflicted sisterhood, the women within it dispossessed, some half crazy from loss, their children either kept from them completely or given to them provisionally, a few hours at a time, hours eked out between Sunday and Sunday, hours long on false cheer, filled with "treats," a half-eaten Popsicle left to melt in a small Tupperware container, one end of the stick immersed in cherry-colored liquid.

I have a sense that the doctor relishes the drama he is creating; like an actor he speaks in a low, modulated tone, so that the judge has to listen more closely: "When I questioned the child, he told me that he tried to wake his mother and that he became frightened because she was, and I quote, 'asleep with her eyes open and couldn't hear me.' "

The buzzing intensifies and I experience a curious out-of-body feeling. I make fists of my hands, squeezing as hard as I can, but I can't feel the machinations of my own body.

When Ben's attorney speaks, I look up. "Doctor," he says, "could you give us an assessment of the mother's ability to parent?"

Again the doctor assumes his low, solemn tone. "I certainly can't suggest that Mrs. Townsend is a bad mother," he says. "In fact, I found her to be loving of her child like any other mother. But she obviously has some psychiatric problems as a result of flashbacks, and she is affected at home, as well as outside of the home." He goes into a litany then about my need for the "oblivion" of darkness and how Jaime has apparently become *acclimated* to this *anomaly* and does not have the normal fear of darkness that most children experience, *at least transitorily*. He makes me sound like a bride of Dracula.

Ben's lawyer turns to study me for a moment before resuming his questioning. "Doctor, would this aberrant behavior and particularly the flashbacks affect the mother's ability to properly parent?"

"Of course it's hard to determine how Mrs. Townsend's going to handle these flashbacks and whether or not they'll impact her in day-to-day life. One could conceive that if the episodes worsened, it definitely would limit her ability to parent, as we have already seen."

Dismayed, I look over at Ben. I cannot believe he's doing this to me.

His attorney moves closer to the stand, so that he's partially blocking the doctor. "Are you able, Doctor," he says, "to give an opinion to this court as to who would be a better parent to child Jaime?"

"Yes," the doctor says. "Although certainly not meant to denigrate the mother and primarily based on the totality of circumstances and evidence, I believe the custodial parent in this case should be the father."

Honora Hudson-Whitman rises. I feel her readiness for the fray. She approaches the stand as one would approach a small yipping dog, with the intention of firmly shutting it up.

But when she speaks, I can hear nothing for the buzzing in my head.

CHAPTER 14

I habitually cheer myself on now: I will not lose Jaime. I *will* lick the melted ice cream that oozes over his cone, will smooth his hair back from his sleep-flushed face and get exasperated when he giggles uncontrollably as I wash his toes. The court decrees it so, after all. Guarantees my time with him. With conditions. Of course. But he *will not* be lost to me.

But I do know that sometimes loss is inevitable, because each February I am reminded of what I lost in Saigon, Tet 1968. I know this: One act can irrevocably change your life. I had gone out hoping to find Ian at Reuters. And that changed everything. Bao-Long died because of that impulse.

Sometimes I'm not sure of the absolute truth here, what images are real and what are not. Memory seems to alter over time. And I'm not sure it matters now. It is in the past. And I can do nothing about it. Other than hope it will illuminate the present.

The trees are radiant. Even in the rain. Maples flare like flame against a nickel-plated sky. As we round a curve, gravel ricocheting off fenders and rocker panels, the stone house comes into view. Callahan downshifts, eases the brake in, slows, and pulls the car into the driveway. It glides through a drift of yellow leaves and stops before the rise of a hummock that is lawn to the ell of the house.

"Tim's already been here," he says. "Smell wood smoke?"

"I don't know why you're doing this, Callahan," I say, wondering what the hell I was thinking when I agreed to come. I look at his face, at the openness that reveals a dogged patience, and I feel like a child who is yet, one more time, going to disappoint. "Really," I go on, "I'm no kind of company."

"Lily, I'm not asking for company. I've got work to do around here, and you've got no obligation to entertain me. It's just a change of scenery, that's all. I thought it'd be good for you to get away for a few days."

I open the car door and step out and find myself ankle-deep in the yellow drift; leaves plaster themselves to the green rubber shanks of my boots. The house, a groundskeeper's cottage—once part of an estate, according to Callahan—is exactly as he had described it: a small cape with an ell, the main house set with beach cobble, the ell shingled in cedar shakes weathered to the color of flint. Callahan has opened the trunk. I go around the car to help carry the bags. He has already taken the heaviest ones, his duffel and a scarred Samsonite that I had before I was married. I take what's left, a couple of bags of groceries.

Callahan stops on the path and looks out at the fields. "It's beautiful up here, isn't it?" he says. "I guess that's why I haven't had the heart to sell the place."

"I can see why," I say. I answer this way only to be polite, because though *I can see it,* I can't feel it right now, the beauty of the fawn-colored fields delineated by rock walls, which I should find soothing but which only manages, by contrast, to make me feel even more despondent: I really should not have left Pointe Blue, and though I know it's irrational to want to be rattling around in an empty house, on a vigil of sorts, waiting for Jaime to come for his first *visit* on Monday, I cannot seem to dissuade myself, even in a place of such peace. Staying in Pointe Blue feels like a sentence that I must serve, part of the punishment being the deep humiliation at having my child's time with me subject to the scrutiny of the social worker appointed by the court, a man whose nose and cheeks bloom red with broken blood vessels. He will interview Jaime and me separately once a week, to see how things are going, to see if I've had some over-the-top reaction to something as innocuous as a backfiring car. And though I have tried to convince myself that I *can* overcome responding irrationally to the incidental static in everyday life and dismiss the odd backfire or sonic boom, I still feel the noose of apprehension around my neck because the stakes are so high: I let myself explore the idea that joint custody won't even be a possibility and that Jaime, devotee of Tonka trucks and all creatures prehistoric, will become more and more attached to that *happy little family:* Daddy and Auntie Rachel, and, of course, cousin Nina. So I must not let my guard down, even when Jaime is with his father. I have to steel myself for any eventuality. Solace, epitomized by the autumn countryside, somehow seems self-indulgent to me at this point.

When I turn back, Callahan is holding the door open for me. Were it not for the light in the downstairs windows, the cobble house would blend into a backdrop of oak and sky; branches, like upturned umbrella spokes, rise above the tin roof; clusters of papery leaves, gone russet in the afternoon light, rattle in the wind. We walk into an entryway, a small white-painted space with a highly polished wood floor. To the right is a living room.

"Have a look around, if you want," Callahan says, "while I take care of these." He hefts the bags and proceeds up a crude staircase that seems like an intrusion in this cozy house. Logs have been laid in the fireplace, mounded skillfully, newspaper rolled and knotted and tucked underneath, proof of a competent fire-starter. Tim Dillard, no doubt, Callahan's closest neighbor up here. Dillard, a woodsman from way back, according to Callahan, had the audacity to refuse to sell his acreage, as fine a hardwood timberland as you'd find anywhere, to the paper company. A man in his seventies, Dillard still goes into the woods with a team of horses to haul out oak and maple that his son fells with a chain saw, a small concession to modernity.

A package of wooden matches has been left conveniently on the mantel, next to a blue agate pitcher filled with faded sea lavender. A remnant, it would seem, of Callahan's wife. I take in the rest of the room: two overstuffed chairs covered in a worn floral fabric, flowers once red now pale salmon, shelves of books on either side of the fieldstone fireplace, everything from Thoreau to the Hardy Boys to a collection of *National Geographic* magazines bookended on one side with an assortment of neatly stacked games and puzzles: Chinese checkers, a thousand-piece jigsaw of the Grand Canyon, Monopoly and Scrabble topped with a cribbage board. Between the windows on the far side of the room is a collapsible green-baize card table, the entire perimeter of a puzzle put together and centered, the box of remaining pieces on the seat of a metal folding chair.

I hear Callahan rummaging in the rooms overhead, so go back through the front entryway and into the kitchen beyond; it is a low-ceilinged room where a wood stove dwarfs everything else: a painted drop-leaf table, four mismatched chairs, an ice chest, a half-pint refrigerator squatting under an oak sideboard, and an apartment-size gas stove. The room, situated at the north end of the house, is evening-dim, though it's not much past three. I set the groceries down and turn on the wall lamp to the right of the table; curious, I open the cupboard door over the slate sink and counter; Melmac teacups in a pale shade of aqua hang from hooks, matching saucers stacked neatly beneath. I imagine Callahan's wife carefully hanging the cups, each facing in the same direction. I can feel her in the kitchen, feel her sorrow, how it manifests itself in the order of the teacups, or the neat line of cookbooks arranged by height, or the canned goods perfectly lined up an inch in from the edge of the open shelves. I understand her preoccupation with order. Isn't that what we do when we're most lost? Create order where we can. If only in our cupboards, facing teacups in the same direction.

I pull out a chair, sit at the table, look out a curtainless window at yellow leaves being funneled and whirled by the wind. Along the window sash, chestnuts and acorns have been lined up, next to a stone shaped like a coin and a child's block engraved with an Old English *R*. And I know she sat at this table, looking out too, wondering how she could possibly inhabit a world without her boy. And this only serves to make me feel my own despair more keenly, the visceral trembling I've felt since the hearing intensifying, making me feel physically sick. So that all I want to do is escape, go back to Pointe Blue and crawl into bed. Close my eyes and make it all go away. The same impulse I had after the Montagnard child died.

I still remember her grandmother, and an aunt, and her two older sisters squatting in grass planted to keep the dust down outside the Intensive Care Unit in Pleiku. Rooted in the red earth, it had sprouted in patchy bunches, sharp-bladed and tough underfoot. The family waited patiently in the hostile grass. In her lap, the grandmother cradled a collection of diminutive green packages: medicinal herbs securely wrapped in tender-ribbed leaves.

Because the child was so badly burned, sterile precautions were observed, the nurses gloved and gowned and masked, the bed linens autoclaved, as was everything else that went into the room. The grandmother was traumatized by the insistence that she "gown up," even though the reasons for the procedure had been explained to her by an interpreter. There would be no skin-to-skin touching, and the sterile gloves, grotesquely large for her small hands, would make *any kind* of touching awkward; the mask over her mouth and nose made her dark eyes the focal point of her face, the pain in them so intense that you had to avert your own eyes, sometimes looking beyond her into the middle distance.

Her small body shuddered beneath the loosely draped gown as she stood at the bedside, listening to the wheeze of the child's labored breathing. The mask seemed to amplify her sobbing. And for what seemed an eternity we stood like that, until I could bear it no longer. I shook my head at her and then untied her mask and lifted it from her face; her cheeks and neck were slick with tears, her nose running with snot. I dropped the mask on the bedside table and gestured for her to remove her gloves. Then I untied her gown and like a child she held her arms out so that I could slip it off her. When I left her she was sitting on the bed talking softly to the sleeping child; at a glance, her black hair, fastened in a thick silk knot at the back of her neck, reminded me of blackbird wings against an evening-yellow sky.

The child was not going to survive; there was no point in insisting that the family follow sterile precautions. The two older sisters, looking more like prepubescent children than the adolescents they actually were, squatted awkwardly next to the bed, as they had squatted in the grass, uncomfortable with the IV tubing that climbed like a transparent snake from where the needle was seated under the child's clavicle, up over the hillocks of pillow, to the bottle of solution that hung from the loop of a metal pole that looked like no tree they had ever seen. The hissing of oxygen, like the hissing of a snake, served to make them wary, as if there were needle-sharp fangs to fear. In order to keep the weight of the bedclothes up off the child, a metal-ribbed cradle had been positioned and secured over her small burned body. The sisters eyed it with suspicion, as if the metal ribs were prison bars. They rocked slowly back and forth, the younger one reaching up shyly to touch her baby sister's toes. In soft girlish voices they began to sing, the rhythm of their song indistinguishable from the rhythm of their rocking, the cadence inherently familiar to any who heard it, Montagnard and American alike, a kind of measure of grief known instantly by the body.

And when they stopped singing, the grandmother stopped wailing. The child's breathing had ceased, the hissing of the oxygen intensified by the sudden stillness. I removed the cannula from the diminutive nostrils and slipped between the bed and the O_2 tank to close the valve, that simple act fracturing the stillness with the grate of metal against metal. The corpsman who had been attending the child untied the strips of gauze that held the cradle to the bed frame and lifted it from the mattress. The grandmother crawled up onto the bed and lifted the dead child into her shallow lap. She rocked and wept, the aunt sharing the anguish, weeping with her, the older sisters, standing apart, gone mute with exhaustion and grief.

Finally, after the sun dropped abruptly behind the mountains, the women left, the grandmother carrying the dead girl. We watched them disappear into the relief of indigo shadow.

That night I sat on a makeshift deck outside my quarters, listening to a barrage of insect sound, an intense and rhythmic clicking punctuated by varying degrees of buzzing. Everything was strange in the green darkness of the Highlands, the hills purely and frighteningly haunted. I sipped Johnnie Walker, straight up, from a coffee cup and tried to make sense of it.

The child had not left the 71st EVAC; I was sure I felt her dark eyes studying me. And at one point, after I went in to lie down on my cot, I felt the hair on the back of my neck stand because I could smell the cloying sweetness of her breath, the scent of dehydration. Instead of blunting my senses, the whiskey seemed to have made me preternaturally aware, my senses so heightened that it was almost unbearable. The smell of human shit plowed into the red fields west of the compound. An abundant and cheap fertilizer. This commingled with the fecund odor always on the wind, the smell of moldering vegetation, a constant process of buildup and breakdown under the lush triple canopy. Add to this the final insult, the aroma of hot iron: the fryolater in the mess hall, grease bubbling violently, burping up french fries and chicken wings and chicken-fried steak.

In the end, I gave up trying to sleep; I dressed and headed back to the ICU unit and spent most of the night reading over patient charts, and then, to achieve the effect I needed—a total absence of original thought—I went on to plod methodically through the literature that had come with the latest shipment of pharmaceuticals: an up-and-coming wide-spectrum antibiotic, a new antimalarial with fewer adverse side effects, and, last, a more effective (the literature exulted) fungicide to combat a particularly noxious type of jungle rot. At daybreak, having dulled my senses with lists of contraindications and possible side effects, I made my way back to my quarters, the sun rising like Lazarus.

Through the thinning trees, I see straw huts. Children squatting before the dead ashes of a cookfire. Stirring with sticks. They laugh. The laughter is musical and infectious. Clouds of ash, created by the stirring, powder the sun-browned skin of their hands.

After a few minutes of watching the children play, wondering how I should approach them, I hear a plane flying low over the canopy of trees behind me, and within seconds it is overhead, and then directly above the village, and as it flies beyond the border of the village, I hear a terrible whoosh, as if the oxygen has been sucked out of the atmosphere, and simultaneously I see a ball of saffron-colored fire and black smoke, and I smell the oily stench of napalm.

In terror, the children run, scuttling into the hut closest. I scramble through the trees and out into the open. But before I can get to the hut where the children are, it explodes into flame, the heat so intense that I am forced backward.

From the tree line, I can still feel heat from the fire on my face.

Powerless to save them, I can only watch the annihilation. In a matter of minutes the village has been razed. Through gauzy rags of smoke I can make out the blackened figure of a child sitting in a drift of smoldering embers, her arms frozen over her head as if to protect it, her body still burning, though there is no obvious flame. I hear the crackle and sizzle of fat, what little she has on her body, feeding the coals. I retch.

I feel the coldness of pine planking under my feet and taste the bitterness of bile in my mouth. I am squatting with arms wrapped across my chest. I don't remember getting up, leaving the bed that Callahan had made up for me in the room next to his. I hear him, his knee cracking as he comes into the room. He squats next to me. "Are you all right?" he says. "A nightmare?"

I nod.

"Let's get you taken care of. You're a wash of sweat." He helps me up. Puts his arm around my shoulders and guides me through the dimly lighted hall and into the bathroom. I sit on a cane-seated chair next to the tub, watching him, his back to me as he stands at the sink wetting a cloth under the running water. I reach out to touch the underbelly of the tub with the tips of my fingers, to deliberately confirm reality, to feel the raised swirl of brushstrokes, the aquamarine paint long since gone chalky and pale. It is the most disturbing night terror yet. I tell myself that I can use it somehow. Take whatever it has to give me. And then let it go. The Montagnards believe a soul can be lost, that fear or grief can cause it to flee the body. As I sit here, watching Callahan, I think they are innately right.

"Here, this'll make you feel better." Callahan lifts my chin and pats my face with the cool cloth. "Must have been one hell of a nightmare," he says.

And all I can do is agree in a sleep-hoarse voice. I close my eyes and smell a kind of faint dusty-cleanness on the wet cloth he uses. And I am grateful for the reality of that smell, and the feeling of coolness on my face, and even for the taste of bile at the back of my throat.

I watch from the window as Callahan pulls into the driveway. He stretches after cutting the engine. He is back from helping Tim Dillard. When he gets out of the car, his deliberate movements tell me that his muscles are stiff. I turn back to the fire I've built, an elbow of oak perched atop the logs sighing as flames consume it. While he was gone, I packed. If he can give me a ride to Bangor, I'll take a bus to Brunswick and from there take a taxi to Pointe Blue. I'm sorry to have to ask this of him and I know he may think it irrational that I want to go back to an empty house, but that's simply the way it is.

Callahan stops in the kitchen to check the stove. Cordwood clunks against the cast-iron belly of the stove as he fills it, the poker making thunking noises as he settles the logs. After he has taken care of the stove, he runs water in the slate sink. I hear him open a cupboard door, take a glass down. He turns the water off then and sets the glass in the sink.

He starts when he sees me. "I hoped you'd be napping," he says. "After last night."

"I'm okay," I say.

"Good," he says, "glad to hear it." And then he nods at the fire. "Fine job, there," he says.

"And I wasn't even a Girl Scout," I say.

He sits on the edge of the sofa, rests his elbows on his knees, leans forward, clasps his fingers loosely in front of him. "I'm not going to ask you to tell me about it, the nightmare," he says. "Suffice to say, I could tell a hell of a lot by the way it affected you."

"I appreciate your sensitivity," I say.

Callahan takes my cue. Changes the subject completely. "So maybe you'd like to take a ride to the post office with me?" he says. "And there's a church supper at the Grange later if you're interested."

———

Callahan has agreed to drive me to Bangor in the morning. He does not question my reasons for wanting to return to Pointe Blue. I am relieved that I don't have to defend my position, though I am also surprised that he did not try to convince me to stay. I can hear him outside, splitting logs for the stove. I turn in bed, away from the windows. I am still cold, despite the blankets. I close my eyes. No use. I open them. Stare at the wallpaper. Which tells me something of Callahan's wife. I study the floral print, a scattering of red clover and dill weed, tiny upside-down parasols set with yellow flowers against a white ground. I notice a hole the size of a silver dollar in the wall just above the baseboard. The rocking chair set at an angle suggests someone rocked too closely. I throw the covers back and get out of bed.

I squat and probe the hole with a finger, touching the exposed tubercular rib of a lath; fragmented horsehair plaster spills onto the floor like coarse salt. I stand. Stroke the arm of the chair where it's worn smooth. And finally, I sit. And rock. She rocked her boy in this chair. I can feel it.

I get up. The chair slips back, rockers grazing the wall. I shiver, out of something other than coldness, I suspect. I check the closet to see if there is an extra blanket. It extends behind the walls on either side of the door. I slide the few clothes hanging there—a red flannel shirt, a gray sweater with both elbows out, and a khaki jacket—over the iron rod to the left. There are shelves at the farther end, sheets folded and stacked. I lift them and find a blue flannel blanket. Something that had been hidden under the blanket falls on my foot. I reach down and pick it up. A baby slipper.

I close the closet door after me, drop the blanket in the rocking chair, and examine the small beaded moccasin, fingering the soft fringe, and I distinctly remember Jaime's tiny baby feet, how I had studied them, held them, amazed at each delicate bud of a toe. Her child will be six for time immemorial.

She will never know him as a thirteen-year-old. Never hear his voice crack. Will never look up at him in wonder that she carried a baby who grew into such a man.

I put the moccasin back where I found it, feeling as if I've stumbled onto someone's private grief.

CHAPTER 15

When I get up groggy from a nap interrupted by an onslaught of twitching muscles and an absolutely believable feeling of falling, I find the house empty. The ashes of a fire smolder under the grate. I rake them with the poker, turning up enough live coals to catch paper. After settling quartered birch logs, bark-side down, on the grate, I crumple the last pages of the *Kennebec Journal* and, using the poker, stuff them under the kindling. The newsprint catches, sending up a crown of flames that engulfs the wood and ignites the papery bark.

Satisfied with the fire, I check out the kitchen. The draft on the woodstove is nearly closed. I use a pot holder to open it fully, then unlatch the door. Logs have been carefully stacked, compacted for maximum burn time. I close the door and adjust the draft again. Callahan's car is gone from the driveway, and I remember that he told me earlier he was going to Four Corners' Variety for the paper and to see the old fellas who still remember when these parts were prosperous lumber towns created by one robber baron or another.

The gauzy October sun has drawn me out. I walk the field beyond the house, up and down the rows, the stubble of corn stalks gone punky and ashen. I feel a sort of schizophrenia, an urge, still, to leave, but complicated by a desire that is nearly as strong to stay until Sunday. As I come upon a sort of no-man's-land between field and lawn, I see a faded red pickup slow down and pull in. I walk through a drift of leaves and across the lawn, to the driveway. The truck idles hard, an ancient Ford with split windshield and bulbous fenders. The driver, an elderly man dressed in wool mackinaw, the cuffs ragged and unbuttoned, leans out the window and says, "You must be Lily."

"Yes," I say. "And you must be Mr. Dillard."

"That's right, but Tim to you," he says, sticking his hand out, exposing a length of long underwear cuff that loosely bands his wrist. His skin is as speckled as ripe fruit, his fingers a mass of dings, the bed of his thumbnail sporting an ink-blue crescent. I take his hand, feeling calluses hard as burls on his palm.

"Nice to meet you," he says.

"Good to meet you," I say.

"Kevin off gallivantin'?"

"Four Corners', I think, for the paper."

"He'll be there for a piece, then," he says. "Can't get out of there without jawing with the boys. They get lonesome this time of year, no summer people to entertain them with their foolishness."

"I know how that goes," I say. And I feel a sense of complicity: two native Mainers who know that "summer people" can be as numb as a pounded thumb.

"Well," he says, "kindly tell him, if you would, that I stopped by."

"I'll do that," I say, "and by the way, thanks so much for making the house nice and toasty for us."

"Figured you were special company. Seeing you were the first since Maggie left, an age ago," he says.

There is an earnestness in the tone of his voice that makes me understand he is truly interested in Callahan's welfare, and that this isn't just idle chatter. "Maggie, Callahan's wife, you mean?" I ask.

"Kevin wouldn't appreciate it, me saying this. But we were all relieved to hear he had a lady friend. Awful thing, losing his boy. Then Maggie up and leaving."

Though I don't want to make the old man uncomfortable, I can't resist asking: "Why did she leave?"

"Don't really know," he says. "She left him a few days after the funeral. Came up here to stay. In fact, stayed through the winter. We tried to talk to her. You know. Tried to help her. But she wouldn't have anything to do with it. Didn't want us interfering with her grieving. Finally, in the spring, she took off out West, to stay with a sister or some such thing. And that was the last we saw of her. How the poor man survived that year I'll never know."

He reaches out to adjust the side mirror then. Shakes his head. "I'll be accused of gossiping," he says, "like an old woman."

"I won't say a thing," I say, "and besides, I asked you."

"That's right, young lady," he says. "You're to blame for me and my jawing."

I smile and he smiles back, his uppers neat as a row of white corn kernels. "You know," I say, "I've never asked Callahan what happened. How his boy died. He seems reluctant to talk about it."

"Terrible. Terrible that." And for the first time the old man looks away, rubs his clean-shaven chin, then thumbs the fleshy bulb of his earlobe. He stares out at the stubble of corn stalks for a few seconds before continuing. "It was an accident. The boy was hiding in the back of his father's truck. Being mischievous as kids will, trying to pull one over on his dad, you know. When Kevin set out for work and took a sharp corner, the boy went ass over teakettle. Came down hard against the tailgate. It dropped open and he fell out." The old man's eyes go dull then, washed-up bottle glass. "And that wasn't the worst of it,"

he says. "It was a car hit him that killed him. One of those station wagons. That was the worst of it."

I feel the blood gutter from my face.

The old man reaches out, braces my wrist with his hand.
"Are you okay?" he says. "Lord, I shouldn't of told you. So
outright."

"No," I say, "I wanted to know. It's just that I didn't expect
that. I thought he'd been sick. That it was leukemia or something like that."

"Well," he says, "dead is dead. Though this way has left his
father with a terrible lot of guilt."

I look at the old man. When I think of Callahan and his
wife and what they have endured, I feel shame. And then gratitude, the kind of guilty gratitude a survivor feels.

"You look like you're digesting that hard," the old man
says.

"I'm okay," I say. I take his hand then, feeling the calluses
again. "I'm glad Callahan has such a good friend."

The old man chuckles. "A good friend he owes for two
cord of stove wood."

I can still hear the loose tailgate of his truck in the distance
as I head up the path. And I remember the cat I hit. The
warmth of its body as I picked it up.

It is after four when I hear Callahan. He comes into the
kitchen, a cold draft in his wake. I can smell the coming winter
on his clothes and in his hair. I close the *National Geographic*
magazine I was perusing distractedly and push it across the
table. "You look cold," I say. "Car not heating up?"

"Car's fine," he says. "I saw old man Dillard out struggling
with a length of poly, trying to cover the north side of his foundation. So I stopped to help. We buttoned it up tight. And then
I set hay bales chockablock along the length of it. The old man
won't ask his son for help. Does things around the house when
his boy's off up in Ellsworth. Says the boy, a forty-year-old

man, mind you, works hard enough without having to do for his father."

"Did he tell you we met?" I say.

Callahan pulls out a chair and sits. "Yeah, well, he told me he was impressed with you. Says that you're as nice a looking woman as he's seen in a long while."

I can't help but laugh at the irony, knowing that I look exactly like I feel: distracted; someone whose mind is elsewhere and whose hair is in need of a shampooing, and toenails of clipping, never mind the little things like lipstick or cheek rouge or the glint of an earring. But I'm glad to hear it, just the same, because I know the old man didn't breathe a word about our conversation.

Callahan sits up in his chair, elbows winged over the spindled back. "He's a man of discerning taste, now, I tell you," he says.

I prop my chin in my palm and look at him, straight on. "What a lot of palaver," I say.

"I'm no palaverer," he says, "not me." A log shifts in the stove. He gets up, holds his hands over the filigreed cast-iron surface for a moment before opening the draft. Then he folds a pot holder in half and uses it to open the door. The hinges squeak loudly as the door yawns wide, revealing the last log nestled in a bed of dazzling coals. After he's filled the stove and adjusted the draft, he puts a hand to the small of his back and stretches. "To bed early tonight," he says. "We have to get up at the crack of dawn to get you to Bangor in time for the first bus. And after I come back, it's the gutters. Oak seedlings growing out of the decomposed leaves up there. Great growing medium, apparently. Last summer I had a crop of sunflowers. Made traffic by the house slow down to get a closer look."

That he does not offer to drive me back to Pointe Blue or try talking me into staying until Sunday somehow disappoints me. But I tell myself that I wouldn't change my mind: I want to be home. I watch Callahan sweep around the stove and I see in his face the son he lost, the boy in the photo atop the piano. And I feel something for him that I hadn't felt before. And it scares the hell out of me. Because it reminds me of Ian. And I don't think I have it in me to ever feel that way again.

CHAPTER 16

I came back to a damp house. The smell of creosote, intensified by the wind blowing down opened-flued chimneys, was pervasive. I set my suitcase down and I put catalogs, flyers, and bills in a pile on the kitchen table; I needed to get my name off some mailing lists. Gone only a few days, I'd come home to a mailbox regurgitating stacks of slick, glossy-paged housewares and seed catalogs. Though that was the least of my worries. The persistent smell of creosote depressed me, one more thing that reminded me of the emptiness of the house. I went into the living room to turn up the thermostat and close the flue. I reached up into the mouth of the chimney, found the lever. The rusty workings resisted, but I persevered until the flue slammed with a clatter.

After the house had warmed, I put the kettle on for tea, and while I waited for the water to boil, I stood at the windows that looked over the lawn and beyond to meadow. To the south the sky was milky, the sun opaque in a scrim of smoke rising from a fiery field just in sight of the house, the Arnolds burning off two seasons' worth of dead grass. I watched father and daughter armed with iron rakes nearly disappear in the smoke, only a red shirttail visible.

Beyond the fields, to the east, the sea looked unnaturally calm at midmorning. It was eerily quiet, the branches of the young spruce trees we'd planted for shade and, more importantly, birdsong paralyzed by the stillness. And the stillness, like the smell of creosote, worked at me, making me acutely aware of the absolutely reliable mechanism of grief industriously grinding away inside me.

"Enough," I said aloud, as if hearing the word would forswear the feelings. And, to further the process of disconnect, I thought of Callahan, of the steadfastness of his friendship. He accepted the peculiarity of my lot with grace, as if he'd heard it all before, so nothing to get uptight about. I had told him about even my most abhorrent behavior in Pleiku. I had seen the life vanish from a boy's eyes, like seeing the crest of a moon reflected in a puddle disappear when the thumping tires of a car displaced the water, and I went from the dead boy's bedside to the high hilarity of a party in someone's hooch, and I drank in order not to feel, losing all connection with my body. I slept with a subordinate that night, a corpsman with a midwestern accent; though opportunistic, he meant no harm, engaging in the act with enthusiasm, at one point cajoling me: "Come on, Lily," he'd said, "you can do a whole lot better than that." He may as well have been engaging in necrophilia. And he happily went on without me and fell asleep almost immediately after he came. I got up and dressed in the dark.

We were hit by rockets later that night. I stood under the drizzle of a lukewarm shower listening to the whine of incoming. I closed my eyes and lifted my face to the water and told myself that if I were blown sky-high, it would be a goddamn relief.

I eyed the pile of catalogs that had toppled and spread like a slick deck of cards. I got up and pulled the basket we used for kindling up to the table and, in one motion, swept the entire lot into the basket.

———

Among the bills was a letter from Ben suggesting that we put the house on the market. I couldn't face the idea of uprooting Jaime, of creating yet more chaos in his life. So I decided to ask my brother for a loan to buy Ben out. I had kept both my brother and mother at arm's length during the divorce proceedings. It wasn't easy putting my mother off, but I couldn't bear to tell her that I was afraid I'd lose Jaime, so I said something I wish I hadn't: "I can't deal with any hand-wringing right now, Mom. I'm sorry, but it's better that I be on my own with this."

In fact, she'd never been the type to hand-wring and had managed to overcome the most difficult circumstances with a level head and an amazing sense of humor, traits strengthened early on in her marriage, dealing with the mad antics of my father. And during my first short stint on P6 at Maine Med, not long after I got home from Vietnam, she handled things with aplomb, acting as if the strange cast of characters, I among them, who peopled the dayroom were no different than people she would encounter at the supermarket.

When I asked Mark for the loan, he offered to fly to Maine to help his little sister deal with her ex-husband: "Asshole," he said. "Someone needs to straighten him out." I assured him that there was nothing he could do in that regard. "It's done, Mark," I said. "My priority is Jaime now. I don't want to create any more chaos in his life." All I wanted, I told him, was a stable environment for Jaime, and the loan would help to create that.

"I am more than willing to give you the money," Mark said, "but I have one condition, and that is that you be honest with Mom." She had been deeply hurt by my behavior, he told me. "It will make her feel better when she understands what your motivations were."

I agreed to the conditions, regretting that I hadn't been honest with my mother from the start.

When I called her the next morning, she was preparing

seed for her bird feeders. "Just let me get the other phone, Lily," she said. "I can't hear on this one."

I waited till she went into the living room.

"Lily, you there?"

"Yes, Mom," I said, "I'm here."

"I'm so glad you called. I've missed talking to you." She paused and I heard her adjust the phone. "I know you wanted to works things out for yourself, and I've tried to respect that, but it hasn't been easy."

Of course, this made it doubly hard to tell her about the custody arrangement and my second visit to P6. "Mom, I've got a lot to tell you," I said, "and please forgive me for not telling you before. I wanted to protect you. I feel like I've disappointed you so much."

After she heard me out, she said, "Lily, let me tell you that you've never disappointed me. Never. And it makes me sad that you were alone with this."

"I'm sorry, Mom. I just wanted to save you the trauma of it all."

She was quiet for a moment, long enough for me to feel a little panicky.

But finally she spoke: "There's nothing to forgive, Lily. Just promise me that you'll trust me next time."

"Yes, Mom," I said, "I promise I will," thinking to myself, There'll be a next time only over my dead body.

"You know what, Lily," she said, "there'll be a time when *I* need *you,* and I have no doubt that you'll be there for me. We've gotten through a hell of a lot in this life and so far we've come out okay. More than okay. But none of us can do it alone.

"We need those who love us to say it'll be all right and mean it."

As I knew she absolutely did.

Overwhelmed with emotion, all I could say was "Thanks, Mom. I love you."

Two weeks after I came home from Callahan's house up north, my mother arrived. She was a comfort, and while I saw my counselor, Lucinda Garvin, and looked for work, she cooked and cleaned and bought red variegated carnations at the IGA. Their spicy scent reminded me of Callahan. And on more than one Thursday afternoon, after I'd seen Lucinda and sat, hoarse from crying, in an ergonomically correct chair, I would find myself taking a detour on the way home to drive past Callahan's house, though I told myself I didn't know why the hell for. I hadn't heard from him since I got on the bus in Brunswick to come home. I didn't even know if he was back. And I was disappointed that he hadn't called me.

It's Thursday the tenth of November at about four-thirty, and this time, for no good reason, I pull into Callahan's driveway. His van's not here. I park and ask myself what I think I'm doing. But before I can answer that question, I see him pull in behind me. And, of course, I feel like an idiot, sitting in my parked car in his driveway. He gets out of the van and comes around to the driver's side. I have the window down and he leans in slightly.

"So, Lily," he says, "how are you? And Jaime? How're things going?"

At least he doesn't ask me why I'm here. "We're fine," I say. "My mother's visiting. For moral support." And almost immediately I wish I hadn't said that.

"I saw you on Silver Street a couple of days ago with her, I think, in the car."

"Yes, we're sidekicks, for the time being," I say.

I have to stifle the urge to ask him why he hasn't called.

"It's still got to be tough, I guess," he says.

I must look desperate, sitting in his driveway in the goddamn twilight. He smiles ruefully, and I think I see in his expression a kind of patience afforded to the mad. Which makes me instantly resentful. Is he one of those men who gets his kicks from saving women in need? I wonder. Who get their thrills solely by coming to the aid of the dispossessed? Who bask in their own benevolence and then disappear because they're on to the next lady in distress? I can't think of another reason why he'd simply disappear.

"Would you like to come in," he says, "for a drink?"

"Okay," I say. Something in me wants to see this through. Irrational or not. Why would he have been so there, so supportive, and then just vanish? Is it just the way he operates?

When we step inside, Max is already at the door, overjoyed to see Callahan and, by association, me.

"Go on, Max," Callahan says, lightly slapping the dog's sleek rump, "upstairs with you."

The dog, in the mauve elegance he's ironically capable of, moves with fleet exactitude up the carpeted stairs. Callahan steps back, allowing for me to go up ahead of him, and I do.

Max leads us into the living room.

"Have a seat," Callahan says. "What would you like, wine or beer?"

"Beer, thank you." I sit in an overstuffed chair, feeling hostile, thinking I should either confront him or forget it altogether, which may or may not be the best strategy. Because if he hasn't wanted to call to see how I was doing, why do I care? How could he have been so supportive, then all of a sudden nothing? Was he waiting for me to call him?

Max backs up against my knees and turns his head to eye me. Absently, I stroke his satiny ears. He closes his eyes and exhales with a groan. "Okay, Max, enough now," I say, afraid the comfort of touching him will diffuse my righteous indignation.

When Callahan returns with two glasses of beer, heads of foam beer-ad perfect, I sit up straight, displacing Max, who acts offended, as if I've done something rude.

"Thank you," I say as Callahan hands me the glass. I sip a tiny bit and lick the foam from my upper lip.

He pulls up a stool and sits in front of me. "You look like you're a little preoccupied, Lily. What's up?"

A perfect in, I think, to tell him exactly what's up. "I just wonder why I haven't heard from you, that's all. It seems out of character. But maybe I'm wrong about that. After all, I really don't know you all that well, do I? And maybe I'm not such a good judge of character."

Callahan carefully sets his glass of beer on the floor and leans forward. "You seem a little confused, Lily," he says. "You wanted to come back to Pointe Blue all of a sudden, remember? We had to get up before daylight to get you to the bus.

"I figured you needed to work things out by yourself. I thought I'd give you a little time."

"What does that mean?" I say. "A little time—almost a month? Look, Callahan, you were there and then you weren't. How was I supposed to gauge that? Just because I came back you thought it was okay to disappear?

"Is this how you work? Busily save whatever hapless female you run into? And then walk off? And *I'm* not hapless, by the way."

He stands. "I never said you were."

I sit forward. Max's ears lift and drop. "I want you to know that I do appreciate everything you've done for me, but I don't need your pity."

Callahan combs his fingers through his hair, then looks at me straight. "So maybe, Lily, you need to stop pitying yourself first. For one thing, stop trying to read my mind. Creating destructive scenarios that don't exist.

"*You've* got Jaime to worry about, remember? Yes, maybe you have to share him with his father at this point, but that'll change if you get your act together and get on with it, for God's sake."

I feel heat rise into my face. My voice shakes when I speak. "You're one to talk, Callahan. Why the hell haven't you gotten on with *your* life? Your wife left five years ago! And maybe, just maybe, you haven't come to terms with the fact that you were driving the truck when you lost your boy. So don't try to tell me about getting on with my life!"

I knew I'd crossed a line the moment the words were out of my mouth, to say nothing of implicating Tim Dillard, the old man up north, the only person who could have told me about how Callahan's son had died. And then I went quiet, because I didn't know how to undo it, how to get back to where we were before I said it. So I left, Max following until Callahan called to him.

"Max, stay!" he said.

My mother was her inventive self when Jaime came. One evening she popped corn and drizzled butter over it, set the bowl on the coffee table, and read while I held Jaime in my lap, his legs folded awkwardly, like a fledgling in a nest grown too small for him. She was at her best dramatizing, transforming herself; as she read *Madeline's Rescue* she became Lord Cucuface nastily banishing the dog Genevieve from the premises. Her rendition was so believable that Jaime sat forward in alarm when Madeline and the other little girls could not find the pup.

My mother put the book down. "Oh, don't be worried, Jaime," she said, "your grandma's just acting, putting a kind of play on for you." She patted the cushion beside her. "Come sit beside me and you can look at the pictures. That'll help you understand the story better."

Jaime unfurled himself, leaving a warmth in my lap, and went to my mother, snuggling in next to her; she put her arm around him and took up the book again and began to read. His instant enchantment reminded me of my own childhood, of how my mother had entertained us, relieved us of a sometimes painful reality by leading us in sing-alongs, a favorite Gordon MacRae enactment of "Oklahoma!" She created delightful fantasy when our father was off in Utah looking for uranium, engaging in his own fantasy, one that eventually caused the demise of his marriage.

I tried to convince my mother that I was coping, that I would be perfectly okay if she went home. "I've got Lucinda, my therapist," I said, "remember?"

She did leave early, promising to come back if I needed her. Neither of us wanted to admit that when Jaime wasn't there, we became unnaturally pensive; we somehow felt an obligation to engage in banal conversation, each trying to buoy the other. And whenever she went out she never failed to surprise me with a present on her return. "I have a little something for you," she'd say: a gift of Revlon enamel in Ravenous Red, or bars of sweet-smelling Portuguese soap as big as mangos, or an Austen novel she was sure I hadn't read, often accompanied by chocolate wrapped in embossed silver foil, or an Almond Joy, a grapefruit knife she thought I needed, and, finally, a celestial map from the used-book store because she hoped to rekindle my childhood fascination with the Milky Way.

And I would try for cheery in the morning, or at the very least industrious, making breakfast, Earl Grey tea served in bone-china cups, eggy popovers on warmed plates. I never told her that I had to struggle each morning when I awoke with a sense of renewed anguish at having Jaime only provisionally. And in the end, the ritual of fixing breakfast was therapeutic: the measuring, the pouring, the mixing, the grinding of coffee beans, the squeezing of piquant Valencia oranges. I'd use a little self-deprecation to lighten things up: "Jesus, Mom, I do have the misfortune of looking like hell in the morning, and I know I couldn't have possibly inherited that from you." I'd plump my hair, a nest of loose knots, and bat my sleep-swollen eyes at her.

And sometimes I felt her anguish mirroring my own when Jaime's father came to pick him up. How she crossed her arms over her chest and with cold cordiality asked: "How are you, Ben?" She watched his car back down the driveway, still holding herself, as if she were afraid she might say something she would regret.

She slept in Jaime's room, and sometimes I would hear her get up and turn on the light. Then she'd be quiet and I imagined her standing in the middle of the room looking at Jaime's shelves, his books, his Matchbox cars lined chockablock along the edge, the stuffed animals on the bottom shelf, bunnies and bears and the odd octopus. And then I'd hear her sit on the bed, not the bed she slept in but Jaime's bed, and I imagined her holding his pillow to smell the scent of his hair still damp from shampooing, and the coppery smell of new pennies he'd counted and dropped one at a time into a glass bank shaped like a bell. I would purposely get up then and make noise, opening my bedside drawer, crossing the floor in bare feet, opening the closet door to get a robe that I seldom wore. I knew she'd hear me and turn off the light and slip back into bed because she wouldn't have wanted me to catch her grieving for us.

I'd go to the bathroom, flush the toilet, run the water, and go back to bed. But I'd feel her sorrow through the walls as I knew she could feel mine. I felt guilty because after a while I wished her gone, so that I could sleep in Jaime's bed when he wasn't with me. Wrap myself in his sheets, bury my nose in his pillow. So it was with a mixture of regret and relief that I said good-bye. When I admitted as much to Lucinda, she tried to assuage my guilt, saying, "It's okay. Sometimes, it's all you can do to feel your own grief without feeling someone else's too."

It was part of the custody agreement that I'd see a therapist. By some quirk, I'd heard about Lucinda, maybe during my stint on P6. I can't remember now. She was married to a Vietnam vet, a man who'd lost an eye during the Tet Offensive. She was like a seasoned vet herself, as if living with one had enlightened her in a way nothing else could have. She had a habit of sitting back, of letting her hands drape gracefully over the arms of the chair, that put me at ease. She was stylish, a big-boned woman who wore hand-hammered silver jewelry and raw silks. At first, I found it difficult to talk, but after a while, with Lucinda's coaxing, I just let it roll.

My nightmares began to diminish, losing their teeth, becoming distinctly matter-of-fact. Oddly, it was sound and smell that made themselves manifest: the luscious plinking of monsoon rains fracturing the surface tension of puddles that steadily deepened. The fecund tang of jungle, of fruit softly overripe, and of leafy mulch slowly simmering in the humidity. The sessions with Lucinda seemed to innoculate me. It was as if I had acquired a kind of immunity. I could count on her logic: "Feelings aren't facts," she'd say.

"I don't have time for a psychotic break," I tell her. "I've got to get a job, take care of my kid."

It was actually through Lucinda that I found out about a position at the well-baby clinic. The job didn't start till late spring, which would give me time to do a reasonable orientation. The doctor who interviewed me, a man standing well over six feet, looking all stringy muscle and sharp bone, thin hair standing like pinfeathers on his nearly bald pate, spent a fair amount of time advising me: "You really should be working on a trauma unit, considering your experience." He persisted in this manner until I quietly but firmly said, "Dr. Beavens, quite frankly I'd prefer not to go back to that. I'd much rather take care of relatively healthy babies."

He ran his hand over his pinfeathered head. "Well," he said, "I guess I'd be happy to hire you, then. I just hope you won't get bored. After all, this is no Vietnam."

CHAPTER 17

I watch Jaime finagle T. Rex and Bronto into adjacent seats of the Fisher-Price Ferris wheel and set it awhirl. They look like roadkill lying on their backs, legs stuck straight up in the air.

"That looks a little uncomfortable," I say.

Jaime studies them for a moment before answering. "They don't mind," he says, " 'cause they're having fun."

I go back to perusing the Burpee seed catalog, a kind of antidote to the late autumn rain. I stop to study the amazing varieties of *Helianthus*. "Do you want to plant sunflowers again next spring?" I ask. "Here, come take a look."

I read down the list I've made: "Cosmos, verbena, night-blooming stock, nicotiana, cleome, sweet alyssum, and last but not least sunflowers. I think we have it all."

Before Jaime can respond, I hear a car. Jaime looks up from the catalog, listening for a moment before pronouncing: "It's not Dad."

But it may as well be. I feel the change in him, a kind of distraction, something that occurs habitually near the end of each visit; it's as if he has to remove himself emotionally from me before his father comes to pick him up. The first time it happened, I tried to cajole him out of it, catching him up in my arms, kissing the soft ticklish spot where his neck meets his shoulder, but it soon became clear to me, when his body resisted, stiffening in my embrace, that detachment was his way of enduring the back-and-forth of his life. His way of adapting, I told myself. Though I hated the idea that he should have to.

And in the way you make small talk to deny the feelings of uneasiness, I say, "I'll draw a map of the garden, and we can decide where we'll plant the flowers. How about that?"

"Will I see the seeds crack their shells like last year?" he asks as he flips through the catalog like a blind man, the pages no more than what they communicate to his fingers: a slick flat coolness. He remembers how we wrapped sunflower seeds in wet paper toweling. They germinated overnight, generating tiny spring-loaded sprouts.

"We'll see," I say. An answer that promises nothing.

This isn't about seeds germinating. It's about wanting to be where you feel at home. And for Jaime that is here, in this house, where he has grown up. It's about the trill of spring peepers, the asthmatic yip of a neighbor's dog, the scent of lilac debauched by cat-piss pine. It's about things that comfort in times of discomfort: the hammering and hissing of radiators on a winter night, the reluctance of taking cold medicine that tastes of turpentine, the way the teaspoon and bottle just sitting on the bedside table seem to ease the symptoms: the sniffing and hacking and blowing of the nose, snotty sounds made into yards of toilet paper, tissues long gone.

But then, it is pointless to think of such things. For now, at least. We must play the game by the rules. So we soldier on, like good men. And when his father comes to collect him, there is no overt resistance.

Not looking up from the catalog, Jaime says, "He's here," more attuned to the sound of his father's new car than I am; the Mercedes, the familiar sound of its diesel engine and the distinct racket of its lifters, long gone. I get up from the table and look out at the new Volvo, all gray gleam, hubcaps like silver shields set against the obsidian of pristine radials. I wish for a bird to fly low and shit on this symbol of the bourgeoisie.

Jamie has his bag ready. He hugs me mechanically before his father appears at the door. Ben knocks perfunctorily, lets himself in, nods to me, and asks Jaime if he has everything.

"All ready," Jaime says, holding up his bag. He follows his father out the door.

"See you Friday," I say. "I love you."

I wave at the window and watch as they back down the driveway, then I return to the seed order, totaling it up, adding tax and shipping. And I know the Montagnard child is here, in this kitchen, watching me with her dark eyes. But she does not materialize, and for that I am grateful.

There were rumors, Ian told me, that a Reuters correspondent had been killed by Vietcong. He figured it was bullshit: Gary Landsdown was in Đà Nẵng and Will McKechney was in Bangkok; that left Bao-Long, and Ian thought he was too shrewd to get himself into the sort of predicament that would get him killed. He had seen Bao-Long in VC territory, had seen him coolly and respectfully talk his way out of one highly volatile situation after another. Once, after they'd been scrutinized by a particularly erudite VC and let go, Bao-Long translated the conversation for Ian. " 'This man Australian journalist,' I say. 'He write truth. About Vietcong. About Americans. That is only way war will end. When people know truth.' " Bao-Long's integrity was irrefutable. Evidently, the Cong recognized this and concluded that he and his friend were better left alone. So that they could write the truth.

They'd walked out of that ville, infiltrated by VC, where only days before the children had been massacred, their bellies bisected, cut cleanly by machete. I imagined the children dying, their small hands trying to hold back the pink bloom of intestine. This heinous act presumably as retribution for village elders allowing corpsmen to innoculate the children against polio. A response that tragically hamstrung the Americans, the idea of winning hearts and minds through acts of goodwill gone dreadfully wrong.

A hard rain, unusual in February, had startled us out of a sleep diluted by humidity. At first, we had just listened to the deluge, then Ian got up for a drink; that seemed to facilitate a kind of febrile conversation. There was no question of going back to sleep. The rain beat out a loud and dissonant rhythm on a profusion of surfaces: metal, stone, glass, and, of course, terra firma itself in all its incarnations.

I looked at the clock on the bedside table and though it was only four-thirty I felt wide awake. I hadn't told Ian about my little Tet foray to Reuters. There didn't seem to be any point now that he was back. I laid my hand on his chest. "Bao-Long's grandparents live near the BOQs, don't they?" I said. "So it would make sense that he would see to it that they were protected."

"That's what I'm anticipating," he said. He reached for his reading glasses then.

I got out of bed to brush my teeth and wash my face. While I was in the bathroom, Ian had propped his pillows behind his head. He was reading the front page of the two-week-old *New York Times* I had found in the lobby. When I got back into bed, he put his hand on my belly and kept reading. I knew he was sleepless because he was worried about Bao-Long.

I was nearly asleep when he put the paper down. I got up on one elbow and reached for the glass on my bedside table. I took a sip of the tepid water and set the glass down.

When I lay back, Ian without fanfare said, "I want you to come to Brisbane with me."

"Okay," I said, mirroring his forthright delivery, "but Bao-Long will be envious. So you've got to ask him too." And with that silly attempt at humor, I felt a shift in the atmosphere.

Ian got out of bed, stood in front of the opened louvered

doors, and watched the rain. "Jesus," he said, "it'll be hard going with this downpour. Cholon will be a Chinese Venice."

He was quiet then, lost in thought, it seemed, still watching the rain.

Monday will begin my third week at the well-baby clinic. Weighing and measuring, listening to the staccato of tiny hearts, and the breath sounds, reassuring in their rhythmic constancy. Some of the mothers are awkward and shy; some are children raising children. One in particular, the first appointment on Friday, really struck me. She toted a toddler, aptly named Noël, into the examination room. The child looked spit-shined, cheeks like polished macs, high-topped shoes freshly whitened, hair clean and fragrant standing softly on end, snapping with static electricity.

The mother, skittish as a feral cat, seemed to calm a bit as she watched me. I warmed the stethoscope in my hands for a few moments before listening to the child's heart. After being quite patient, letting me do as I would, she caught the device, first eyeing it, then turning it over with her baby-doll fingers. This moment of pensive examination gave me a good opportunity to talk to the mother: "How's Noël doing at home? Eating? Sleeping okay, is she?"

"A woman came from the state," the girl confided, her voice gravelly, sanding her words flat. "The old lady down the hall called them because Noël was crying all the time. I told the woman that Noël was teething and that, at night when she was fussy and couldn't sleep, I took my pillow and blanket and crawled into the playpen with her."

I imagined her tucked up in the slatted pen, the baby sitting in half-light like a miniature Buddha.

"Now when she cries," the girl continued, "I take her into the bathroom and close the door, so the old lady won't hear her. Sometimes we sleep in the tub."

It was there, in the way she held her body, arms straitjacketing her chest: the fear of losing her child. When I finished the examination, I said, "We'll help you figure things out with Noël. In the meantime, you can get her dressed. Your very lovely and inquisitive baby." She wasted no time, guiding the child's stockinged feet into a pair of bibbed overalls. Unlike most babies, Noël didn't cry as she was being dressed. Instead, she watched her mother's face intently, as if taking cues from subtle changes in her expression.

The girl sat on a child's play stool, Noël in her lap. They were perusing *The Children's Encyclopedia of Dinosaurs.* I thought it a reflection of her keen intelligence, the degree of absorption Noël exhibited. She was obviously intent on taking it all in, the picture of a plesiosaur swimming in a primeval lake. I pulled up the other play stool and sat next to them. "Looks like she'll be a good reader," I said. "Such curiosity."

"We have Dr. Seuss at home," the girl said, not looking up from the book, almost as absorbed as her daughter. "We read a lot."

"A good mother, you are," I said. She looked up then and smiled as if I'd given her a great compliment. "In fact," I said, "I'll call DHS, if you like. Tell them that Noël is a healthy and well-taken-care-of baby." And then, as if on cue, Noël said, "What's this, Mama?" She had turned the page to find a chart describing the geological strata of the Paleolithic period.

"Rocks," her mother said, "old rocks."

I watched them a moment or two before I did my doctorly duty: "I'm going to send you home with some medicine for the teething pain," I said. "And we'll make another appointment to see Noël in a few weeks."

The girl left with samples of cherry-flavored chewable vitamins, a tube of anesthetic oral gel, and packets of orange-flavored analgesics, baby riding high on a cocked hip. I'd written my home phone number on a piece of paper ripped from a pad, one of the half dozen left by a particularly fervent pharmaceutical salesman. "I want you to call me if that doesn't do the trick," I said.

In the afternoon, I pulled Noël's file. There was no phone number. Only an address: *351D State Street*. I'd leave a little early. Make a house call on the way home.

CHAPTER 18

The humidity was even more oppressive after the unseasonable rain. But the atmosphere in Saigon had nothing to do with weather. The VC and NVA had done a real number on us. The tension was as thick as the soupy air, everyone struggling with their own small and sometimes absurd terrors, fearing the VC would keep crawling out of the sewers and end up under our beds, or in our closets, or maybe even snake their way up through the pipes and into our cool porcelain bowls, upon which our asses would be firmly planted.

During curfew, which began in mid-afternoon, Saigon seemed a city haunted: the streets empty, the quintessential effects of a ghost town on display: a fluttering litter of paper gliding on the funk of a putrid wind. There was no trash collection; the already squalid avenues and alleys grew even more so. Liberally dotted with dog and human turds alike. And the quiet was devastating, sporadically punctuated by the engine noise of jeeps, MPs enforcing the curfew, or, incongruously, the ethereal tinkle of Buddhist chimes, a sound beautiful and strange in the midst of the unrelenting collective dread.

After Ian left to find Bao-Long, I sat on the balcony and sipped scotch. Anything to keep the anxiety at bay. The VC had taken Cholon, as they had the American embassy. And although we had reclaimed the embassy, Cholon was a whole other story. The scotch unfinished, I found the deadly quiet and my own company unbearable. My rationalizations simply stopped working: That Bao-Long knew how to deal with the VC no longer gave me comfort. I feared the worst.

I headed for the lobby.

Journalists, NGOs, and all types civilian milled around aimlessly or sat as if stupefied on rattan furniture. The smell of fear in the guise of sweat-saturated clothes and dry-mouth halitosis was pervasive. I went into the dining room. Sat by myself, drinking tea, what little scotch I'd had already working its magic: a kind of numbness in my joints and an illogical resolve to believe that Ian was somehow invincible.

I pretended to read a *New Yorker* magazine that had been left on the chair. It was over a year old and on its cover were orange and black oddly shaped jack-o'-lanterns with no missing teeth. I heard scraps of conversation from the three men sitting next to me: "They say Tan Son Nhat's still burning. And the VC have Cholon sewn up. And the fucking American embassy. Can you believe that?"

And all the scotch in the world finally couldn't keep me from feeling the terror that vibrated in my gut. I stood up abruptly, hitting the table so that the teacup rattled in its saucer. The men glanced at me and I wanted to tell them to shut up, to just shut the hell up. As I walked back to the lobby, I decided I would find someone who really knew what the situation was. Fuck the rumors.

The lobby felt claustrophobic, more people than before, talking and shifting in their seats or standing, rocking back and forth, their arms folded tightly in front of them. I focused on the stairs. I had to figure out how to get to the Caravelle. As if someone there knew exactly what was going on.

The door of the room was ajar. I thought that in my distraction I'd not closed it. So when I opened it fully and saw Ian sitting on the bed, I was startled. When I saw his face, I knew Bao-Long was dead.

"Oh no, Ian. No. What happened?"

"They found Bao-Long's body in the park close to Reuters. He never made it to Cholon. He died shortly after the offensive began. The same night. He promised me he'd stay at the office till I got back. Someone had to be there. He knew that."

I heard the pulse pound in my ears as I asked him how he'd found out.

"Lananh. The Saigon police told her. And, of course, she had to identify his body."

There was an urgency behind his words, as if he were compelled ultimately to hear them, so he could properly weigh their gravity.

"They liked Bao-Long," he said, "and respected him. Both sides. Their people and our people. He maintained his integrity and decency through it all. Admirable, when you consider that so many people are corrupted by it. They see the worst and it makes them feel privileged to witness it, and they only want more. And it's not for fucking humanity that you do it, it's for your own fucking ego, the adrenaline pumping so hard that you practically levitate. You become your own God. All-powerful." And then he rubbed his face with his hands and went quiet.

My joints, already numb, tingled, a sensation that forced me to sit in the chair opposite the bed. And I knew I had to tell him. But I couldn't imagine how. How could I tell him about my complicity in Bao-Long's death? As I watched him, I realized that I'd been given a reprieve, for the moment, that his grief demanded that I stay quiet, that I simply act as a witness to his need to self-denigrate, the need to deny his own decency, how he had repeatedly put himself at risk to tell the stories of people ravaged by the war, the stories he had told me: how after a firefight when a ville had been razed in a frenzy to find what could not be found, dozens of Vietcong had melted away, even their dead disappeared as if a sort of Rapture had occurred, if one believed in such phenomena: people, bodies and all, being instantly delivered to heaven, their clothes, sneakers—flip-flops, in this case—left as they had fallen, because what had formerly filled them was now paradise-bound. Ian was profoundly affected by something he saw in the debris of smoldering ash, a huge white goose blackened by napalm smoke, its yellow eyes alive and knowing, in the way a dumb animal knows; it had nestled itself, feet tucked under, against the body of a dead child.

"I hadn't allowed myself to cry, up to then," he'd said. "But this pathetic bird huddled close to the dead child, which it must have trusted, made me bawl like a goddamn baby."

Everything else was dead, he told me, pigs still in their sty, a white dog with milk-engorged teats, an old woman with teeth bared in a death grin; he had to save the goose, the only thing still living; he had to do something redemptive, even marginally redemptive. When he tried to pick her up, she hissed viciously and lunged at him with her blackened beak. When he tried to talk to her, to soothe her, she pushed her sooty body deeper into the hollow created by the child's knees, which in death were pulled in toward her chest.

The goose put up such a fight that he finally decided that he must honor her need to stay with the child, to find solace in the small body gone stiff with rigor mortis. He had to convince himself that that in itself was an act of redemption.

Now he only wanted to take Bao-Long's death and use it to mirror his own fallibility. But speech finally failed him, and in a kind of torpor, he poured scotch liberally into his empty glass and drank it straight off. And then he lay back on the bed and closed his eyes.

I took a bath, washing perfunctorily, hardly aware of my own body, distracted by the panic that made my throat narrow and my pulse race. As I dried I heard the crow of a rooster in the barnyard that was Saigon. I brushed my wet hair back and secured it with a barrette. I did not bother with makeup.

Ian seemed to rouse as I dressed. He turned on his side, facing the wall. I had the feeling he was awake but didn't want to talk.

I sat in the dining room for a long time sipping watery mango juice and watching the Saigon police, the white mice, patrolling. When Ian appeared at the table showered and shaved, I was not surprised. Nothing about him surprised me anymore. He sat across from me and politely said no to the waiter when he was asked if he'd like to order.

"I'm going to the office to pack up Bao-Long's belongings and take them to Lananh," he said. "And try to make arrangements to send her money. She is a proud woman and will probably refuse to accept my help. I'll have to come up with a way to convince her. Maybe tell her that, for me, it would be a way of honoring Bao-Long's memory and his commitment to his family. And that would be the truth." He looked at his watch then and rubbed the face of it with his thumb. "It won't change things, I know. And maybe it's my way of dealing with the guilt. I shouldn't have insisted that one of us stay at the office and that it, presumably, be him because he could speak the language and knew how to deal with the VC. And by then we knew the city was crawling with them. It was a given. He'd lived a charmed life up till then. Do you see that?"

"Yes, he did," I said. "Live a charmed life. And would have continued to had it not been for me." I looked down at the table because I couldn't look at him. "I went to Reuters after you left me that night. I panicked. Wanted to see that you were safe. So I went to Reuters." I glanced at his face and saw mild confusion; I looked down again, simply so I could continue.

"You could have gotten yourself killed, Lily," he said. "I thought you'd have known better."

I made myself look at him then. "I didn't get myself killed, Ian—"

He interrupted before I could continue. "Was Bao-Long there?" he asked.

"Yes," I said, "and he was worried about my safety and insisted on bringing me back to the hotel. We came through the park. We were being followed. Bao-Long pushed me under the branches of a tree and told me to stay till he came for me. I never doubted that he'd return. And just before dawn, he did. And he brought me back here. He made me promise to stay. Said he knew you were okay, that you would be back 'directly.' Though I knew that he *was* worried about you."

"He must have gone back the way you'd come. Through the park," Ian said. "That's where they found his body. In sight of the office."

He stood up then, walked to the balustrade that bordered the terrace, his back to me. He fished in his pocket for a cigarette. And when he lit it, I understood that I couldn't bear to hear what his silence already told me. I slipped away from the table.

A few minutes later, he came back to the room and out onto the balcony where I sat trying to numb myself with warm scotch. "It's not safe out here," he said. I didn't bother to tell him that I didn't particularly care. That a stray bullet through the head was not the worst thing. That death would be a goddamn relief about now. He spoke again, repeating his warning, and when I didn't respond, he took my hand and pulled me up out of the chair.

On a bed still rumpled from an oppressive sleep, he undressed me with a gravity that reflected his grief. And when he lay naked beside me I couldn't look at him, so I closed my eyes. His touch was tentative at first, his fingertips barely grazing my hip; the muscle of my thigh contracted as he traced it with less constraint. And then he said, "Please, Lily, look at me." I opened my eyes and saw absolute despair. The kind of despair that cannot be relieved in the way he was trying to relieve it. He kissed me, bruising my mouth with his insistence. I could not respond. And in a kind of frenzy, he made love to me, his unsupported weight suffocating. I cried silently, tears sliding over my temples and into my ears. Out of sheer persistence, he came, more from anguish it seemed than pleasure. And I loathed him for how he made me feel, even though I knew I was in some way responsible.

And it was almost worse after, when there was nothing to say. Because we both knew it was over.

I had come to care about Noël and her mother, Etta. Her name, short for Henrietta, seemed old-fashioned, of another generation, a generation that might have served her better, a time when young women had babies, not careers; a time when, if a young woman was lucky, the townspeople would help her if her husband deserted her. Neighbors rather than a bureaucratic institution like DHS. Or maybe I'm being naive. Dr. Beavens—or Jack, as he likes to be called—cautioned me. "You're too personally involved," he said. "These young girls are sketchy, notorious for disappearing without a word. I don't want you to be disappointed."

"I understand that," I said, knowing that he'd had a lot of experience and knew better than I what the possibilities were. "And I will accept the consequences. I'm realistic here. But just maybe Etta is different. Anyway, we have to give her the benefit of the doubt, don't we?"

And I truly believed that Etta *was* different. Many of the other young women who came to the clinic *were* sketchy: Some came with babies nursing bottles filled with Coke or Kool-Aid, always of the red variety. Others had no compunction about screaming at their toddlers in the waiting room: "You just wait till we get home, Mr. Man! You just wait!" And still others seemed to go into a sort of fugue state in the examining room, hardly able to undress their children. One toddler had exhibited signs of abuse, a constellation of red weals revolving around a protruding umbilicus, looking suspiciously like cigarette burns. And as I had contacted DHS to defend Etta, I had also reported the suspected abuse of this sad child, all wide eyes in a sallow face.

On my first house call I found Etta's apartment, a rabbit warren of a space: a long narrow hall leading to a high-ceilinged common area that was bedroom, living room, and, at the far end, a kitchenette, an afterthought of jerry-rigged counter of cracked gray Formica, suspended pressed-wood cupboards whose doors hung ajar, slack-mouthed, a tiny stove with two burners, a Lilliputian oven, and a round-shouldered refrigerator circa 1950. Despite the decrepitude, the place was cheery: Artwork probably from a nearby Goodwill store decorated the walls. Though shot through with cracks, the plaster was freshly painted in a deep shade of lavender, suggesting the landlord had bought cheaply in bulk. A framed poster—van Gogh's "Sunflowers"—and five no-names, a riot of flowers in plastic gilt frames, were perfectly spaced. A double bed, made up with white sheets and yellow pillow slips and a faded flannel blanket, was pushed against the wall, three overplump throw pillows of faux tapestry propped for effect, making the bed double as a sofa.

And in the middle of the room, a white net playpen, the centerpiece of the home; it was cushioned with satin-trimmed baby blankets and inhabited by a motley gang of stuffed bears and a homemade soft-bodied doll with yarn hair, embroidered periwinkle-blue eyes and a red bow mouth. Above the playpen was a chandelier of white hobnail glass, the original Victorian fixture long gone, only the elaborate plaster medallion left. From the light hung a mobile, an assortment of motifs cut from greeting cards turning gently in the draft coming from the bay window that dominated the room: Glittery snow scenes caught the light; blowsy roses of soft apricot and paradoxical magenta slowly revolved; floating above, a second tier, kittens with angora pasted on.

Noël, thumb in mouth, toddled up to me and pulled me by the hem of my coat into the bathroom, a windowless room lighted by one working fluorescent tube next to a medicine-cabinet mirror; the room had once been a closet. Like the kitchenette, it too had been jerry-rigged, a tub fitted next to the outer wall, a sink the size and shape of a shoe box, a commode squeezed between the two. Noël blithely climbed up onto the lid of the commode, stood, reinserted her thumb, and pointed to a bowl of goldfish centered on a shelf over the back of the toilet. "Eggs and Green Ham," she said, talking around her thumb. "Mama just cleaned them."

"How pretty," I said, watching the two fish swimming round the small bowl, flashing copper in the fluorescent light. "Their names, then, are Eggs and Green Ham?"

Etta stood in the doorway watching us.

Noël popped her thumb out of her mouth to clearly enunciate: "Yes, Mama said I could pick their names."

"What a good mama," I said. We watched the fish a few moments more, and though the bathroom appeared spotless, despite the rusted bowl and sink, an acrid tinge of ammonia hung in the air, in the tub a pail of diapers soaking.

Etta squeezed by me and said, "Noël isn't night-trained," as though she'd read my mind.

"She's young yet," I said.

Noël bobbed her head up and down enthusiastically. "I say, it's okay, Mama! Ooh-kay."

Etta lifted Noël and propped her on a jutted hip. Noël, with one small hand, turned her mother's face and grinned around her thumb conspiratorially. "Okay, Mama?" she said.

"Okay, Noël," Etta said.

I followed them into the living room. "Well," I said, "I wanted you to know that I called DHS and spoke with your caseworker. I told her that Noël was well taken care of and definitely well loved."

Etta smiled, shrugged Noël higher on her hip, and seemed to stand taller. "Thank you, Dr. Townsend. So much."

Noël was having none of the sentimental talk. With her thumb completely out of her mouth, she said. "Let me down, Mama. So I can get my books."

She proceeded to take my hand and lead me to the bed. I sat while she lay flat on her tummy on the floor, rummaging around under the bed, finally scuttling out with a bunch of dog-eared books: Dr. Seuss. Of course.

Noël became a welcome element in Jaime's life. He missed his cousin Nina when he was with me, and I hadn't the heart to leave Etta and Noël solely in the clutches of an incompetent state. So on the nights Jaime was with me I invited them to dinner. Etta stood in the kitchen, shy and awkward until I handed her a bunch of carrots and a knife. "You don't mind helping, do you?" I said. "I'll do the onions."

With something constructive to do, she relaxed into the rhythm of peeling and chopping while Jaime and Noël loaded the Fisher-Price Ferris wheel with dinosaurs.

We talked about her hometown, the Forks, a town close to the Canadian border, where the post office was located in the postmistress's house, and where deer came at dusk to nibble at gardens. Not to be too idyllic here. After all, it was the small-minded prejudice of the town that drove Etta out after it became obvious that she was pregnant. And by a *summer boy,* no less.

I remember at one point when the children were under the table, heads together, coloring in a giant coloring book Etta had brought as a gift. "I can still smell Robert's hair," she said, speaking of Noël's young father. "I cleaned his grandparents' summer house, and they used white soap and creamy shampoo in tall glass bottles."

It was the one and only time she had spoken of the boy. Before I could respond, she had changed the subject, obviously trying to cover the shame she felt.

"You do it different than my mother," she said, "chopping onions."

"I learned this from a guy I dated a long time ago," I said. "You want to try it?"

She put down the knife and stood next to me.

"First of all, set it on its root end and begin to cut." I demonstrated the technique, slicing vertically one way and then the other way, not quite through the onion, creating a grid. "Don't cut into the root because that's what makes you cry.

"Now, turn it on its side and cut off a little slice so you've got a flat place. The onion won't roll now when you cut into it."

After I finished, I passed her a fresh onion. "What do you think? You want to try it?"

She was tentative at first but ended up with a perfectly diced mound.

"Great job," I said. "You're a natural."

She smiled wide and said, "Thanks."

It struck me that her success with the onion wasn't such a small thing.

CHAPTER 19

I stand on the cellar steps. The light is reflected on the surface of the water, which seems to ripple, lapping back and forth, a kind of tide, the sustained torrential rain too much for the sump pump, apparently. Though the furnace squats on a raised cement pedestal, I'm not convinced it's out of harm's way. And I don't relish putting on my Wellies and slogging through the black water, upon which floats a flotilla of unrecognizable objects, one of which looks decidedly like a drowned mouse.

I retreat back up the stairs and into the kitchen, where Jaime and Noël sit at the table, eating alphabet cereal before bed. Etta is enduring a long bus trip to Jackman, where her mother will pick her up and, from there, they'll drive the short distance to the Forks. Her father, a man ravaged by lung cancer after a lifetime of working in sawmills and smoking cigarettes, is dying. Etta, though white-faced and quiet, was nonetheless stoic, grateful that I offered to take Noël. "It's a long weekend," I said. "The clinic is closed until Wednesday. We'll make cookies, listen to music. We'll have a good time. Don't worry. You've got more than enough to deal with." I didn't tell her that it would be a relief to have Noël when Jaime went to his father's.

I often stayed late at the clinic. "Don't you have a life?" Jack would ask, eying me like a Jewish mother. "Other than administering to our little ragamuffins?" He scolded me affectionately for working long hours, but he was no different. We'd go out for a late lunch sometimes to talk shop and then he'd say, "Well, got to go pick up some groceries for Irma. She's invited her mother for dinner." He'd sigh and roll his eyes. He often grumbled affectionately about his wife, a petite woman who came up to his chest. A former nurse, she sometimes came to help out at the clinic, the babies always soothed by her substantial bosom. One afternoon, I saw them kissing, his hand cupping her bottom through the white uniform. I was touched by their obvious affection for each other, but, at the same time, I was made acutely aware of my own solitary life, not just the lack of a partner to love—that went without saying—but the simple camaraderie I longed for: perusing a used-book store together; one going out for bagels on a snowy winter morning while the other sips coffee in bed; the pointing out of something the other one misses: a cicada just out of its chrysalis, the moon coming up under the dark flounces of a colossus pine, a sprinkling of dainty turds left by a miniature dog being pulled along on a leash by a master oblivious or embarrassed.

Once after our particularly gregarious pharmaceutical salesman had dropped by, Jack said, "Good-looking fellow. Seems quite intelligent, despite his line of work. And since you don't seem to have a life, maybe you should respond to his obvious interest in you."

"I'm sure he's a great guy, Jack. But I'm really not interested."

"You got to get out sometime," Jack said. "You're not getting any younger."

"Oh yeah, thanks," I said, "just what I needed to hear."

In actuality, I secretly hoped Callahan would call, but I felt my face flush with shame every time I thought of what I'd said to him. I even wrote a letter of apology but couldn't make myself mail it. I figured he had no interest in me and, frankly, I didn't blame him.

"Mum," Jaime says, "can we listen to the *Star Wars* tape? Noël's never heard it."

"If you put your bowls in the sink," I say, "I'll put it on for you."

"Okay," Jaime crows, collecting Noël's bowl and spoon, taking it along with his to the sink. Noël smiles around her thumb. "Okay," she says. "Okaaay."

I settle them on the sofa, covering them with a blanket, and put the cassette in the tape player.

Back in the kitchen, I tell myself that I could test the theory that Callahan has no interest in me. I have a legitimate excuse to call him. "What the hell," I say aloud, and head for the phone. I dial, then purposefully uncoil the black cord while I listen to Callahan's phone ring. On the third ring his answering service picks up. "Oh," I say, "sorry. This is Lily Townsend. I've got a flooded cellar, I'm afraid. Does Mr. Callahan have any time?"

"Let's check, Mrs. Townsend. Could you hold a minute?"

"Sure," I say, feeling my heart in my throat. Before she returns to the phone, I realize I can't go through with it.

Then she's back. "Mrs. Townsend, Mr. Callahan is not available. Norm Trafton is taking calls; shall I send him?"

No need to waffle anymore, I think. "That'd be fine," I say.

"It'll probably be within the hour," the woman says.

"Thanks," I say.

I sit at the table feeling both relief and disappointment and even a little paranoia: Maybe Callahan has told his service that he won't accept calls from *Lily Townsend*. Amid a chorus of whistles and clicks from R2-D2, I rinse the kids' bowls and place them in the top rack of the dishwasher.

Noël's blue eyes are dreamy, her hands wrapped around

the fat tummy of Jaime's octopus as she listens intently to the tape, to the grunts and clicks and the voice of Princess Leia, screaming mostly at this point. It's the first time I've seen her with her thumb out of her mouth for more than a minute or two.

Norm Trafton arrives on time. No-nonsense, he slogs through the water in the cellar. After a minute or two I hear the sump pump sucking furiously. When he comes back upstairs he stands by the door and looks at me as if he wants to shake his head and call me ditsy. "Hate to charge you seventy-five dollars for that," he says, meaning the pump was simply not plugged in tightly. "But it is an after-hours call, Mrs. Townsend."

"It's worth my not having to swim through that," I say, refusing to take the bait, be made to feel foolish. I take my checkbook from my bag and write out the check, hand it to him, and say, "Thank you." He nods and I watch him head for the back door, his boots sounding squishy. "By the way," I can't resist asking, "do you know when Kevin Callahan will be back?"

"I wouldn't know," Norm Trafton says. "He's a mystery to me, that one."

With that, he leaves and I'm left with the impression that Callahan is an anomaly in the trade. At least to this fellow plumber.

I have to wake Jaime when his father comes. After they've left, I carry Noël to Jamie's room and tuck her into bed. I thought it would be comforting to have Noël in Jaime's absence, but as I look at his empty bed, his favorite rabbit propped against the pillow, I realize that isn't the case.

I hear a little voice from the downstairs hall and realize Noël is calling me. I glance at the clock. It's a little after eight in the morning. "Coming," I call.

It's Saturday, I think, as I make my way downstairs. Isn't

it? Noël's no longer in the hall. And when I come into the living room, I have a surprise. Noël is stationed next to Callahan.

"Who's this little darling?" he asks.

"Did she let you in?" I ask. I feel shy and exposed, but even with gritty eyes and snarled hair, I can't keep from stupidly smiling.

"She did let me in," Callahan says, grinning. "A morning person, I guess." And with that I see the nest of blankets on the sofa, peopled with a half dozen stuffed animals and Noël's cloth doll.

"I'm sorry," I say, "but I'm not sure why you're here." I try to sound straightforward, but it's useless. I can't keep the silly smile out of my voice.

Callahan pats Noël's blond hair, hers too a mass of tangles. "If you give me a cup of coffee, I'll tell you," he says.

"Let me put on some clothes first," I say.

He nods in agreement, as if to say, Yes, you look a little wild, but that's all right.

"Maybe Mr. Callahan will get some cereal for you," I say to Noël.

"Okay," she says, smiling around her thumb. "I know where the Cheerios are." She takes charge by slipping her hand into Callahan's and leading him into the kitchen.

I watch them disappear, Callahan looking like a kindly giant with little Noël.

I groan when I see myself in the mirror. And go to work, brushing my teeth first, then my hair, plopping a little face cream into my palm, massaging it in quickly, dotting a little lipstick on the apples of my cheeks, rubbing it in. Not to much effect, I think. My eyes still swollen from sleep.

I slip into a pair of jeans and a black cardigan with tiny buttons that I fumble with, leaving the first few undone.

I see them before they see me. Noël is sitting with her back to me, spooning cereal into her mouth, a glass of orange juice next to her bowl. Callahan is standing, perusing the newspaper that he must have picked up on the porch.

I stand in the doorway with hands on my hips. "So you're going to tell me why you're here," I say. Callahan puts the paper down and leans against the counter. I open the freezer and, after a little search, find the coffee beans behind a carton of vanilla ice cream.

"Answering service said you'd called. And that they'd sent Norman Trafton. That could be a disaster right there. So I figured I'd stop by to make sure things were okay."

"I'm embarrassed to tell you," I say. "The sump pump wasn't plugged in."

"Bet that little mistake cost you," he says.

"Seventy-five dollars," I say.

He just smiles, folds his arms, and watches me as I grind the beans, then spoon the coffee into the filter, add water, and flip the on switch. Like magic, the rhythmic drip begins, accompanied by the clink of Noël's spoon.

And then the clinking stops abruptly and Noël says, "Lily, can I listen to *Star Wars* again?"

"Are you finished with your breakfast, Noël?" I ask.

She picks up the glass, drinks the last bit of orange juice, wipes her mouth with the back of her hand, and says, "Yes."

"Okay, then, sweetie, come with me, and we'll see about Princess Leia." I lift her up, she puts her arms around my neck, and I nuzzle her hair. "We have to teach you, Miss Noël, not to open the door to strangers." She nods her head vigorously and smiles at Callahan.

"I'm no stranger, Noël," he says. "It's the next guy you have to watch out for."

After I rewind the tape and tuck Noël into her nest, I go back into the kitchen. Callahan has just poured two mugs of coffee. They're steaming on the table. "Milk?" I say.

"No thanks," he says.

I pull a chair out and sit down. "So what can I do for you?" I say.

"First of all," he says, "tell me about this little waif."

I'm glad for the distraction, so proceed to tell him about Etta.

"You have a good heart, Lily," he says after I finish.

"You wouldn't think so, sometimes," I say.

I know that he knows what I'm talking about. And when he doesn't respond, I take a sip of coffee, and, of course, I manage to spill some. "Goddammit," I say, and get up to grab a cloth. But he stops me by putting an arm around my hips. He holds me loosely. "I understand why you said what you did," he says. "I understand. It's okay."

"I'm really ashamed," I say. "You can't imagine how much."

He holds me more tightly. I touch his hair, and I feel so much. Everything conflicting. Relief. Desire. Fear.

And then the earth continues on its axis: "Pleeezzzz, come turn the tape, Lily!" we hear, a surprisingly strident little voice from the living room.

After I fast-forwarded and turned the tape, Noël impatient for her favorite part—Princess Leia's rescue—Callahan left, but not before asking if Jaime and I would like to have dinner on Sunday. "Max would be thrilled to have the company," he said.

"In that case, we'll be happy to come. But only if we can bring something. Dessert, maybe? Apple pie? À la mode?"

"À la mode is good. Max hasn't had vanilla ice cream in a while. I try not to indulge him."

I had to laugh at that; Max, though maybe not treated to ice cream regularly, was incredibly indulged in a "man and his dog" kind of way.

I stood in the driveway and watched him back out. He waved before disappearing down the road.

"The thing about your tirade," he'd said, referring to my meltdown on that awful afternoon, "was that you *had* a point. But I didn't see it at first. I was angry. I was thinking, Who were *you* to criticize?

"It came to me at five A.M. the next morning, in the cold light of day, that you were right, I hadn't gotten on with my life. Going to work every morning to keep body and soul together wasn't living. I hadn't accepted Will's death, or my wife's leaving. I'd been in a kind of limbo."

He was quiet then. Like you are when you've surprised yourself. And said something you hadn't, exactly, intended to.

He was standing at the counter, had been getting ready to leave, and I was standing next to him. I was struck, mostly at the sound of his boy's given name. There was such intimacy and ache in it. On impulse, I put my arms around Callahan and hugged him. I could smell solder and copper filings and a faint spiciness. He held me tightly; the sound of his breathing, quiet and rhythmic, was somehow reassuring. We stayed like that momentarily, till Noël called again, this time asking that the volume be turned up. When I went to move away from him, I found myself caught, my hair curiously twined around his coat button. As he carefully uncoiled the errant strands, I joked, "There are easier ways to catch a woman, you know. Don't you think this is just a little bit extreme?"

After he's left, I rinse the coffee carafe, dry my hands on a damp dish towel, put the milk away, jockeying for space between the apple juice and the barrel-shaped jar of grape jelly. Then I rearrange the refrigerator magnets: multicolored dinosaurs, all in a row, an exhaustive collection of teeth, wings, armor, claws, spikes, crests, and fins; a mix of the Triassic, the Jurassic, and the Cretaceous I ordered from a museum catalog. I line them up by reputation: T. rex, brontosaur, stegosaur, iguanodon, diplodocus, plesiosaur, and, of course, a merry band of pterodactyls. I can identify them instantly because Jaime insists we name them every time he returns from his father's. It is a ritual he seems to require, something that feels real, something he can depend on. An indispensable part of each visit. Now he's teaching Noël the who's who of the dinosaur world. Sometimes she speaks clearly, repeats him precisely; other times she speaks around her thumb, which sends them both into convulsions of laughter.

I'm okay now, for the most part, with living in Pointe Blue, comfortable with its small-town rhythms, its familiarity, and even with the fact that I live close to Rachel and Ben, because essentially it's good for Jaime. And I'm hopeful that in six months or so, after demonstrating that I am capable of absolutely unimpeachable mothering, Ben may be open to renegotiating the terms of the custody agreement.

But for now, to get through it, we make the commonplace uncommon: When I read to Jaime, he often falls asleep in my lap, and instead of carrying him to his bed to nap, I put the book aside and hold him until he wakes, rocking slightly, my chin resting lightly on his head, humming "I'll Be Home for Christmas," because it just feels good, even though it's not yet the season.

I look for her in all the usual places: at the far end of the IGA parking lot, or in the shadows of my bedroom, or beyond the driveway, near the spruce trees where chickadees, winged flashes of black and white, trill and flit. But I don't see her anywhere.

Oddly, I miss her. Though not enough to wish her back. There's no way to explain it, rationally. Let's just say that I lost my soul in Vietnam. And let's say I got it back the first time I saw Noël and Etta in the clinic when my life began to be about the living again, instead of about the dying or the dead.

The Montagnard people are known for their love of children. They are inherently bound: A baby sleeps with its mother at night, curled in the concave space of warmth made by the curve of her body, and by day rides on her back, safe and snug in woven blanket and hat. I remember that not long after being assigned to the 71st EVAC, I saw a beautiful child in the city of Pleiku, helping her mother gather sheaves of straw rice; she was about Jaime's age, dark eyes accentuated by a fringe of bang. "Aren't you just beautiful," I said to her, impulsively touching her cheek; her skin, a deep caramel color, felt like warm silk. First she giggled, then shied away from me. The mother, young, maybe fifteen, looking like a kind of mythical highland Madonna, smiled quizzically, turned, and spoke softly to the child and went back to work. There was an innocence about her that I later saw in many other Montagnard people, a quality that even the war couldn't diminish.

I walked on but turned once to look back. I was struck by the incongruity: They, mother and child, were like extravagantly beautiful flowers, out of place on the side of the road, squatting in the red dust, as a military truck passed, assaulting the still air with grinding gears.

About the Author

Cheryl Drake Harris lives in Gardiner, Maine, with her husband.